The Fall

Glyn Pope

To Katy
lots of love
gp xx

The Fall
Glyn Pope

First Published 2007 by CameronAdams
France

Written by Glyn Pope
Copyright C.2007 Glyn Pope

ISBN - 978-1-84799-147-8

For Jill
I used to live alone before I knew you (LC)

ONE

Following Mr. Newstead's instructions Michael caught a flight from Heathrow to Charles de Gaulle airport in Paris. Using the metro he went to Paris Nord railway station and took a train southwest to the city of Angers. There he stayed in a large hotel across the road from the station. He booked and paid for three nights although he knew he would not be in the building for all of them.

It was late October. There were plenty of tourists about, some foreign, but mostly French. Michael's mother had been French, his father English. He had inherited his mother's tongue and was as devious as his father had been. He could blend in easily with the locals. He should have been born forty years earlier to be of some use to the resistance, or the occupiers.

The following day after breakfast he wandered around Angers blending with the tourists. He went into an art gallery at the theatre. He didn't like this modern nonsense. The red and white colours reminded him of a head he had smashed smearing the blood and brain. He sauntered out again into the main square and decided to take a walk around the outskirts of the town. He quickly found what he was looking for in a moderately crowded car park. People could be so stupid. He'd once seen a car with its door wide open waiting to be stolen. This was just as inviting as the driver had left the keys in the ignition. Michael drove out of Angers, confident, as though he owned the car. He went on until he reached the small town of Doue and then parked up to check the route to St. Aurélien. He drove on main roads, then streets until he was going along country lanes that were to narrow to take more than one car until he saw sign to the village that was his destination. He parked in the main square along with the two or three other cars. He was French in a French car. He had nothing to hide. Through his windscreen he could see the name of a bar 'Chez Max' that boasted meals and rooms. Adjoining it was a shop. Behind the bar a middle-aged man looked up and watched Michael getting out of the car, his spectacles reflecting the yellow from the overhead lights. Michael went into the room, nodded to the few assembled customers, ordered a rosè, lit up a Gitanne leaning against the bar as if it were his local.

"Tell me," he said to the barman, "Are there any properties for sale in this village. I'm on the look out for a client. An Englishman." He raised his eyebrows as if to say I'm sure you don't want the English living in a charming place like this.

"Ask the mayor. Maurice!"

With that, a short and rather plump man swayed their way clutching his drink. "You want to buy?" Asked the official looking at Michael.

"Maybe." He paused and took a sip of his drink. "I'm looking."

"There are very good flat conversions near the boulangerie." The mayor had an interest in these and he could make some money if they were sold.

"The boulangerie?"

"Out here," he said waving an arm in the general direction, "Right. Right again and up the main street."

"Yes." Michael nodded.

"Up the main street past the Bar Mary…"

"You don't drink in there," the barman laughed, "Come back here."

The mayor sighed as if he were being interrupted at a council meeting. "Straight on until you come to a cross road and there you will see them on your left."

"Thanks. I'll take a look." He was familiar with all this. He had done his homework in England. He knew the way to Jonathan's house, which was where he intended to go. He finished his rosè and cigarette and with a 'see you later' left the bar. He went up the quiet street and found the flats. He had a look at them as if he were intending to buy and then took the long route to Jonathan's house. The village was very still and quite deserted. After the boulangerie he met only one man to whom he said 'good evening'. Jonathan's house was about one hundred metres into a side road. Michael could see that there was a light on in the bedroom, so his prey was at home. The house opposite was in darkness and the rest of the houses were spread hundreds of metres into the receding countryside.

Jonathan lay on his bed staring at the ceiling. It was Easter. He was looking forward to a well deserved long weekend. It felt good. He had been nearly a year in France and quite a few months in his own house. He was deciding whether to decorate or garden or perhaps even both. He took the plunge and went for both. Stephi, with whom he had lodged for a while, joked that he'd be better employed looking for a wife. No, he'd been through all that. That was why he had fled England and was here. That could wait. Stephi had gone away on holidays with her family to Italy for ten days to look at the art galleries and churches. He'd waved them off when he'd returned from getting his baguette that morning. He'd been asked in the shop if he was going on holiday; "I might," he'd answered even though he knew he had no intention of doing so.

Michael looked up and down the street for a second and third time until he was sure it was deserted. He opened the heavy iron gate to Jonathan's house and closed it carefully behind him. He went cautiously across the gravel to the front door and opened it. He had no doubt it would be unlocked. People hardly locked their houses in villages like this. In the hallway opposite him was a wooden staircase. He padded quietly and carefully up the stairs.

Jonathan thought that he heard the gate, a crunch, then the door and footsteps on the stairs. This place was too silent at times he decided. It made his imagination work overtime, until he suddenly became aware of a bulk filling the doorway. He turned his head and looked half expecting it to be Ahmed, the local joker drunk, playing a trick to scare him. But it wasn't.

"Who...?" But no other words came. He was rapidly approaching terror. His throat felt paralysed and he could not speak.

Michael walked round to the foot of the bed and stood looking at his victim. "How many French bitches have you screwed on this then?" He paused as if waiting for an answer. When none came, he went on. "Why do people like you with perfectly good lives, a great country to live in and a nation to be proud of, a monarchy to look up to want to live in a fucking rat hole like this?" He paused again as if giving him the opportunity to answer.

Jonathan, now terrified for his life, rolled from the bed and ran from the room. Striding Michael followed him. Jonathan reached the top of the stairs and began to run down. He tripped over his own foot and fell. His head hit the stone floor. Jonathan's neck broke and he was dead in an instant.

Michael had touched nothing except the front door knob. He knew that must be covered in fingerprints. He would leave it. He would never be traced. He took a last look at the lifeless body feeling disappointed that he could not have played some more games. He left the house walking across the garden listening all the time for any signs of life in the road. A car passed. When he was sure it had gone he walked quickly back to the bar and his car. He opened the door to get in and the barman called, "Everything all right?"

"Oh yes," he replied, "Could not be better. Goodbye."

Michael drove. Abandoned the car where it would not be found for a long time. He was back at his hotel in time for dinner and in England by the following afternoon. As agreed he didn't telephone Mr Newstead. He would find out soon enough.

Jonathan's body lay undiscovered for about ten days until Stephi returned with her family. She went to visit and knocking on the front door saw his inert form lying on the stone floor. He must have fallen down the stairs was the official decision. He was missed for a week or two in the village. He was replaced within a day at his school. An English family bought his house. They were never told the tragedy that had happened there. They changed the layout of the house and Jonathan's existence.

After the police had left Jonathan's parents alone with the news of their son's death the pair sat in silence.

Jonathan's mother spoke, "You don't seem very surprised,"

"He was never alive anyway. Not really."

"Did you have anything to with this?"

"How could I?"

"I don't know. But I don't know a lot anymore. I don't know you that's for sure. We live. You'll die. I'll live alone a lonely old woman's life. I'll die. And no one will remember anyway." She enjoyed the feeling persecuting herself like this.

She would look through the d
later to see if she knew anyone
she would put herself out to go t
to Jonathan's burial either.

So that's how it all ends n
cry. But it's all been said before. 1
there to be a mighty explosion in J
against the stone floor. Choose the ɛ
dead before he was born. He ha
unimportant. He was a fantasy born o   ̲ ̲ wished for
by Rick. Rick owned him. Only fant̲ ̲ ̲ ̲ end as an individual
might hope to have some kind of control over. There aren't
always happy endings. The hero in the story isn't a character
from a saccharine film. So as Rick was over fond of saying,
'don't live in my dream because it's a nightmare'.

TWO

Just a few days later Rick was standing in the kitchen,
staring out at the dusk, finishing off a bottle of wine and was just
about to open another when his wife Lesley appeared beside
him.

"Drinking up the French wine are we?"
"There's nothing else to do..."
"There's plenty."
"Like what. Talk to you?"
"There'll be none left for Christmas."
"Who cares about Christmas? Anyway Tescos 'll have
plenty."
"I don't think you'll be here at Christmas."
He held onto the bottle and looked at her, genuine
surprise crossing his face. "What do you mean?"
"We just don't get on anymore. You drink too much.
You don't like my friends. I'm not even going to bother with the
party anymore."
"Well there's a relief. What party anyway?"
"See what I mean? If you drink anymore, sleep on the
sofa down stairs. That'll make you feel great for school in the

...in about that instead of your stupid ideas." She strode out of the room. He reached for the corkscrew. ...an't use your grandpa dying as an excuse any more. He ...just a very old man."

"Bossy cow."

He gazed out of the kitchen window for a moment and caught his reflection in the light against the already darkening sky. He suddenly remembered a party last Christmas. He always liked to go to Philip and Elizabeth's Christmas drinks and last year they had wanted to take Christine. Why did his mind play tricks like this remembering what he didn't need to remember? It occupied his mind unnecessarily. At their lunchtime gathering on Christmas Day there was always plenty of smoked salmon and wine to break up the time after opening the presents and eating dinner. Before the festive celebrations, he saw them deciding who could be invited. The pair of them sitting uncomfortably in their straight-backed chairs.

"You look cross dear," he had said.

She looked over at Phillip still holding the phone close to her ear. "That was Lesley on the phone. Asking if her friend Christine could come to our Christmas do." They held a Christmas event annually as if they were Lord and Lady inviting the surfs.

"Well?"

"Well? I think we've got enough people coming and anyway why should we invite their friends?"

"Ah yes."

"She said she thought we'd like her. Seems like a bit of a wimp to me. Any meaningful conversation would blow her away."

"Oh." He wondered if his wife felt threatened for some reason.

A while ago when Lesley and Rick were flavour of the month with Elizabeth she would have said 'Of course, bring who you like. I'm sure we'll love them.' But Elizabeth discarded people like broken toys and anyway now she was trying to build up a relationship with the local prospective parliamentary candidate. He'd already been for a meal and she liked to believe that he had promised an invite back. This worried Philip a little as he had always voted for the country party.

"From what I gather," she said sitting down on the sofa still cradling the telephone like a small rodent, "From the Handsworths is that they hardly see anyone else now."

Charles and Diana came rushing into the room from the garden, after scratching at the French windows that Philip had opened for them and up to Elizabeth tails wagging frantically.

"I think you love those corgis more than me." Adding as he left the room, "Perhaps they're wife swapping," Philip was smiling.

"That's not funny. Come to mummy. That's right. Anyway she doesn't have a husband. I don't know what happened to him." She all too easily remembered, with the guilt that only a child making their first confession would have, the wife swapping sessions that she had been involved in. Changing partners at bedtimes. Sometimes having foursome sex, a night of frenzied animal behaviour. Changing back again in the morning before the children woke. Pretending all was normal and that she wasn't exhausted.

The whole world seemed to be at Philip and Elizabeth's gathering. This irritated Lesley no end.

"We could have brought her along."

Why he thought. We do see enough of her.

"Elizabeth has completely cooled off towards us."

" I wouldn't let that worry me."

That day for Rick was one of knowing the confusing emotions of lust and passion again. He saw a woman that he could only gaze at with a longing from afar. His eyes followed her each move. She was tallish, slim, vivacious, flowing auburn hair, jeans that hugged her frame, eyes that sparkled and a laugh that could have charmed a cadaver. He couldn't approach her. She didn't look at him once. He wished that he were a hunchback so that she might notice him but he was invisible as polished glass. He watched as she chatted away to a local head teacher who was equally as besotted. Rick had no idea who she was, where she lived, what she did. Had Christine been there, she could have told him.

Now he stood in his kitchen wondering then where all of the time had gone. It was only fifteen years or so that he had been at university with his life ahead and the thought of anything being restrictive was plainly ridiculous. He wondered what had happened to it all, the excitement, the freshness, the new boy from whom he felt that everybody expected great things. He should have at least been a senior teacher by now but already the younger recruits were beginning to catch up and he was becoming cynical like the old teachers that he said he would never become, and the cynicism would only count against him. It wasn't like running Rag Week anymore, which was the problem. He wasn't the hero anymore who people wanted to hang around. He suddenly remembered visiting a satellite college of his university as the Rag chairman and it was as if he were a pop star bestowing his benevolence on the minions.

And now his wife, it seemed, didn't want to be part of his life either. He wasn't the most important person in her life. He never had been. He'd never been the most important being in anyone's life. Perhaps that's the way it was. He remembered being with a girl to whom he had sworn undying love. They were arm in arm crossing a busy road when he looked to the left and a huge lorry was bearing down upon them. He realised that if he didn't get her off the road they would both be dead. On the pavement tearful in his arms she was unable to speak. He held her there the hero that had saved her from sure death. Three weeks later she was screwing with his best friend. From then on when the alarm went off in the morning it was always himself that he thought about first and he knew now it was the same with all people. He wasn't a hero. He could understand that Lesley had had enough. Realistically he'd had enough of her as well. There was nothing else to do, here, in their lives. They had reached a dead end. Maybe he should have married someone else. Why did he marry Lesley? Why did he stay with her and have children when he realised after six months that she was the wrong person. Why did he go in so deep, destroying not only his own life but also hers, his children's? He thought about Tara. What she was doing now, who she was married to. Did she have children? Did she ever remember him? He met a man on the beach once who told him that there was a seal out in the sea.

Looking over the man's shoulder for the seal was like looking into the past. You couldn't actually realistically see it. It had gone now. There was no point in actually conjuring up a thought of Helen. He thought about her everyday. She had cursed him that he would never forget her and how it had worked. How he longed for that time back again. The Sunday afternoon with Lesley waiting downstairs, the real witch. It ached so much in his chest that he believed he knew what a heart attack was like. Ached so much because he could not turn back the past and start all over again. He took the bottle and went and lay down on the sofa. When Hannah woke him in the morning half of the wine was left in the bottle. He desperately needed a cup of tea with plenty of sugar. As he was making it Lesley hissed at him as if she were a poisonous viper, "I'll speak to you later." At that point he decided to call school and tell them he was sick. Fuck school. Rick knew that he shouldn't have taken up the post there within hours of starting his new job as Head of Department. Yes, it was more money but with a bigger house and a higher mortgage it was less money. It had the kudos, but his department was under the umbrella of Humanities where they had lumped together religion, geography and history for some reason. It could be argued that Religion had more to do with Literature, and Geography with Science, but if you can't teach, teach people how to teach so the idea of putting them together came from some distant figure in a far place off learning. The head of humanities was also the head of geography who was by all accounts an arrogant poker faced man going by the name of Roger Fox. At Rick's interview Fox's opening gambit had been 'Tell us Mr. Sharpe, what is your philosophy of humanities?' Rick had two responses: one that he didn't know, and the second how long have you got? But he hadn't really any idea so he went for the former. He burbled his way through an answer and with help of an ally on the interviewing committee gave the appearance that he knew what he was talking about. When he'd gone for his interview in his first teaching post he'd walked into the room and a dear lady, the chairwoman of governors, had said 'now here's an interesting man. Mr. Sharpe tell us about your experiences at Taize in France.' That was the difference. One was interested in him as a human being and what he had to offer to the school. Mr. Fox was just saying 'I'm not interested in you.' He only wanted everyone to know how clever he was with his smart question. Rick knew now that he should have realised at that point that he was dealing with a pompous idiot that wanted the educational world to believe that he was god's gift to the curriculum. He should have withdrawn and gone back to his first division school with head teacher who had rightly been mentioned in the honours list, his female head of department who had treated him respect and had promised him the sixth form to teach the following September. He saw now that it was her attempt at keeping him. But here he was stuck in a third division dump of an ex secondary modern school turned comprehensive that still carried the stigma and always would. The head teacher was a man who didn't know his arse from his elbow. The only other member of Rick's Religious Studies department looked and behaved as if he'd been raised from the dead to make up the numbers, a head of history who'd been happier living in the utopia of communist Russia. And of course there was the token female teacher who rushed off at three forty five to get her husband's evening meal ready. Maybe she was the most realistic. Treating the job as a job. Knowing what was important to her. Rick would sit year after year, term after term, day after day in his classroom looking at a pile of marking that meant about as much to him as it did his students waiting for his lift home. In the winter it was dark early. In January it would rain, it couldn't even snow. Christmas and other holidays never gave any relief to the monotony. 'There's no money' she would say. Where did it all go? Rick never felt he spent any. When his lift finally arrived he went home, saw to the children when they were babies. Bathed them and put them to bed. Then he went to bed himself just before one of them woke and the whole cycle started over again. Now he could not cope anymore. He hadn't coped for a long time. It was just that nobody recognised it. Nobody cared enough to recognise it. He thought about half term. It had come and gone. It would be Christmas again soon. Christine had gone and seen her mother somewhere up north. He expected that she had seen Louise as well. Perhaps he could have gone with her. He had gone into her empty house and fed her cat. It rubbed herself against his leg. Her house was cold and very lonely. He felt just like it. He listened over and over again to old songs full of nostalgia, missed opportunity really and realised that he was alone and had been alone for a very long time.

His family left for their respective schools and he sat around drinking the rest of the bottle of wine in the empty house. He picked up a photograph from the dresser. It was of himself holding a baby. The baby was not his. He thought that it might be his niece Naomi and that the photograph had been taken at his sister's house. He looked very happy, very handsome, his hair quite long. A woman at one of their dinner parties had told him, whilst peering at the photograph through thick lenses, – 'God Rick. If I'd known you then, who knows? You look like Cat Stevens. What happened to him?' 'Well, wouldn't you now?' He'd added without going on to say that she was a frustrated middle-aged middle class housewife and that he would have never done her any favours.

He switched on the radio. A girl was singing 'It's not supposed to hurt this way I need you I need you more and more each day'. It might have been Helen singing when he'd rejected her.

He sat down glass in hand. It was probably because he was drunk, but he started to cry.

"Wot no work today Rick?" the man behind bar asked as he was pulling him a pint of the local cider later that day.

"One of these Baker days you might have heard about. We're supposed to be working at home." Rick lied between sips of the cloudy sour apple liquid wondering if the man had smelt the rest of the bottle of wine on Rick's breath when he had entered the bar.

He picked up his glass and walked to a nearby table and sat down on the fake leather that had long lost any pretence at care and comfort. The whole place was worn and had the stale smell of a century of drinking, smoking and body smells. The floor covering was dirty and pock marked with the dropping of butt ends. Lying on the seat next to him was a newspaper. He picked it up expecting it to be the usual gutter trash bought by the clientèle who frequented a place like this. To his surprise it was The Observer and not Piers petty minded junk that was the published meat and gravy for morons.

Rick leafed through the pages without really taking any notice of what he was looking at until a face caught his attention in recognition. He read the name under the photo William Hall. He went onto read the curriculum vitae that went with the article. Born the same year as Rick. Went to the same grammar school as Rick. Passed similar examinations. Then of course their paths parted. William got a first degree in biology and became an accountant. A midlands firm as a financial analyst employed him. William went to Paris two years later, ten years after that he was European controller, then he was a finance director for an European supermarket chain before returning to the United Kingdom to take on the job as the chief executive employed by Euro tunnel. The article was all about William's meteoric rise to the pinnacle of his career at a relatively young age. From his photo in the paper Rick thought that he looked like a happy man. He certainly wouldn't be half pissed in a back street bar with his life falling to pieces. They had been acquaintances at school. They had had similar opportunities. One of them had made the wrong choices. Rick put down the paper and went to the bar to buy another drink.

A few hours later he left the bar and walked home. He stood outside his house and looked across at Christine's. He sauntered up the path, pretending he didn't feel drunk, to her house and went around the back and tried the sliding French door. It was open. He went into the house that he knew quite well and walked around touching various items. He went upstairs and into Christine's bedroom. He felt very tired. He lay down on her bed. Feeling cold he got beneath the unmade duvet. He felt warm and comfortable as though it actually were Christine that loved him and were lying beside him. The next thing he knew was the gate slamming shut and Christine's voice shouting for the children to get a move on. He leapt out of bed and down then stairs out of the French window and hid by the side of the house. He waited until he heard her front door close and moved slowly down her drive. If she saw him he would pretend that he was on his way over not on his way out.

When he finally got home his wife was waiting for him. He was aware that the children weren't there. They had obviously been sent to friends' to avoid the showdown. The house was strangely silent in an eerie kind of way. Lesley was very calm.

"I just want you to leave. You are not happy. I am not happy. Together we are not making the children happy. I've packed you everything you need. I've drawn you a hundred pounds out of the bank. And you have your Visa. You will be responsible for that. So go. You can telephone later, in a few days. I've just watched you come back from Christine's. Why don't you see if she will have you? No don't. I don't want you just across the road. Ring me in a few days. Don't come back here. I mean it. It's the end for us. I'll talk to the children later. I am divorcing you."

The word divorce took him aback but he didn't show it as in his heart he knew it was the end. A large part of him was relieved. Without saying goodbye he picked up his bag and left the house. Like he was in a previous life again and every mistake he'd ever made had been made perfect.

Across the road Christine happened to be looking out of her window and saw him leave. Without being told she was well aware of what was going on.

He walked down the road without looking left or right into the town to find a bed and breakfast for a few days of lying on the bed or sitting in a bar. He was in shock.

THREE

After a breakfast of coffee and croissant, now that he had moved to France, Jonathan decided that he must get a job. This was not to be a holiday. It was the place where he was to work and live. He asked for directions to the local secondary school and went straight there. He found the office and enquired from whom he believed to be the secretary if he could see the principal. He made an appointment to meet with her the following day after explaining that he hadn't come to enrol children. He didn't look that old did he? Now the day could be a holiday so he wandered all over the small town, which didn't take him very long. He took his time over a long plat de jour and bought a new shirt, socks and underwear. He returned to his hotel in the late afternoon and slept for an hour before repeating the same exercise before he went early to bed.

The following morning he was tense. He tried to rise as late possible. He knew to avoid the wine at lunchtime even though the French often didn't and arrived promptly at the school at three o'clock as appointed.

Madame Maulin was a middle aged sleek woman. She was the epitome of charm itself. She didn't ask why a young Englishman should turn up in a country town out of the blue wanting a job. In fact she seemed almost relieved to see him.

"I arrived," she went on, "From my holidays this morning to find," she waved a piece of paper at him as if he could read the flapping words, "This! Our English assistant will not be joining us this term or ever it seems. One of your country men has convinced her of staying in England after all." She gave him a welcoming smile her eyes looking at him expectantly.

"Oh." Was all he could think to say.

"We could, I suppose, manage without one. But now you are here. A French language teacher in England you say."

"Yes."

"You have your teaching authority with you?"

"Yes, and my passport for identity."

"Good. You cannot teach here. Are you aware of that? You do not have the authority. But you can be an assistant teacher. You would like the position I expect?" She smiled. "You are all I've got so a formal interview seems pointless."

"Oh yes." He nodded his thanks.

"You seem to have been sent by God." He felt his nervousness begin to lift. "The salary is not the same as teachers receive. It is about half. You don't mind?" She didn't wait for an answer. "I must check your background to make sure that you have no criminal record. Can you provide me with references from your last school?"

"That might be difficult. I left very suddenly."

"You weren't in any kind of trouble were you?"

"No, no." Almost surprised at the question. "Nothing like that. I just left."

"Term starts in five days. If I haven't heard about you by then from your last place of work, start and we will be watching you very carefully. Do you understand? Believe me, the care of my pupils is personally important to me." She looked directly at him.

"I understand." And he added a little too dramatically, "I will not fail you."

"Well we are not fighting the English in one of our old battles!" That broke the tension that had built up in the heat of the afternoon. "Where are you staying?" Jonathan named the hotel. "You will need somewhere permanent. The hotel will be too expensive. I will introduce you to the teacher of English. She may be able to help." She paused. The interview seemed to be over.

"Thank you. When shall I return?"

"Oh yes. I forgot, on Friday at 10am. All the staff meets then."

He left the school with a tremendous surge of joy. He could hardly believe his luck. He decided to celebrate.

That night Madame Maulin told her husband about the Englishman who had turned up out of nowhere and had gone some way towards saving their lives so that they could fulfil the curriculum as required by the French authorities.

"If he lives up to my expectations then he will be very good."

"You have a penchant for attracting these males. Is he good looking?"

"Of course! But not as handsome as you Didier." She kissed him lightly on the cheek and then returned to her Phillippe Delerm.

"Good book?"

"Yes. He is a very good writer. I wonder if I could get him to come into school and speak to the older students. I don't know why, but I think he is a nice man who would if asked."

"Hm. Maybe a first priority would be to find out more about this Englishman who just turned up. How do know he's not some sort of mad axe man or more seriously a man who could compromise the children. It could reflect very badly on you. What was he called?"

"Jonathan something or other...don't tell me my job. But you are right. I will telephone the school that he claims he taught in England first thing tomorrow morning. It's always so busy at the beginning of a term."

"And it never gets any better as the term goes on. Thought about retiring?"

"No. But I am thinking about sleeping." She closed her book. Turned off her bedside light and said, "Goodnight. Don't read for long."

On Friday the receptionist intercepted Jonathan as he entered the school for the meeting of all the staff. 'Madame Maulin wants to see you,' she told him. He hoped beyond hope that it was not bad news. He knocked on her office door. He entered. She didn't ask him to be seated. He stood like a child ready to be reprimanded and expected the worst.

"I have talked to your employment in England and they tell me, as you said, you left very suddenly," he went to speak but she raised a hand to stop him and carried on, "There is no question of your conduct within the school. There was no problem. But I repeat I cannot be let down. We cannot arrive at school and find that you simply do not turn up. Do you have something to tell me? That I should know about?"

Jonathan explained everything that he was afraid of marriage. That he was just not ready. That it had nothing to do with his teaching, which he enjoyed. She seemed fairly satisfied with his answer and asked him whether he had written to his fiancée and parents explaining how he felt and where he was.

"No." He shook his head sadly genuinely distressed.

"You owe it to them. And they may be worried."

So he wrote. He never received a reply from anyone. He assumed that he was never forgiven.

FOUR

June rattled round the empty house like the remaining dead body in a forgotten mortuary. Even though it was a council house on a busy council estate in the middle of a big city populace she would always feel alone, now. It hadn't been long that her husband Bill had been alive. In his final illness though he'd been hard work. Just a few weeks before Bill had died she'd lost her father, though he'd been batty for the last year of his life. Fortunately she'd been able to off load him onto her daughter in the 'granny flat' and still had what remained of the old man's money, as she was next of kin, rather than share it. She wasn't going to go and live there. Not that they would want her anyway. A least she had his bit of cash. She had quite a lot of money now and enjoyed seeing the three pensions enter her bank account and the amount going in always greater than the amount going out. She could offer her niece's trips to New York all expenses paid and pull out at the last minute blaming the doctor for saying that she wasn't really up to it. She had contentment about her as long as she looked good, benevolent and impressed people. June would leave a will. She'd seen to that. Her solicitor was Mr. North. She liked Mr. North and he liked her. He always knew who she was and would say '*Why* hello June,' as though it was his greatest pleasure in life to see her. She was obviously a very important customer. She never paid him anything. He had told her that it would all be settled when she died, 'Long may you last,' as though he were proposing a toast and laughed, 'By the deeds of the will.' And when June fell out with one of her children he was always happy to change the will, 'No trouble at all,' he would say.

June had got her funeral arranged as well with the local family firm of undertakers Witts and Wutteridge. Went back ages they did. Their whole name conjured up images of top hats and plumed horses in Victorian times. Mr. Wutteridge had been to see her and it was all done. A small amount was paid from her bank each month into a fund that the firm controlled and it was all guaranteed and paid for. She could die tomorrow and the family would have no worries. He, Mr. Wutteridge, had seen to Bill's funeral as well. Her Father's had been in the north so they had to have someone else. It wasn't a very good funeral. Rick having a tantrum and behaving, as he was still five, because of an argument with his wife about his drinking. It was the last time he'd seen Bill as well. But Bill didn't really know what was going on. She knows that Rick was drunk on her father's funeral just like he was at Bill's. She hadn't been with Bill when he died. She hoped that he didn't feel too alone. On the way to the crematorium in the black family car Rick was talking to his brother about some book by Bao Ninh, Why had that name stuck with her? Because it upset her that they weren't watching Mr.

Wutteridge leading the procession down the road in front of the hearse walking regally and carrying a top hat. She could feel the eyes of her neighbours on her. Poor June they were saying, one day that will be us and we will bear the sorrow honourably like the Queen Mother and June. She didn't hear them laugh as the procession was rounded off with her son-in law following up in a Lada. It was probably going at top speed they said.

Sometimes in the night though she woke and there was silence pervading her every pore and she wished that she could hear a baby cry out. She wished she could have the family life, the fun, and the laughs all over again. Where did it all go? Will she sit in a chair she wondered, incontinent and confused? Is life only about looking back to the previous best and reliving it?

FIVE

Helen knew that she had little or no hope of even gaining his attention. She was not much over seventeen; he was twenty-one. All the difference between a child and an adult she believed. He had the assurance of maturity whilst she had barely left school. Though still at night she would lie in her bed thinking only of him and agonising warmth spread through her body. And there was of course also the other female. He'd had a long-standing relationship with a woman. She was a nurse Helen thought. They were always seen together at university gigs and discos. It was common knowledge that they were living together. Rick's girl, Tara, was tall quite elegant with a figure that had everything in the right place and proportion Helen thought. They appeared to be devoted to each other. And she, Helen, at the local sixth form college on a secretarial course, in her opinion had none of these attributes. She was of very average height with shoulder length black hair that did nothing for her and to cap it all she wore glasses, which for Helen was a total put off for any member of the opposite sex.

A notice had appeared on the board of her college:
'Wanted for Rag Week next term. Any helpers with great ideas...'
It went to a lot of other blurb about raising money for charity and so on.

Added in hand at the bottom was written, 'We desperately need a girl Friday/secretary who can type'. Rick Sharpe signed it and put chairman by his name. This was the boy Helen had been infatuated with for so long. Rick. Helen's heart pounded as she read the notice and she felt as if she'd had a sudden rush of nicotine. The notice gave a telephone number to ring at the Teen University students' union office. She searched through her bag for change so that she could call. She must get that job before anyone else. She wasn't sure what being a 'girl Friday' entailed but she could certainly type. She would then be at his side probably once a week for the next few months. She had no change, only a note. She looked around the area, there were plenty of students' but probably most of them broke.

"Can anyone change a pound? " She shouted out to anyone who cared to listen.

People stopped and looked at her as if she were raving.

"What's the problem Hel? '

'I need 10p. I've got to make a phone call. It's urgent. "

"Can't change a pound. Don't have that kind of money." He laughed and she didn't. "But you can have this." She snatched the coin from his hand. "Hey, patience. You'll owe me a pint Hel. Perhaps tonight?"

"Yeh. Thanks. Okay." Helen bolted over to the phone box as though her life depended on it.

He yelled after her retreating figure, "See you at eight? In the bar?"

I wouldn't be seen dead with the spotty youth she thought.

As always whenever it was desperate there was someone using the phone looking as though they were to inhabit the box until it became Friday. Finally Helen stood very close to the door and coughed twice to make her presence noticed. After an eternity the receiver was returned to its cradle.

"Ta," said Helen to the rather large and ugly blonde in an afghan who ignored her striding away full of self-importance. Helen's heart was pounding with anticipation. Two minutes from now she could be speaking to Rick. Tall, broad shouldered, hippy haired and charisma exuding Rick. Her fantasy. She lifted the receiver. "Bugger", she thought. She hadn't written the number down. Great secretary she'd make. She left the box and went quickly back to the notice board. Fumbled for a pen in her bag and wrote the number on the back of her hand.

"Goin' for that are you?" said the spotty youth. "You must be crazy. Looks like hard work for nothing. See you at eight. Students' bar at the Teen." He thought he ought to make sure that she'd heard.

"Yeh okay," replied Helen with no intention of being there.

Back at the phone she rang the number.

"Students' Union Office," said a rather officious voice that sounded as if she'd been put through to a traffic warden's convention.

"Is Rick Sharpe there? Please." She sounded as though she were pleading with him.

"No. Sorry. We do go to lectures sometimes you know."

"How can I get hold of him?"

"Fancy him do you?"

Blushing she replied firmly, "Certainly not!"

Laughing the anonymous voice said, "It's just that you said you wanted to hold him. Only joking duck."

Stumbling over her words now Helen replied, "No. I just want to speak to him."

"Well he's not here."

"Any idea when he will be?"

"Hang on." She heard him shout away from the mouthpiece, "Stevi. Some girl wants Rick. Any ideas." Helen then heard a female voice in the background. "Stevi says that Rick told her he was going to the bar at around eight tonight."

"The bar?"

"The bar here, at the Teen. You might see him here tonight."

"Right. I want to be the Rag Week Secretary." She said rather too enthusiastically.

"Oh. Bully for you. " She detected more than a hint of sarcasm in his voice and she felt foolish until he added more kindly, "Do you know what he looks like?"

"Yes." No doubt.

To be sure of seeing him Helen arrived at the bar soon after seven. That was after a shower; her mothers' Avon perfume. Her hair brushed until it shone. Wearing the bra that an aunt had bought her for Christmas and was supposed to do all the right things to her breasts. Though what it did for her she couldn't rightly see. Her lecherous uncle said 'give us a fashion show then' as she had unwrapped the gift. He'd already had too much too drink early on Christmas day. She'd put in the back of a drawer. No male had seen her wear it yet and the way she felt probably never would. Hug fit denims that she didn't realise showed her newly formed figure as if she were naked and a loose cheesecloth shirt that contained the promise of what may be.

"You look a bit dressed up," said her mother, "Seeing a boy?"

"All dressed up and nowhere to go," laughed her Dad.

And no one to see Helen's mother thought. Though she didn't know whether she was pleased with that thought or not. "Don't be too late," she said.

"No, home before the last bus. You don't know who will be on it," Added her dad because he felt that he had to.

Yes I do. Jack the Ripper lives down our street, thought Helen.

The bar was virtually empty and Helen bought herself an orange juice and sat down. Time passed slowly. The bar had a clean and polished feel to it after the lunchtime session. Slade were 'Far Far Away' on the jukebox. She looked at her watch repeatedly and every time someone entered she looked up hoping it was Rick and finally at five to eight the spotty youth came in.

"Hey Hel, you're here waiting! I could have got here earlier if I'd known!" He sounded extraordinarily surprised. "My mates said you wouldn't turn up. Won a bet I have. What you want to drink Hel?"

"Nothing. I'm fine." Please go away she said inwardly.

"Naw. Come on," the youth retorted, "It's our first date after all."

I'm going to be sick she thought. "Okay. An orange juice."

"Naw. Something stronger. Girls like Babycham," as if speaking to himself. "A Babycham," he shouted across to the barman, miming a cowboy in an old Western movie that he'd watched by himself on a Saturday morning at the children's cinema, "And a pint for me," he added firmly. After paying, he put the drinks on the table. "You don't know my name do you?" He said to Helen.

"No."

"Malcolm."

"Oh. *That is nice.* I owe you ten pence. Here you are."

"Naw. Forget it Hel. Feeling generous tonight." Self-conscious he chortled at his own feeble attempt at humour. She left the money where it lay on the table. "You do typing don't you? Click click." He mimed a typist and laughed. Helen didn't. He acted out something else. "Guess what I do?" Helen said nothing. She lacked the confidence to say a wanker. "I'm bricklaying. Good eh?"

"Oh."

"Great to see you though Hel. Didn't think you'd turn up. My mates said you wouldn't. I've won a bet."

Suddenly she felt a change in the atmosphere sensing that Rick had arrived. She looked over at him. He hadn't noticed her. He was dressed in yellow cotton trousers, red platform boots and a t-shirt showing Dylan circa 1965 in a pink jacket. She would have never approached Rick and it would have been a night of frustratingly beating a pillow into fitful sleep asking herself why she hadn't spoken to him but now she would do almost anything to get away from Malcolm.

"Excuse me I've just got go and have a word with someone."

"Oh yeh the rag bloke. Don't worry yourself Hel, I'll still be here when you get back."

Helen got up from the table hoping that Rick hadn't heard Malcolm and walked towards him. He had his back to her sipping from his glass. His broad shoulders covered with his clean long hair and his trim figure made her feel weak at the knees. She stood behind him for a moment though it seemed an age until he became aware of her presence. She would learn to recognise those shoulders anywhere. He turned round and looked down at her.

"Sorry. Am I in your way?" he said, smiling.

"No. You are Rick Sharpe? The one who put the notice up about Rag Week?"

"Yes. Are you the secretary? God I hope so. Stevi mentioned it. That you might be in here tonight."

"Well I saw you needed someone from the secretarial course to help out."

"Well anyone really. No one wants to volunteer for anything that might involve work. And you're willing?"

Aren't I just? "Yes."

"That's great. We can never get anyone to do that."

"It'll be a good experience for me."

"Yes, I'm sure. Look, can I get you a drink?"

"No thank you. I've already got one." She gestured towards Malcolm and the Baycham. Malcolm smiled and waved and she saw her mistake.

"Ah, okay. Well look we meet two weeks on Friday, at the Student union offices, seven-thirty? Can you make that? She nodded. "Great. Well I won't keep you from your boyfriend. Essays to write myself." He finished his drink in one long draft. "Bye."

"Bye Rick."

"Ah yes. What's your name? Sorry I should have asked earlier."

"Helen."

"Helen I'll endeavour to remember." She already loved the way he said her name. "Bye then Helen. Till next time." He turned and left the bar with a friend.

"Who was that?"

"Just some chick that's stupid enough to be the rag week secretary."

"Well, she can be my secretary when she likes. Hope you know what to do with her."

"I'll think of something."

Helen walked back to Malcolm. At the sight of him anger churned inside her.

"Okay then Hel. Got the job! Finish your drink and I'll get us another and then we could go and get some chips to celebrate so we'll always remember our first date."

"My name's Helen. Hell is where I wish you would go to." She paused. "Or quicker, go and jump off a high bridge." She allowed that to sink into Malcolm's brain. "And I hate Babycham. Here. You have it." She poured the glass of the stuff into his lap and left. "You won't forget that."

Rick spent most of his nights with Tara but still kept a room near the centre of town. After his meeting with Helen he, unusually for him, went back to his own room. He shared a house with six other girls; his own room with a good friend who was a homosexual. They were surprised to see him and after some banter about being a single man again he went to his own room, lay on the bed and let the songs of Leonard Cohen drift across the atmosphere and pass through his mind. He didn't feel as content as he should. He had a long standing relationship with a beautiful girl whom he thought he loved; he was Rag chairman which was good for the ego and he was working hard enough to gain a reasonable degree in Theology. He turned the record over, switched out the light and lay down again and watched as the occasional car headlight caught the posters of Laurel and Hardy and Don't Look Back. 'Tonight Will Be Fine', the singer told him but somehow it wasn't. Rick was asleep when his friend Jeremy returned from his job at the cinema and was surprised to see Rick there. He turned the stereo off pleased that he hadn't brought anyone home with him.

In another part of town in another room in another bed Tara lay awake listening for the footsteps on the stairs. Rick usually rang when he couldn't come over. She missed him. She wanted his strong arms around her body. He usually held her all night long. Tara should sleep; she had an early shift in the morning. Perhaps she would wake in the dawn and find him there.

Helen also lay awake like a child waiting for Christmas morning. Perhaps this was only schoolgirl infatuation and she should snap out of it, she told herself. Wondering if she should have Malcolm as a boyfriend but to allow that spotty face near her was repellent.

And as Malcolm was drifting off to sleep he was wondering if he did indeed understand girls. After all he'd only lived with the opposite sex, his mother and his grandma. Grandma had died now. Not so long ago and so he still missed her. And aunts had come to visit. But they had dominated him. So yes it went without saying that he understood the fairer sex. His mother screamed with rage at him sometimes and he didn't know why that was. But she still loved him. She told him so. When she came into his bedroom and said that she was sorry. Even though he was nearly eighteen and just about finished his apprenticeship. He didn't tell people who didn't know him that he was a trainee apprentice. He told them that he went to the university. They didn't usually ask what it was that he was studying. Really he was just like that student bloke they had met earlier in the bar at the university. Well he hadn't met him, Hel had, but that student bloke had thought that he was Hel's boyfriend. Hel's boyfriend, he liked the sound of that. He knew that inside she fancied him, she just hadn't seen it yet but he had. She certainly hadn't liked that student type with his long hair and red platform boots, a right queer. It was written all over her face. She just needed the experience, that's what all this Rag Week stuff was about. He couldn't wait to introduce her to his mum. Mum this is Helen. She is on a secretarial course at the university. He would tell his mum that he had a girlfriend in the morning. Cheer her up before she went to work. She'd be able to tell her mates. Malc wouldn't treat her the way that his 'dad' had treated his mum. He had left her before Malc was even born. He sometimes wondered if he passed him in the street and that they didn't even recognise each other. Or had they? Perhaps he was the man that he had said 'morning' to but he hadn't known was really his dad. But he'd said 'morning' to plenty of men early in the day when there was a feeling of bonhomie that didn't last beyond eight thirty. That man had left her with nothing just grandma. They never talked about granddad and he never asked. The three of them had lived in a two up two down-terraced house. Two years ago they'd moved to this new council house. Their old house was still waiting to be knocked down to make way for a new road scheme. He had heard that student's were squatting in his old house. Malc had loved that home even though he'd had to share a room with his mum until he was thirteen. Some nights she didn't come home. At school he told the other kids that his dad had a job in Saudi Arabia and that he sent home lots of money. Malc told them that he only came home during the holidays so consequently 'friends' were never invited to his house. He couldn't show the lack of father but also couldn't display the palace that he supposedly lived in. He lived a lie or quite simply where nothing of significance was ever spoken about. He'd had a lonely childhood but the two women had doted on him. His mother worked at the lager factory mixing chemicals for the populace to drink and grandma was always there when he came home from school. His mother had wanted the best for him and had pushed him towards a job that needed training. Like all parents she believed that she had spawned a genius but ultimately came to the realisation as she read between the lines of his reports, 'tries hard but…' or 'should have a stable future…' The careers teacher knowing all about Malcolm's lack of academic brainpower suggested bricklaying, 'People always need somewhere to live' he told their eager faces at the final parents evening before Malcolm left the school to go to the technical college. Yes, as he lay there not sleeping because of his excitement at the day's events. Who would have thought it? She turned up, that said everything. They would make a great pair. They would get one of those new houses in the west of the town. Or perhaps he would even build one. He would work hard perhaps having his own business one day. She could be his secretary or even a school secretary. He could say 'my wife's a secretary' and people would be impressed. After a few years she would stop working and they would start a proper family. They had a funny way of showing you that they really did fancy you. Helen was playing hard to get he decided. He'd bought her a drink but had left the bar looking as though he'd wet himself. Well it showed some emotion, he thought, and perhaps she just didn't have his experience. Malcolm would pass her a note tomorrow saying how sorry he was.

In an English exam Malcolm wrote how his father would always buy his mother flowers. His father was different from other men. Other men were jealous because of their wives and the burden of demanding children. Malcolm alone listened to the silence and watched the flowers wilt.

The next morning when Rick went down stairs to make a cup of tea Stevi was already there. She feigned surprise.

"Oh, you slept here last night. Getting a bit fed up with nursie are we? Stopped wearing the uniform?"

Rick gave her a look as if he didn't understand and wouldn't sully love that way anyway. "No. I just had some work to do."

"Oh yes." Stevi had a way of answering a question that wasn't exactly sarcastic at all but somehow showed that she knew that you weren't quite telling the truth. "There's tea in the pot Rick. Drink up and I'll give you a lift in when I'm dressed."

Stevi was a mature student. By mature this meant that she was about six years older than the usual student. Stevi was the matriarch of the house in her incense smelling Biba room. But she also got them an incredible reduction on the rent. Each only paid about £3 a month.

"So," said Stevi as she stood leaning against the kitchen side wrapping her silk dressing gown about herself, "You really imagine spending the rest of your life with this nurse..."

"Tara."

"Yes, Tara," She mused half gazing at a corner of the room as if she saw a vision there. "Semi detached suburbia. Two and a half children."

"Two and a half?" He was speculating which half they'd get.

"Yes it's the average family size. Dope brain." Stevi was a sociology student.

Rick smiled. "I was wondering."

"Well?" She hugged the mug to herself as if to warm her.

"What?"

"Rick you're evading the question."

"Yes. Of course." Rick didn't sound desperately convincing and they both knew it. "Sounds okay to me."

"You haven't lived boy. Perhaps you never will. Hurry up and I'll give you that lift." She swept regally out of the kitchen with her toast and tea.

Malc still in a state of excitement rushed downstairs to catch his mother before she left for work at the factory.

"Mum, guess what? I've got a girlfriend."

"That's nice. What's she called?"

"Hel – Helen." He'd decided that Helen sounded more sophisticated. She nodded whilst adjusting her lipstick in the mirror above what should have been the fireplace in a house of paraffin heaters. "I'm going to ask her to marry me."

"That's nice. Bring her for tea and I'll buy some Mr Kiplings," she said as she picked up her handbag and hurried out of the house so as not to miss her bus.

Rick looked out at the unkempt garden and the tenement houses. In a window he could see a mother fiercely brushing a child's hair. He stared and wondered.

SIX

Rick leant against the cool pale tiled wall in a London underground station people watching and dreaming. His wife and children were buying rail tickets and getting the information as to which line they needed. He'd never understood the system and considered that in all probability he would have been hopelessly lost without his family. There were more people here he thought than you saw when his small town centre, where he lived in Devon, was at its busiest. Quite suddenly the sight of five surgeons coming through the barrier, dressed as if ready to operate there and then, finally completely captured his attention taking him off his guard. One of them approached him waving a bucket under his nose. As if in a past dream the mask spoke "Wanna buy a Rag Mag?" Rick felt through his pockets and found a pound that his wife had missed and dropped it into the bucket taking the proffered comic. He didn't bother to look at it. The 'surgeons' were so young. He was old enough to be their father. He felt poignant nostalgia for their high spirits. He felt embarrassed for them as he remembered himself just years before. How foolish he must have looked and behaved believing that he was so important, but was really very egotistical. He didn't really like to remember the past. It held too many memories, painful, yet a time that he would love to live through again. He would have changed the way his life turned out if he had known the future. Thinking about how that time now often hurt him. And he did think and fantasise. He would wake alone in the night full of remorse and regret. He walked over to a bin and dropped the Mag in.

"What was that?" his wife demanded when he returned to her where she was waiting full of importance and impatience. Her face now slightly plump and quite red to what it had been when he first knew her.

"Nothing. Advertising bumf. Do you know where we're going? As usual I don't."

Jonathan had lain awake all night. Or at least for Jonathan it felt like that. Stars in his hallucinations were even appearing onto the ceiling of his bedroom. As the gloom gave into some kind of light he knew that it was time to leave his bed. It was the day of his marriage. This bedroom, the smallest in the house, had been the favourite of the children that had lived there. On its wall were posters from a previous era, skeletons of Grateful Dead and a Pink Floyd concert for 2/6d. This space was tatty now like the rest of the house, though his mother might have favoured the words 'lived in'. It was kept in a state worthy of people who preferred to spend any extra money they had at the pub. He got up, dressed for the day, splashed some water on his face and gave his teeth a cursory brush. Downstairs in the kitchen he waited for the kettle to boil. He looked at the decoration. It had been orange gloss for as long as he could remember and it had needed a second coat first time around. You could tell that from the swirls and green showing through in patches. It would be easy to wipe down his mother had said but that clean was well overdue seeing the amount of fried food that had been prepared in the room. Nothing was state of art. He laughed at the phrase. The room and its fittings were still like the council had put in a couple of years before he was born. Quite longing for a cup of sweet tea. He didn't have a hangover. His mother hadn't allowed the party to drink too much the night before, not with the day ahead. The dog moved around in a whining anticipation of a walk. One of his masters was dressed already. Jonathan switched on the radio. 'Wide-eyed and legless' he sang, 'I've gone and done it again.' As he stood sipping the scalding tea he heard the toilet flush and footsteps on the stairs. The top step always creaked giving the game away. How many times he had silently entered the house and made it to top of the stairs before his mother shouted, "Is that you Jonathan?" He often wondered if she was expecting someone else. His father entered the room, his chested a mat of hair. There was nothing modest about the flies of his pyjamas.

"Turn that off. You'll wake the house." He waited until the song had disappeared. The old man was chewing on his gums. "You alright boy?"

"Yes fine. You want a cup of tea?"

"No I'll wait until the teasmade."

"Might take the dog for a walk. Be nice and quiet this time in the morning."

Jonathan wanted to ask him what he'd done with his life. He was sixty-three and probably only had ten or fifteen years left to live at the most. Did he feel that he had achieved anything? Was getting married and having children enough? Was there really point to it all? Were they any different to the insect that was trod underfoot? His Father would look at him though with a pained expression that said 'Everything I've done I've done it for my family, all the sacrifices that I have made'. Or was it just that you couldn't think of anything else to do Dad? His question would be misunderstood though.

"Okay." He ambled off back upstairs to his bed.

Jonathan put his jacket on and patted his pockets. He had all he needed. He checked them again. Attaching the lead to the dog and shushing him as the animal went into a frenzy of excited barking, they left the house and walked down the street. Most of the curtains were still drawn and it was if the whole world had forgotten to wake up. A cat looked with disdain at the dog and licked her paw as if to say no one chains me. I go where I like and I'm still fed. At the bottom of the street the hill overlooked the city. Smoke rose from an industrial chimney. He stroked the dog's head and rubbed him behind his ears as he loved. He tied the dog to a nearby fence and walked towards the smoke.

When the man at the bottom of the road left for work that Saturday morning he saw that there was dog tied to the railings of his house. Initially ignoring it he realised that it was

Jasper from up the road. He hurried back into the house and called one of the children to take it back.

"What's it doing there?" asked his wife as if husbands know the answers to the origins of the universe.

"No idea. Must go. I'm late already."

A few minutes later the doorbell rang at Jasper's house and Jonathan's parent's looked at one another as they sat in bed sipping scalding tea.

"Who can that be at this time in the morning. Post?"

"Lover boy," said his father. "Forgotten his key. Mind you he's got a lot to think about today." He went downstairs and opened the door. 'Come...' He stopped as he realised he was talking to a child and Jasper wagging his tail in recognition.

"Me dad told me to bring him back."

"Bring him back. Where was he?"

"Tied to our gate."

"Tied to your gate?"

"Yeh. Bye." The boy thought he'd leave quickly as the man obviously had something wrong with him where he had to repeat everything he said.

"Hang on a minute." He went and got the child 50p. He shut the door, patted the dog, went upstairs and told his wife what had happened. Jasper must have got away and someone tied him up there they decided. "Jonathan ull be out looking for him. Do you think I ought to go and look for him?"

"And have everybody looking for each other? No I'll get his brother up in a while. He can go. Let's give him time to get back home. Pass the time a bit for him anyway 'till he has to get ready." She took another swallow of tea and placed the cup back on her bedside cabinet with a satisfied look on her face that expressed to the world all was well with it and would be well.

In the city Jonathan made his way to the railway station. He wanted to get away as far away from the bottom half of England as possible. A single ticket, to stop and pause, think for a few days, make decisions.

"What now?" his mother exclaimed as the phone rang. "This is like Clapham Junction today." Though she would have been disappointed if it had been otherwise.

Jonathan's father got out of bed and went downstairs saying "Well it would be today," in a resigned voice but enjoying the situation all the same.

She lay in bed and listened.

"866334. Jonathan? Where are you? Jasper's here. Yes, he's okay. *I am listening.*"

"No Dad. You haven't let me say anything yet. I can't do this. I've got to get away. I'm at the train station now and the train is about to go. I'm sorry." Without giving his father the opportunity to reply he put the receiver down and went to board the train leaving him standing in the hallway looking at the 'phone as if it were somehow to blame.

"Who was that?" Shouted Jonathan's mother from her bed.

Sitting in the carriage as it gathered speed was like a rebirth tugging him easily from everything that had lain in his way in the past. It soon left the city to the suburbs and into the countryside. The east line would take him north. He had bought a ticket to Edinburgh but he could get off anywhere. That would do for the moment.

SEVEN

As Jonathan was travelling North Christine lay in her bed wide-awake listening for the sound of her parents leaving the house. Firstly her father left. She even heard her mother say "Sh. You'll wake Christine and Steve. He's got a long journey today." And she laughed to herself. If they knew why she was awake. Finally the front door clicked silently as her mother went after him. She waited fifteen minutes to make sure that she had gone and definitely wouldn't return. She watched the clock his hand moving very slowly. One day, she thought she would only have fifteen minutes left to live. But that was a long way off. She thought about Steve and how she had first met him. It was on a cold and rainy October morning Christine sat without company in the campus coffee bar sipping a cup of tea sitting as close as she could to her target. Listening to him talk with a group of friends he was deliberating on the excellence of the newest Crosby Stills Nash and Young offering. That afternoon Christine bought her first ever cassette and second hand player, hoping that it would work, from the a junk shop and taking it back to her room she listened intently so she virtually knew every song word for word. Fortunately she liked it. If she hadn't she would have probably had to look elsewhere for the father of her children. Many years later she would have cause to reflect that might have been better for all if Steve had been expounding on the excellence of Showaddywaddy on that day.

Within weeks they were an item and living together. She knew enough to play hard to get for a while so that he was about to explode, and sensing when she lit the short fuse she moved out of university hall and into his bed-sit. Her Father should have paid her grant and didn't, so it meant that two really did live as cheaply as one as Steve received the full grant. But her parent's weren't totally mean. They saw the benefits in some ventures. They had paid for Christine to go to America to visit her English cousin, who had newly settled there and needed an English visitor from 'back home'.

The time had passed. She knew that Steve would be sleeping. He could fall asleep on a washing line. She went via the toilet to his bedroom and stood by his bed watching the gentle rise of his chest as he slept on his back. He looked far from dead. She slipped her long t-shirt from over her head and stood teasing the unconscious male. Gently she slipped back his bedclothes and saw his erection. She wondered for a moment what he had been dreaming about. She would wake him with a surprise. Quickly and deftly she sat astride him and slipped his penis into her vagina.

"What…?"

"Oh. Where you asleep? Come on we haven't got long and you've a train to catch. And I expect you'll want breakfast as well."

EIGHT

In a large modern middle class home in the Midlands of England as the train did its job carrying Jonathan north there was a chaos of organised activity. The room was full of furnishings as synthetic as the people themselves. Then there was silence as the 'phone rang. The family stopped what they were doing as if they were caught in a photograph. Jonathan hoped Lesley in an excited anticipation of the years to come. Her mother picked up the 'phone and listened for a moment before giving it to her husband saying, "He wants to talk to you."

"Who?" enquired Lesley looking directly at her sister, "Jonathan?"

"Wait. Jonathan's father," her mother mouthed and moved over to her daughter sensing the news that any bride dreads. Her Father replaced the 'phone in its cradle quite deliberately and carefully controlling his fury.

"The bastard..."

"Who?"

They all knew whom. She was just hoping.

"The bastard's done a runner. I'll kill him. The money I've spent..."

"Money! I want my Jonathan."

He moved over to his daughter and him already dressed to give his speech. He hadn't touched her for many years so he didn't know how to.

"I know my baby. And you shall have him." Though in how many pieces he hadn't decided.

When the train got to Durham Jonathan decided to get out but the train pulled away before he could gather his thoughts properly so he had to go onto Newcastle. 'The fog on the Tyne is all mine all mine,' he sang to himself. He looked around and the station was cavernous like one would expect the epitome of a Victorian station to be. Its throb of artery seemed to be life itself almost as if the focal of the universe were there.

He decided to stay. And after a pint of Newcastle Brown he thought that he should look for somewhere to sleep that night. After he had settled that he could start to make his other plans, if there were any. As he left the station bar a girl was waving to someone on a train as it pulled out going south. She turned and they virtually fell over one another.

"Sorry. That's okay," they said at the same time and laughed.

"Actually," Rick said, "Are you local? Do you live here? Not in the station, I mean the city. Are you a, what do they call them? A Geordie?"

"That's right pet. A Geordie. I can tell you're a foreigner."

"Would you know of a good place to stay and that's not a chat up line."

"It wouldn't make any difference if it was. I'd still knee you in the balls if I didn't like it. We're like that here." She smiled to show she didn't mean it but might if pushed. "There's the station hotel next door. But it's expensive. Nice though. If you like that kind of thing."

"Fancy a drink there? You could show me the way."

"Ah, go on."

They left the station and he followed her lead to the hotel. They went into the bar and were silent until he asked her what it was she would like to drink.

"Gin and tonic."

He brought the drinks back and appraised her for a moment. She was small. Not a lot over five feet, very long dark hair and really quite beautiful.

"You don't have much luggage for a travelling salesman. In fact you don't appear to have any."

"I'm not a travelling salesman."

"No? You surprise me."

"I was to get married today."

"Now you do surprise me. Here a bouts?"

"Cheltenham Spa."

"Never heard of it. Though anywhere south of Durham doesn't exist. Good for the waters eh?"

"Probably, but not today I think."

"So a jilted bride and what are you, hardly a fiancé? Bastard? I'm getting married in two weeks. I was just waving bye bye to mine. He won't jilt me. He knows I'd have his balls."

"You do a lot with balls don't you."

"Either way. I enjoy it."

They sipped at their drinks neither now knowing where the conversation was going. Two years ago they might have gone off on a date and got married. What is it, he thought, that puts people along certain tracks and makes them get off at certain stations and meet and marry certain people. Surely if the human being is unique there should be the infinite number of opportunities to experience everything.

"Penny for your thoughts," she said.

"I was just thinking that this place does look expensive."

"Well you've all day. In fact from the sounds of it, you have the rest of your life to look."

A well suited smart haired young man passed them at that point and almost with a sneer said, "Why hello Christine. We don't often see you in here."

"Hello Marvin. I just about made it with the dress code today."

"Oh I say. New boyfriend?" Giving Jonathan a smile that turned his stomach.

"No. Friend from university."

Full of disbelief, "Oh yes."

"Do you know what a university is Marvin?"

"Of course and I'm not even a long haired layabout. I work," and looking at his watch as if he had an appointment that would save the world said, "Must rush. Can't stand here all day gossiping. Bye."

"That was a bit short wasn't it," said Jonathan, "Not a friend of yours I take it."

"Well at least I haven't left him at the altar. Mind you I did tell him to jump off the Tyne Bridge once."

"Why?"

"He wanted a date. He's a friend of my brothers'. My brother and his friends all look as though they should belong to the Young Conservatives."

"I take it then, that your brother didn't go to university."

"Goodness no. He's in Australia making a fortune. That's what he would like anyway."

"So his bed's empty."

"No. No." She said emphatically. "I've known you for," she looked at her watch as if checking the time precisely, "Twenty minutes. You obviously aren't a very nice person." She smiled sweetly. "Well maybe."

"I could be the friend from university. Just turned up."

"Get me another drink and I'll think about it." He returned with gin and tonic. "I wanted ice and lemon. I was too polite to say first time." He gave her a look but returned, as requested, to the bar with the drink. "Here's what we'll do," she said pausing to take a sip, "Hang around here in the town for the day. There's plenty to see. If you haven't found anywhere else ring me at five. Me mam 'ull be home from the post office then..."

"Takes her all day to buy a few stamps?"

"She works there." She looked at him and didn't smile.

"Carry on."

"I'm trying to." He grinned, falling in love. There was something familiar about this girl. "And I'll tell her you've just turned up. You can only stay for a couple of nights."

"Okay."

"Here's my number. But it will only be a couple of nights," she emphasised again. "Or I'll blow your cover and my dad won't take kindly to that." She finished her drink. "I'm going."

"How will I get to you?"

"If you're lucky me mam 'ull come and pick you up. If not a taxi." Looking at him as if to say you've got a brain, use it. "And buy something that looks as if you have some luggage."

NINE

Helen was eating a packet of crisps and drinking a can of fizzy drink in the last of the warm September sunshine, when she became aware of a gawky lanky boy towering over her spreading a chill.

"Malc asked me to give you this."

God, this is like primary school she thought. She took the envelope from him and opened it. The missive read, 'Dear Helen, Sorry about last night. I didn't realise that you didn't like Babycham so if you go out with me I'll buy you something else. Lots of love and kisses, Malc. PS. My mates call me Malc so you can to. I won't call you Hel again. Love again Malc.'

The graceless boy was obviously waiting for a reply. She looked up at him and said, "Tell him what I said about the bridge, I meant."

The boy looked delighted. Malcolm's lack of conquest would obviously be common knowledge amongst the trainee builders that afternoon.

Helen screwed up the letter and threw it away. Still one love letter was better than none.

After an hour of staring into space in the university library Rick went over to Tara's that night. He let himself into the house and as he opened the door to her bedsit he shouted, "Only me."

"What happened to you last night Rick?" Tara was still in her uniform. The sink a jumble of dishes though she'd been home sometime. She smelt faintly of chloroform.

"Sorry." He kissed her on the cheek as she moved away. "I finished late at the library. An essay to meet a deadline."

"What about?"

He thought for a moment. "Theories for the existence of God." Rick was studying theology. She didn't pursue the subject any further. "You look a bit done in. Why don't we both go and have a bath and then go to bed?"

"No. You wash the dishes."

A year ago she would have been dragging Rick into the bath with her.

She bathed. He washed the dishes. Rick stood with his arms nearly up to his elbows in the warm suds whilst Melanie went to Carolina in her mind. Rick went with her. He remembered well meeting Tara. Philip, a friend, took eight of them, in his van, to the Chichester folk festival. Tara was the only non-student who went along with a giant of a man called Bob. Bob was in his early thirties, a very mature student. He had designs on Tara, then just nineteen. Late on the first night she fled the tent containing Bob who was a hair's breadth away from raping Tara and literally bumped into Rick. She was desperately upset. All that night they wandered the streets and on a park bench she sang to him 'I don't eat animals' and told him that she was a vegetarian as the sun began to burn away the early morning mist as he said, "Let's go and find bacon and eggs. Bacon for me. Eggs for you." They could have been the only two people alive in the world. At the dawn they made their way back to the festival site and slept on the staging until the smell of coffee woke them. Rick was terrified as the huge figure of Bob bore down on them and he expected to be knocked flat. Rick tried to talk to Bob, but Bob didn't want to listen. He was only angry because his pride had been hurt and afraid that Tara had been accusing him of attempted rape. Rick tried to tell him that Tara was frightened, that she wasn't ready. But Bob only fumed in his fear and fury. Tara stuck by Rick as her knight and protector. Rick wondered what a broken neck would feel like as Bob glowered at them for the rest of the festival in his burning anger. Finally they arrived back at Teen after witnessing a couple having sex in the back of the van as the rest looked on, or didn't, as the case may be. It could only be called sex like animals. There was no love there. Rick wondered if Tara remembered that.

"Rick. Wake up. I've called you half a dozen times. I wanted a clean towel."

" Clean towel? You'll be lucky. Sorry. You know, I was just thinking about when we first met."

"Hm. I don't think I'd forget Bob waiting outside at six in the morning after we'd spent the night together," Tara replied.

"He must have been there all night. I thought he was going to kill me. I said hit me. I won't hit you back. I'll just fall down."

"He got over it though."

"It was his pride and once he realised that no one was very interested...What do want to do tonight? A flim? `Pat Garrett's` on, stay in, eat out, and make passionate love...?"

"I don't know. I'm on early again tomorrow so I don't want to be late."

"Goodo!" Tara didn't smile. "Why don't you go out and buy some eggs and bread and we'll have an omelette."

"Coming with me?"

"No. I'll stay here."

Later that night in her bed Rick embraced and caressed Tara.

"Rick I'm really tired and I've got to get up early."

"Oh. I'm sorry."

"I'm sorry to." She kissed him quite tenderly.

He lay for a while and soon could tell from her breathing that she was sleeping. He slept.

The next he became aware of was the girl shouting, "Get off. Get off! What do you think I am a piece of meat?"

"I'm sorry Tara." He was breathing heavily and felt groggily confused. "I obviously felt randier than I thought.

But it was like sex in the van.

"I'm sorry Rick. It frightened me. It must have been talking about Bob."

"I'll get you some coffee."

That Saturday The Troggs' and a disco were on at the Teen. The place was packed to see the original punk group. Though there wasn't a lot else happening in the dead end town. Rick went with Tara. The *sophisticate's* hated them. There were no pretensions from Reg Presley who looked like he should be in an armchair by his fire at home with a pipe, slippers and a mug of cocoa watching 'Come Dancing.' Only the lead guitarist succumbed to the fashion of the day with his daglo trousers and top and silver platform boots. There was a great deal of heckling from the gathered crowd and equal amount of insults flowed from Reg to the audience, but the anthem 'Wild Thing' was like an electrical storm which the crowd could not ignore.

The disco afterwards went on until after one in the morning and Rick stood with Tara on the sidelines as an observer. He only danced to 'Spirit in the Sky' and the 'Gene Genie' so he took to the floor twice as the chords pounded through his whole body as he and Tara moved almost in harmony.

Helen went with her friend Fiona but lost her to a potential mate early in the evening. Alone she joined a group from her college but remained on the outer reaches of the circle. On her way to get a drink she pushed past Rick and Tara in the melee.

"I'm sorry," she said as she accidentally trod on Tara' foot.

"Helen!' said Rick feeling high on alcohol, "Hello. Having a great time? Tara this is Helen my secretary." Neither girl said anything.

"I was just trying to get to the bar."

"See you Friday then."

After Helen had disappeared into the crowd Tara turned on him and said, "At times you are so pompous and egotistical. My secretary," she mimicked him sarcastically, "My secretary. You love it don't you?"

Humiliated Rick answered, "Well you know..."

"Yes. I know."

Helen leant against the side of the room like a wallflower, music pounding through her like a headache, lights flashing like a migraine. She wanted to be somewhere else looking for another wallflower, searching for calm and security. 'What's my name Virginia Plain' the singer said over the bodies gyrating together. She wished that she weren't plain and that there was a body she could gyrate with in love. Preferably Rick's.

"Hey. Helen. Didn't see you here. Having a fab time?" Why did everyone need to know whether she was enjoying herself? It was Malcolm. Helen said nothing. She had a feeling of a sort of dread as nausea. "Great disco isn't it. Can you ask the DJ to play *me* a record?"

This is an escape Helen thought. "Yeh. Why not? I'll be back. Wait here."

"Sure thing Helen."

As she walked towards the DJ she thought well at least he's learnt something. I'm not Hel. She laughed out loud and people looked at her as if she were drunk. At the console it was crowded but she pushed her way to the front and asked for her favourite record of the moment though she was only about ten when it came out. "Yeh that's right," she said, "Let's Spend The Night Together. For Malcolm. No. It's from no-one." Helen disappeared back into the crowd carefully avoiding Malcolm.

The Stones sang later not registering in Helen's mind until she heard the familiar voice: "Hey Helen. Great record. You played it for me. Let's spend the night together! Do you mean it?"

Helen couldn't cope with this. "I'll be back in a minute," she said to Malcolm.

"No. It's okay. I'll come with you." Malcolm wasn't going to lose her for a second time that night.

"I'm *going* to the toilet. I'll be back."

Helen fled. It was too late for a bus. The time was later than she realised. She knew her mother would be waiting up angry and worried. She hoped her Father was asleep. She couldn't afford a taxi. Cutting across the town wouldn't take her too long. Walking down the hill away from the college she heard the sound of a motor approaching. She turned round and stuck out a thumb, a stupid thing for a girl to do at that time of night. The transit stopped.

"Where're you going?" a voice said.

"The town centre," Helen replied.

"Yeh alright. Get in."

The man in front squeezed across to the driver and Helen moved in beside him.

"Where you been?"

"The university. A gig and a disco."

"Yeh. Who was on?" The driver kept his eyes fixed in front of him as though he were paranoid about leaving the road.

"Some group of old men for old men. The Troggs."

"Oh Yeh. I remember them. Still a good group?"

"No. They were crap."

The driver laughed. She realised who she was talking to. Helen wanted the ground to open and bury her.

"Better take her to her front door Trev," said Reg, "At least she's honest."

Tara lay awake long after Rick slept. She was on lates for the week. Two o'clock until ten so it didn't matter if she slept until after lunchtime. She was very confused in her thoughts. She knew with the instincts of a female that her relationship with Rick was threatened. She had seen this Helen, the way that she had looked at Rick coolly and nonchalant as if she didn't care but she was like a fruit, ripe and for the taking and she wanted Rick to prick her and penetrate her aching flesh. And this girl was to spend more time with Rick that she ever did. He would have to have the self-control of an ancient monk to resist her. But perhaps he did. Maybe she was being unfair. Conceivably he could see through her too and only loved Tara. Somehow she didn't think so.

Helen lay awake long after Tara slept. She'd met her adversary. She didn't think that she could possibly win against such a beautiful girl when she in her opinion was small and ugly. She had no idea how to anyway. They didn't teach that at school, the art of seduction. I got a grade 'A' in seduction. She wondered how they would examine it and the thought made her laugh. She thought about what it would feel like to fail it. She would fall short. She knew that before she even started the course whereas Tara probably could write volumes about it. Rick, like a fool, had no idea of what was going on she concluded. Maybe boys were like that, stupid. Tara and Rick looked so much like the perfect couple that Helen was left without any hope.

When Tara awoke Rick had gone leaving a note saying that as she was on lates he'd see her next weekend, though condescendingly, she thought as she read between the lines of the scribbled note, he might be able to come across and see her on a couple of mornings. He'd never done that before. He'd always been waiting for her when she arrived home. Maybe he had a lot on and she believed it would help him sort out his essays and plan for Rag Week. Tara wanted to believe that. But it would be lonely coming home to an empty room.

The week felt strange to Rick without Tara but refreshingly free. He caught up on essays and prepared himself well for the Rag Week meeting that Friday. Stevi of course noticed that he was 'at home' all week. She didn't comment, yet. On Thursday Rick went drinking with his room mate Jeremy before going onto Tara's bedsit.

"You finished with this Tara then?" Jeremy had never met her.

"You finished with your latest boyfriend Jeremy?" retorted Rick.

"No. It's just that when you're home I can't bring my friends round."

"Why, do you then?" asked Rick.

"No."

"Well what are you moaning about?"

"If I wanted to," Jeremy replied almost whiningly. More upbeat he went on, "You want to think yourself lucky I don't fancy you."

"Thank God for that. I'll stop sleeping on my back all night." They both laughed.

"No, seriously," said Jeremy, "Are you getting a bit fed up with this husband wifey bit with Tara?"

"You been talking to Stevi?" Jeremy smiled. "No I'm not!" Rick picked up his glass and took a swallow of the black liquid replacing it firmly to the table. "I don't know." He looked at the bubbles rising to the froth. "Another drink Jeremy? Then I'll go home to the wife."

Before he left Rick went to the toilet to avoid a painful walk. 'Gay' men and women frequented the pub they used. When he returned Jeremy told him that one of them had liked his new boyfriend.

"Oh no. I think I'd better go and prove I'm a man."

"I am a man," Jeremy sounded angry. "I'm not so different from you. I have the same physical urges. I fall in love. Or at least I wish I could fall in love. That's the problem I have the physical urges and when they go there seems to be nothing left. I think I'm afraid. I think I'm afraid of women. I think I'm afraid to fall in love." He had never spoken at such great length to his friend or anyone for that matter. Rick didn't know what to say. "And I think it's wrong to like the same sex. Or at least I don't think it's wrong. But I feel that I'm being judged all the time. I like men's bodies." Rick really didn't know how to respond. "You like Tara's body? You like seeing her naked? Well."

"Well. Yes."

"Does she like seeing you naked?"

"I've no idea. I think men's bodies are peculiar."

"You don't think about that. I'm sure she does like to see you naked. I expect you'd be happy to end up a fat slob but still want your wife to be, well have a wonderful figure."

"I've never thought."

"I don't believe you and if you haven't you should have. You should. If Tara like's your body, then there's nothing wrong with me liking men's bodies. Ask her. Sorry I'm going on and not making much sense."

"No I'm the one that should be sorry. Any time you want to talk." Fully intending never to he added, "And I'll ask Tara."

"Yeh I should think so." He laughed. "See you."

"Okay okay. I'm going."

He walked to Tara's that night her room being in a house on the fringes of the town. It was refreshingly cold. A winter's night with the thought of Christmas approaching. He stuck his hands deep into his greatcoat pockets and his head into his collar like a tortoise. When he arrived it was lovely to be out of the cold into the warmth of Tara's room with Cat Steven's beautiful voice filling the room. She was so happy to see him.

"I'm sorry Tara. I was just getting worried about essays and the meeting tomorrow."

"You should have told me. I thought that you didn't love me anymore..."

"Listen, Cat Stevens is saying it for me." And they both kissed and hugged as Cat sang `How Can I Tell You'. Later close and warm in Tara's bed they traded their lust. "Tomorrow night I'll come straight round after the meeting. I'll get a Chinese on the way."

"Oh yes. You're meeting with your lovely secretary."

"I'm sorry. It was very pompous."

She nestled into him and they slept.

TEN

Jonathan found an art gallery that showed only 'modern' art. That is art from the last six months it seemed, as he looked around at the exhibits. It was quite empty even though the entry was free and there was a peace upon the place as if he were in a church. He noticed the time and realised that he would have entered and left the church by now, made his vows and being the butt of innuendo at his wedding breakfast. He moved into a room and on the floor were hobnail boots or perhaps they were army boots carefully arranged covering the whole of the floor. He looked. It all suddenly felt very claustrophobic as though the boots were trampling all over him.

Lesley's Father was pacing up and down the long lounge floor sipping regularly at a whisky and soda, which he had been drinking since the telephone call from Jonathan's father that morning. His face was now very red. He should have done his youngest proud by now and here she was sitting weeping on the sofa like a forlorn film star. And like the film star she had always had what she wanted, a good private education, clothes, a car at university where no one else had. Everything. And now that animal, that filth, which could not see the preciousness that he was marrying into, had done a runner. He would kill him.

"Dad. Do sit down," said her mother, "Do you want something to eat? You ought to put something into your tummy. With all the alcohol you've had."

He glared at his wife and then looked fondly at his daughter. "I'll kill him."

"Dad. No." In despair Lesley went from the room to be alone with her grief.

"*Now look.* Watch what you say."

"Well I will."

"Now you don't mean that. I'm getting you a cup of tea and a sandwich."

In the hallway mam shouted upstairs to Christine that the phone was for her. "Someone called Jonathan."

"Jonathan? I wonder what he wants," she lied. She placed the receiver to her ear. After the play acting of 'what a surprise' she said, "I'll go and ask me mam." She looked towards her mother who was standing in the doorway of the kitchen clutching a tea towel in one hand and a cigarette in the other. "A lad from university's at the station – can he stay for a couple of nights?" She tried to hurry her. "He's in a call box. He could have John's bed."

"John didn't like what was left in his bed last time. When you had that party."

"I'll check carefully. And if he's by himself I doubt that's going to happen. Can we go and collect him?" Christine's mother made a face that looked as if she'd been asked to climb Mount Everest without any equipment. "He's got luggage."

"I suppose so."

When they reached the station Christine looked and then said, "There he is," as if she were meeting a long lost friend.

"Bit enthusiastic aren't you? Has Steve met this..." she searched for a name.

"Jonathan. Of course, they're mates." She brought him back to the car and he got into the back. "Me mam."

"Hello. Thank you." He realised he didn't know the surname of the family he was about to stay with and really he ought to have done.

"I thought you had luggage?"

"I have," and patted his pocket like Benjamin in The Graduate, "Toothbrush," but it was lost on her.

Jonathan's parent's asked each other the same question they could not answer again and again – Where is he? Why?

"The 'why' might be fairly obvious," his father said.

"Hm. Stage fright."

"Marriage fright." He tried to laugh but really there was nothing to laugh at.

"But where. Perhaps we should report it to the police..."

"He's twenty –two..."

"Twenty-three." She corrected him.

"Not nine, and late home from school."

"Do you remember that? Three hours late. Bin out to Bradgate Park and turned his watch back and pretended it was still only four thirty." They smiled at the memory and wished life were still that simple. "You sent him straight to bed and his sister smuggled milk and biscuits up to him. He did better than the rest of us."

"Always did land on his feet."

"We'd better eat. I'll get something. You listen out for the phone." As if making a simple meal that neither of them wanted would stop her hearing the long desired for call.

"Some more Jonathan?"

"No that was delicious Mrs.." He paused as if trying to remember her name. "I'm useless on names. Aren't I Helen?" He looked at Christine and smiled.

"Mrs. Milton," said Christine's mother. "You can call me Emma."

"You coming to the wedding then Jonathan?" asked Christine's Father.

"No. I'm not able to. That's why I thought I'd play a surprise visit now."

""You're a friend of Steve's then..."

" Yes, but more of Christine's."

Steve would ask Christine's father who the hell Jonathan was in a fortnight's time and later the same question would be put to Christine over the years. Even though she told him the truth, he never believed her.

"Do you like a drink?" Christine's father suddenly asked him.

"Oh yes."

"We'll have a walk round to The Robin Hood then."

The Robin Hood, thought Jonathan, here in Newcastle.

"We'll all go shall we? You coming mam?"

After an hour or so Christine's parent's left them alone in the bar and went home.

"Why did you call me Helen? Earlier. You called me Helen."

"It was just the first name that came into my head that's all."

"Another drink. Then we'll go and tomorrow you'd better decide what you're going to do."

His father could not sleep. Lesley's father could not sleep. They lay staring at the ceiling like Jonathan had done only twenty-four hours earlier. Both of them wanted know what had gone wrong. Both of them were angry; one of them wanted to put it right, the other death for Jonathan by slow torture.

ELEVEN

Rick and Helen spent Friday in animated anticipation. Rick because it was his first meeting as the Rag chairman and he wanted the whole event to go well and Helen because she would physically be close to Rick. At the very least she could play an important role in his life supporting him in what he was doing.

The woman behind the scenes who made sure that all was well, minutes kept up to date, letters to write, coffee when he needed, just like she'd seen secretaries do for their bosses on the television. Mind you she knew that in some of those programmes they got up to other things as well. She thought all of this as she showered and dressed that night. Unconsciously looking at her most attractive without realising her whole naivety in the affair. She arrived for the meeting quite early after all the 'good lucks' from her parents. They were proud of her and saw this role, as being something for her benefit but that would also reflect on them as parents. "Make sure you buy a Rag Mag this year," her father would tell the men at his local, "My daughter's the secretary." Helen went into the bar area at the university in excited trepidation. Rick was already at the bar with a few other members of the committee.

Rick was determined that the meeting would go quickly and efficiently. That he would stamp his authority and make it patently obvious that what members committed themselves to they would do and if necessary he would chase them up. He said as much to Helen when he took her aside for a pre- meeting pep talk in the corner of the bar. Helen would have agreed with Rick regardless of what he said. But she also hated inefficiency, which was one reason why she would make an excellent secretary. With Rick she was determined that she was going to make the best impression. Minutes well kept, letters written off quickly, prompt replies to those received.

"Can you do shorthand?" he said. She affirmed that she could. "So you'll be able to keep minutes quite accurately. Don't waste time writing down a load of rubbish. Just what is decided? Don't forget she who keeps the minutes controls the meeting." She wasn't sure what he meant but nodded and smiled. "We'll try and meet outside of these meetings to keep on top of what's going on. Okay with you?" Helen showed her agreement. "I don't know when but we'll sort something out. We'd better go in. Sit at my right hand Helen so we can work as a pair." And very self-importantly added pompously, "Be my right hand."

Full of their initial enthusiasm the students' were falling over themselves to volunteer for 'jobs'. Rick tried to point out the pitfalls of each position and what he expected of them.

"Yes, Rag Week is fun", he said, "It's got to be. But remember the intention is to raise money. And we have to be totally committed and efficient. There's nothing others will like to see more is us make mistakes, fall flat on our faces, fail. That's the main reason why I intend, with Helen's help, to take full responsibility for the major event of the week." Helen hadn't realised this but still showed her approval. "The final event. The Rag Ball." He spoke a little too dramatically.

"I thought I'd be best to do that. I assist the university social secretary. I have the contacts and the experience," said Dave, totally put out by this news.

"I know Dave, but we have plans for the evening." Again Helen nodded even though she had no idea what they were.

"Would you like to share them then with us?" Dave asked.

"Of course. I intend to book a very well known band..."

"That'll be expensive..."

"It'll bring in a large audience who will pay..."

"I think we should discuss this. In my experience..."

"Well we're not. I'll take full responsibility. You'll be answerable to me. I'll be answerable to myself."

"Who are they anyway?" asked Dave.

"Him. Richard Thompson."

"Never heard of him," somebody said contemptuously.

"Late of Fairport Convention," another replied wanting to show off their knowledge.

"That's right and amongst the more cultured," Richard spoke sarcastically, "He'll drag them in! And with a finality that ended any further discussion he said, "Is there any other business?"

"Yes," said Fiona, a friend of Helen's, "You probably all know that there's a squat just off the town centre in one of the terraced houses. The council plans to knock it down in a couple of years..."

"Is this relevant to Rag Week?" Rick asked.

Fiona gave him a stare that told all that he didn't at all awe her. "It might be. Wait and see Rick. It would make great accommodation for students' as would a number of the houses there. But the council say no. A few students' are squatting at the moment. The council can only evict from a squat if they know the occupant's names so we plan to put in different students' each night. And Rick, you scratch their backs and they'll scratch ours."

"Any volunteers then let Fiona know after the meeting. I can make next Friday night."

"Thanks Rick. Very kind," added Fiona smiling sweetly at him.

Helen registered Friday in her mind.

"Oh, sorry folks one more thing. Sorry to keep you from your liquid refreshments with only half an hour to go before last orders but," and he looked at a piece of paper as if reading it for the first time, "Helen and myself have been asked to attend a Rag Week conference in the New Year at Aberdovey University. Well it doesn't actually name us just invites Rag Chair and secretary." It didn't in fact say that, but invited a representative so any one of them would do but Rick wasn't letting on. "That alright with everybody? I'm sure we'll pick up useful tips from the larger universities such as Leeds." There were murmurs of assent and Helen squirmed in her chair. "That's okay then. I'll call the meeting to a close."

But Fiona interrupted him. "May I see the letter?"

Fortunately he hadn't already given it to Helen or she would have immediately passed it onto her friend. "Well it's full of all the details, travel arrangements etc. I don't want to lose it or hold the meeting up any further. Helen will do you a copy and have it to you by the weekend. Off we go then. The bar calls." He got up and left before any one could say anything else.

As the group left the room Helen asked Rick for a word.

"Good meeting eh Helen?"

"I didn't know about the Rag Ball thing. Who's Richard Thompson? I had to pretend."

"You'll love him. I didn't think that you'd mind."

"I don't, but if we're to work together you've got to tell me your plans. And what about this Wales thing? I don't know if I can go to that. I'll have to ask my parents." And you'll have to ask Tara's permission she thought, she's not going to be thrilled you going off with me for the weekend. Though I quite like the idea. For the moment she fell short of telling him not to walk all over her.

"All expenses paid. Should be fun. Do that interfering bitch Fiona a heavily edited version of the letter. You'll see why." He passed her the letter.

She was feeling angry. "Fiona is probably my best friend."

"Oh right sorry. She just gets on my nerves. I can't stand this entire righteous bit that she comes out with. She'd probably go to Wales and come back with armfuls of notes for us to pay attention to, rather than just using it as a free holiday. We must keep on top of them though. Its all very well making promises for this, that and the other. I must see they keep to what they've said they will do. We have some letters to write. Can you do them and pass them to me for signing?"

"Of course."

"I'll try and get to you. Do you have a phone number?"

Helen gave him her home number.

"You okay with everything then? I'll talk to you later in the week."

TWELVE

After only one night of Christine and her parent's hospitality Jonathan decided not to return to the Midlands and the possibility of reconciliation. The wedding date had passed and he could not, would not, be caught for fifty years and five children, working nine till five every day at a job he didn't like with a wife that he'd fallen out of love with and her him. He would not be responsible for all that.

He waited till Christine's parent's had left the house for work and then told her as he was biting into a piece of toast.

"I'm going back..."

"To sort everything out?"

"I don't know. I might go to France."

"To France?"

"To start again."

"To run away." It felt like she'd known him for years.

"Want to come?"

"Jonathan even if I thought you were being serious..."

"I am."

She guffawed and carried on. "Do you seriously think that I would go with you? I'm two weeks away from my own wedding." She paused to take a sharp intake of breath. "To a man I love and have faith in. You've just left your bride waiting at the altar. What do you think she feels like today? I wouldn't even consider it. Well we aren't all idiots. I think you'd better go now." She went to the pile of records and selected one. "You can ring yourself a taxi. Leave the 10p by the phone."

As the car arrived he was standing in the hallway listening to America. He shouted bye and thanks but he didn't think that she heard him, as she didn't reply.

THIRTEEN

Stevi asked Rick if he intended to go to the squat. Jeremy interrupted them that he certainly didn't, 'could be anything there that he could catch and anyway he preferred his home comforts and he wasn't a student anymore anyway.' Rick couldn't decide. He wished now that he hadn't volunteered on the spur of the moment, but had taken time to reflect. He didn't like the idea either, it was all too 'let's pretend we're having a revolution and when its all over run home to Mum for a hot meal and have our washing done'.

"I think you should," said Stevi. "You'll expect support from them for your events in Rag Week beyond the ones that they'll definitely support like the discos. Its no fun you know touting Rag Mags on the street or getting a float ready. If you put yourself out they'll put themselves out..."

"All right. All right. Don't go on like you're my mother. You've convinced me. I'll go."

"When?"

"Why do you want to know?"

"So they'll know when to expect you."

"I'm pinned down in other words. Friday. In fact I had already said Friday. I was just hoping everyone would forget. Tara works late then. I think. That suit you?"

"Fine by me."

He decided to leave it as late as possible before he went to the squat that Friday so that he wouldn't have to speak about

the revolution with too many people. They might all be in bed, if
they had such things. They might have even locked the door so
that he could say that he turned up but no way could he get in.
He went down to the pub with Jeremy for the early part of the
evening. He liked it because it was like being in an Andy Warhol
film, should he dye his hair blond? He decided not. The
atmosphere was warm and smoke filled and scented. After an
hour or so Jeremy said he had to see one of his friends and Rick
didn't want to be alone very much. It was no prejudice on his part
just that he didn't want to have to repulse any boarders. He
looked at his watch it would soon be kicking out time anyway.
He would walk and window-shop on the way. He finished his
beer quite slowly without looking at anyone and left standing for
a moment in the door looking right and left as though he didn't
want anyone to see him leave. He turned and walked in the
direction of the squat down the main street to turn left and look
in the second hand record shop window. He expected that
tomorrow he would go in and buy something, even if he couldn't
afford it, as he did most weekends. He knew where his feet
would lead him; that he would have to do make the right moves
and be seen to be part off the student movement, no matter how
he really felt. He also liked the idea that he was to turn up and be
some kind of hero giving his valuable time to them. Along the
terraced street he found the house candle lit amongst the boarded
up rest and not really showing any kind of welcoming or warmth
to any who wanted it. He hoped that he had the right place and
that it wouldn't be full of alcoholic tramps. He had been told to
go around the back. It was very dark. He wished that he had
brought a torch. In fact he hadn't even brought the things he did
have like a sleeping bag. He wondered where he would sleep. He
counted aloud the empty houses down the back alleyway until he
found the right one. Fortunately a light was showing in the room
that he took to be the kitchen. He went down the yard and
pushing open the back door shouted, "Hello." He jumped when
Stevi almost immediately spoke back.

"You made it then. Almost given up on you."

"Went for a drink with Jeremy. I didn't know that you
were going to be here."

"I'm a woman of many parts. Want some wine?"

"No I'll turn in." He thought the sooner he went to sleep the sooner he woke and could get out of the place.

"Sure? I've put you in the front room upstairs. You can't miss it. It's the first room you come across."

"There's no one else in there? If there is I'll go home."

"No, I don't think so." Stevi laughed.

"What are you laughing at?"

"You. You are just so sociable."

"I just don't want to have to talk to anybody."

"Don't worry. I don't think that you will be talking to anybody. I've put you a sleeping bag in there."

"Thank God for that. I wondered what I'd sleep in."

"Thanks to me you certainly won't get cold."

Helen stood by the window in the cold room. She was feeling very alone. Fiona who she was supposed to be spending the night with in this awful place had gone off with some bloke. She just wanted to go home, to her own warm bed and waking to the sounds of downstairs and a proper Saturday morning breakfast of bacon and eggs cooked by her mother. She didn't have anyone. No one wanted to be with her.

He went up the stairs and pushed the door to the bedroom. A figure immediately turned and looked at him making him jump for the second time in a few minutes.

"Shit", he thought, "I'll have to find somewhere else to sleep or go home. I can't stand this." He hoped Jeremy hadn't brought anyone home, if he had he could always go onto Tara's. She would like that.

The figure gave a slight gasp. "You made me jump." It was Helen.

Tara opened the door to her empty and cold bed-sit. She wished that Rick was there waiting for her with a coffee.

It was Rick. What was he doing here? That was his sleeping bag. Obviously she 'd better go. Or should she stay. A decision. Fate or planned. She wanted him. He spoke.

Tara squeezed the kettle under the tap above the sink full of dirty dishes. They would have to wait to be washed up. She would do them before Rick came round tomorrow and she would clean the room up.

"I'm supposed to be sleeping in here. At least I think it's in here. I'll go and check with Stevi."

Tara undressed quickly. Too tired and cold to wash. She would bath before he came over.

"It's ok. It'll stop anyone else coming in."

'I wonder if Rick feels the same way,' thought Tara, 'It's not nice sleeping alone.' She curled herself into a foetal ball.

Downstairs Jeremy whispered to Stevi in the kitchen, "How's it going?"

'I could get a taxi over to him. Surprise him. Of course he's at that squat thing. That's why he's not here. He'll hate that. I wonder if they'd know where the squat is at his place. I could always go there. That would surprise him.'

"Well he hasn't come down yet. And we'll stay a while to stop anyone else trying to sleep in there.

In the dim light Rick stripped off to his underwear and slipped into the sleeping bag.

Tara lay staring and listening intently, she was sure that she could hear the key in the door. It must be Rick.

"Where are you sleeping?" he asked.

I want to get into that bag with you. Now! I'm very cold. Make me warm.

'I'm cold,' thought Tara, 'I should have got a hot water bottle.'

"I don't know. Stevi told me not to bother to bring a bag. I'm cold."

He thought just for a moment. "Get in here. If you like."

'I wish I had him here to sleep with me. Why does he volunteer to do these stupid things?'

They laid not touching as far as it is possible not to contact in a single sleeping bag. The candle was throwing all sorts of interesting shades on the wall like a shadow watching them. There was a knock on the door. He shouted for whomever it was to piss off. Stevi opened the door a few inches "Just checking," she said "That everything was all right. Shall I blow your candle out?" she went on, "Save you getting out?"

"Yes please. And I want to talk to you in the morning."

"I don't think that I shall be around. Goodnight. Sleep tight."

Come on do something.

"I'm hot," said Helen.

"I'll get out. I'm sure I can find somewhere else to go. I can go home."

"No it's alright. I don't want to be by myself."

'I hate being by myself in this room. Do I love him enough? Do I show it properly? I will from the next time I see him. Tomorrow. Today.'

Do it.

In what seemed like no time at all she was naked and Rick was kissing each part of her feeling a passion that he had not felt before. They didn't sleep, or at least the pair of them weren't aware of sleeping.

He dreamt. You are all women especially today Isis and Mary. Chopped corpse dying on a cross you resurrected me.

Tara finally slept but fitfully and dreamt but in the morning she couldn't remember her dreams other than it involved Miss Secretary's nasty face saying you don't know do you, do you, do you, do you...?"

In the morning when he knew daylight was there he looked at his watch. Close by there was no sound from anywhere else in the house. It was eleven thirty. He kissed Helen again and later he asked her when he could see her again.

"Do you really want to?"

"Without doubt." He kissed her again.

He turned onto his back and she leant on her elbow and looked into his face. It was as if they were seeing each other for the very first time. "Helen you are on the pill aren't you?" He didn't want to go through that movie again.

"Bit late to think about that isn't it?" She laughed, "What shall we call him, Richard? Just to let the world know who the father is? Yeh. Don't worry yourself. For medical reasons, not sex. Though it came in useful."

"Its just I never thought. Tara is."

Tara. "Anyway what about Tara? What are you going to do about her? That is if you're going to do anything about her. But you can't have us both"

"I'll tell Tara." He was silent for some time. "I want to be with you. Only you"

"Turn away," she said modestly as if the night hadn't existed, "I have to get up and go home. I'm supposed to be meeting Fiona. I think I shall have to give her a call and cancel. She'll only want to know the sordid details anyway."

"Sordid?"

"No. It was lovely. I shall never forget." She stopped what she was doing. "Rick. Do you think we were set up?"

"Set up?"

"Stevi, Jeremy. Me in this room. Your sleeping bag here. You said that Jeremy wouldn't come within a hundred miles of this place."

"Jeremy was here?"

"Downstairs when I got here."

"Maybe. It doesn't matter anyway. Come here."

"No. I've got to go."

"I'll tell Tara and ring you later." When he awoke again later he was alone. It was after two. He remembered that he should have been with Tara a couple of hours before. He hauled himself out of the bag and back to his own place for a bath and to eat and coffee.

"Nice night?" shouted Stevi from an afternoon film as he entered the front door.

"As if you didn't know."

"Sometimes love needs a helping hand. Doesn't it Jeremy?"

Rick stood in the doorway to the room and looked at them both and smiled like a conquering hero.

"You look tired," Helen's mother was saying as she sat with a cup of cooling coffee in front of her at the kitchen table. "Helen? Knock knock, anyone there? The lights are on..."

"What?"

"I was saying that I've been accepted on NASA's next manned flight to the moon. You look tired."

"I was miles away. Yes Fiona and I didn't sleep very well last night at that squat. I wish I hadn't gone."

"Your Dad and I didn't want you to go. I don't know why you went."

"Rick thought it would be a good idea for...."

"Do you do everything he says?"

'Well not quite,' she thought.

"You've got your own mind you know. I don't want to see you get hurt." She ignored that as if she hadn't heard it. She'd never get hurt. "He is nice though...Any way Fiona has something or other do with it so I was helping her out."

"Rick's nice is he?" Her mother looked at her and smiled. "He's got a girlfriend hasn't he?"

Helen felt herself beginning to blush. "Fiancée I think." She'd lost her virginity many times with him in fifteen hours and it was supposed to be painful she'd been led to believe but it wasn't. It had been unbelievably wonderful.

"I'm going for a sleep."

She watched her daughter leave the room and thought how young she really was on the threshold of adulthood. She felt there was a communication that was not quite being made with her offspring. She looked out of the kitchen window and saw her husband coming up the path to the house in the rain. He saw her watching and shook as if he were freezing cold and ready for a hot meal. Still after all these years she loved him as she had the first time they met.

When Rick finally reached Tara's bed sit after sleeping, bathing, and eating he could hear 'Suzanne' droning mournfully on out of the stereo. He let himself into her room where a candle was already burning and he wondered if he would ever have the energy to perform the sexual act again, ever again. She hadn't heard him, or feigned not to do so, and he leant and kissed her cheek. She turned and kissed him full on the lips moving his hands to her breasts, "You're late!" She spoke as if he were a naughty boy. "But you're here now. Shall we eat later?" she asked.

"Are you and Mum going out?"

Helen's Father looked at her Mother and asked his daughter why.

"If you were, I thought I might come with you."

"Well yes we are..."

"Down to the Hounds though" said her Father as though this might put her off and to make sure that she knew they weren't going to a disco.

"Okay. But I want a real drink. I'm a woman now."

Her Father raised his eyebrows as if he were terribly shocked. "Well actually Helen, we do want a talk with you. Might be a good opportunity." He looked at his wife. "Go and get your selves ready then, both of you. Then we'll go. Don't be long."

In her room Helen looked at her reflection in the glass and wondered what this chat was going to be all about. Surely they could not know about last night. Maybe it was about getting pregnant...but you didn't talk about such things in the local pub and anyway mum knew that she was taking the pill. She couldn't see her father putting his darts down and saying 'oh by the way are you on the pill or you should be saving your self for the right man you know' was very unlikely. She soon found out though.

In the pub her father asked her what she wanted to drink and bravely she asked for a gin and tonic with ice and lemon and to her surprise he went to get her one.

"Your Dad knows you drink at the college. We were young you know. As long as you're not silly." She laughed and Helen laughed politely along with her.

"What's all this about then?"

"Nothing to worry about. It's very exciting."

She felt some relief. "Well I didn't think you'd bring me down to the pub for a chat about the bird's and bees."

"Well you know all about that. As long as you're not silly." Oh dear was this going to be mum's phrase for the evening. Her Dad brought the tray of drinks back and sat down.

"Well?"

'Let me quench my thirst first love. I'm parched." He was obviously excited but was keeping a cool and calm exterior.

So it was Mum who almost bursting with excitement said "Your Dad's been offered promotion!"

Oh was that it. But she'd better not appear to be indifferent and enthused. After all it would mean more money in the house. Not that they were poorly off. "That's great. Really great. Well done Dad."

"But wait you haven't heard the half of it. You tell her Dad."

"It's in America!"

"America?" She spoke as if she'd never heard of America let alone know where it was.

"There I knew you'd be thrilled."

"But when will we see you?" Then the consequences began to dawn.

"No love. Don't worry yourself about that. We all go to America. It'll be a great opportunity for us all."

"We're just going! You aren't asking me if I want to go?" This wasn't going as they were expecting. "You don't think I have anything here that I don't want to leave behind?" She was looking at them in anger.

"Calm down love. We can talk about it." She was raising her voice and people were beginning to look at them.

"Talk about it. In other words persuade me. No, not even that. Tell me I'm going." She picked up glass and for an awful moment her mother thought that she was going to throw the contents at her father. "Tried to buy me with this eh? I'm in love and I won't leave him."

Her parents looked at her in amazement and then at each other. She left her drink and ran from the pub.

"What was all that about then?" said Dad

"Rick."

Rick found it easy to have sex with Tara that weekend, as the flesh was somebody else's. He breathed out deeply as he rolled onto his back on the Sunday morning.

"Are you alright? You've seemed very quiet this weekend though you have made up for it in other ways." Her fingers stroked his already stiffening penis. "I haven't known you this good for some time and I thought you were going to leave me for that midget secretary of yours!"

Without speaking or kissing her he mounted her again.

FOURTEEN

Jonathan's grandpa stood on the balcony of his high rise flat. Floor twenty-six was where he lived. He was smoking a cigarette. He didn't smoke. He'd given up nearly fifteen years earlier when he was sixty-four and hadn't smoked one since then. But today was different. He had gone to the newsagents early and bought ten. He'd smoked four already. He looked across the city. Busy. Always busy. It never stopped. He'd moved here a lifetime ago it seemed. Then it was exciting. It was where Mary wanted to be. It was new and glowing. After living in bed sits, flats, terraced houses (running from landlords with the rent unpaid) the gas cottages in the war that might be bombed any time. Those huge gas cylinders in the factory at the bottom of the garden would have gone up and you wouldn't have known a thing. Then before this high rise Dartford road with its allotment and garage nearby. He'd liked the allotment. But this was prison on the twenty-sixth floor of this building. Three rooms, a poky corridor they called a hall and tiny bathroom. They'd almost gone back to the beginning. All new it was twenty years ago, now the concrete was tired and very grey. He took a long drag on his cigarette and thought that it felt good. Perhaps he would have a gin later on though that would entail a visit to the small supermarket down below. Commitment was what Jonathan didn't have. He'd been committed all those years ago. He'd married a woman three years older than himself and *she'd* had a five-year-old illegitimate daughter, Jonathan's mother, who'd hated this 'new' dad in the beginning. But she'd grown to love him as most people grew to love him because he was a kind and gentle man. Jonathan had been the diamond in his eye, the son that was never to be. Jonathan had said 'grandpa' to him when he was a few months old when he'd been babysitting; he knew no one believed him but Jonathan *had* recognised him. He'd been alone now for nearly five years after his wife had died. The flats had all changed. The neighbours and that feel of companionship had gone. It was full of social problems now, the out of work and drug addicts. He was the only one left. They were just waiting for him to go then they would knock them down he thought. It would have meant a great deal to him to see the boy married yesterday. It would have been final, like the last page of a book or when 'the end' shows on the screen but it would have been a happy ending. He could have prepared for death then. He was eighty and had had his fair share. He'd better forget the gin until he'd seen how Jonathan's mother was, he'd have to drive there. Strange that no matter how old you got you still cared for your children even if they weren't your own blood.

His intercom from downstairs buzzed. He thought of ignoring it. He didn't really want to speak to anyone but when you were eighty you answered or they battered your door down assuming you were dead, at least that's what he hoped would happen.

"Yes," he spoke into the machine.

"Grandpa? Is anyone with you?"

Jonathan. Grandpa felt a surge of relief. Perhaps it would be all right after all. "No you'd better come up. You have some explaining to do."

The flat smelt of old people. Why do houses get like that Jonathan wanted know. It wasn't plain dirt or lack of washing, was it just a special dust that settled and gave off the smell of old age?

Jonathan rang the doorbell and pushed the unlocked door open. He knew that Grandpa would be waiting for him. He walked down the darkened corridor and the few paces into the almost startlingly bright living room. Once there would have been his grandma there, beaming, a face creased with smiles thoroughly delighted that he was visiting. Now it was his grandpa sitting regally looking cross or at least trying to. He was obviously pleased and relieved to see the boy.

"Hello grandpa. You haven't told anyone I'm here?" He looked around as if he expected other people to be in the room.

"No."

"You okay?"

"Hardly."

"Have you been smoking?"

"I think that's the least of our worries. What *are* you up to?"

"I couldn't go through with it. I couldn't get married."

"Me me me. Is that all you think about? What about Lesley? Your parents? Her parents..."

"And we spend our lives in a marriage that was only done for the sake of others."

"It wasn't arranged. Not like the Patel's daughter Sunni. She ran away you know. She was never seen again." There was silence as they both thought about the Patel's girl and if she was dead. Whether she'd been murdered for running away. It had been rumoured. "Why leave it so long?" he went on, "The decision must have been growing in your head for weeks."

"I was staring at the ceiling all night and there were so many stars and then dawn came and I realised that I hadn't seen them all."

"Oh I see, all that poetry stuff. Too much education. In my day you were grateful for what you'd got. What are going to do now? You want me to come with you to your mother's?"

"No. You haven't seen me. Grandpa, I'm going to France. I want to start again. I'm a French teacher. I can use the language. I need some money Grandpa."

The old man looked to heaven. "Well there's a surprise. Something else that you think just grows on trees. How much?"

"Five hundred pounds. To get me started. I'll send it back to you."

"I don't know why I'm doing this. I'll write you a cheque for a thousand. Don't expect any inheritance."

"No. I'll send it back."

"No. I'll die soon. You know when you are going to die."

"Well let me know!" Jonathan smiled.

He left the room and returned a few minutes later waving a piece of paper. "Here you are. Don't lose it."

"Thanks Grandpa. I could never thank you enough. I think I'll have to go."

"Get to the bank?"

"Something like that." Jonathan went to hug and kiss him and the old man's final act was to push him to the door telling him not to be so silly. "You know Grandpa. It's always felt like you were the first person I spoke to," were Jonathan's final words.

Grandpa returned to his balcony to watch the receding figure

Jonathan banked the cheque and caught another train taking him further south. He needed to pick up a few items, not least his passport, before he caught the ferry to France. This meant a stop off at the house that Lesley's father had bought for them; though it wasn't them, it was her house. The house was solely in her name. She wouldn't be there. He hoped beyond hope. He just wanted to disappear.

Lesley's father had been all for travelling down there that morning because that's where he thought the 'foul rat' would have gone to, but his hangover was from hell.

Her mother was more circumspect. "Leave it," she said, Jonathan was obviously no good for her anyway. "Better to end it now than in five, ten or fifteen years. It's only pride that's been hurt. And all things heal."

Jonathan slipped into the house without him seeing the neighbour peeping through her nets. Without realising it she would have something to tell Lesley and her father when they arrived the following day. He picked up his passport and was intent on leaving the same way. Of course as he opened the door so did his neighbour.

"Jonathan!" she exclaimed, "The newlywed!" She gave him a wink full of innuendo. "We didn't know you were back."

"Yeh. Just going to get some food."

" You should have said. We would have got you some things in. Everything go alright? The wedding lovely? Just as you'd hoped."

"Yes. It was wonderful. I'd better press on."

"Can I pop in and see Lesley later?"

"Of course. She'd like that."

"I want to hear all about the great day."

Later on the ferry to France as he watched the coastline disappear he knew that he would never go back to all that. He bought some writing paper and envelopes and wrote a letter of resignation to his school. He didn't try to justify himself or lay blame. He didn't want to. That was why he couldn't write to his parents or Lesley.

Back home his father was not angry now, only inconsolable. He couldn't understand how the boy who had been given everything and had the perfect life laid out before him should disappear. He got to loath the phone ringing, as it was never Jonathan.

Grandpa threw the cigarettes away and decided not to buy the gin

In France at the port of Roscoff Jonathan found the train station. It was just a matter of following the rails. He asked at the office where the next train went. He was told Marseilles. He asked for a town en route that would make a good holiday destination. The clerk told him that he had relatives who lived in Bressuire and that was very pretty, quite small but big enough.

"A single ticket?" said the man making sure that he had understood the Englishman, "You are not coming back?"

"That's right. I'm not coming back."

By the time he reached Bressuire a few hours later of watching French countryside interspersed with towns and a couple of cities it was dark. He crossed the large station square and went into the nearest bar and asked for a glass of wine.

Sipping his drink he enquired after a room. He was pointed in the direction of a nearby hotel. Later he lay down on his bed and suddenly realised how tired he was. He looked at the style of his room, which was quite Breton in style, though he was miles away from Brittany and even further away from Britain. Many hours later he awoke fully clothed having slept like the unconscious. He undressed and got into bed and slept again until the sunlight swept into his room.

FIFTEEN

Rick, but more so Helen wanted the relationship begun in the squat to continue. Not only did she feel that she had more to lose but also it was as if she loved the boy. She didn't know if the love was reciprocated or was just a good night for him. Helen was determined not to go to America with her parents and wasn't even going to tell Rick about it. She told them she was going to get a flat and stay here. They believed they would win her round in the end, either that or stamp their authority. The parents and child also spent the time circling one another politely as if in a dance.

On Monday morning Rick told Tara that he had a lot of work on that week so thought that he really wouldn't be able to see her until the Friday.

"But you'll ring won't you. I love you. You know that don't you?" She sounded almost plaintive, whining.

"I'll call. I won't make promises as to when. Sometimes there's such a queue for the phone."

"But you love me?"

"Of course."

"Say it then."

That night in his bed-sit he was sound asleep when one of the girls woke him. At first he did wonder what it was she wanted as he mind regained some kind of consciousness. Shaking him she went "Rick. Rick!"

"Yeh. What is it?"

"There's a guy downstairs and he won't go."

"What do you mean he won't go? Just tell him to piss off."

"Come and throw him out."

He got dressed woke Jeremy and went downstairs. The boy was sitting at the table in the kitchen.

"Look friend," said Rick, "Just go and then we can all be off to bed."

"I want to use your bathroom."

"Well..."

"No Rick." He was interrupted by one of the girl's who whispered to him, "He wants to shoot up in our bathroom."

"I see. No mate you gotta go. Like now."

Rick looked more closely at the boy. He had a paper bag with him from which the point of a syringe was sticking. He smelt as though he had never changed his underwear. His clothes were filthy and his shoes were without laces.

"You can't do that here. If somebody, like at the uni found out we could be in real serious trouble. It's not soft drugs you're talking about."

"Just let me and I'll go."

"No."

"I had a nice place to live and a girlfriend once you know."

"Yeh. I'm sure that you did."

"We were going to get married. Then she left me for someone else. I only loved her."

"Why don't you get some help?"

"I will. Just let me go to your bathroom."

"No. Who let this guy in?" Rick asked no one. And no one admitted responsibility.

The circling conversation seemed to go on for hours.

"Come on. I want to go to bed."

"When I've been in your bathroom I'll go."

"No."

Finally he agreed to leave when it was nearly dawn. As he went down the hall he fled up the stairs and locked himself in the bathroom. Rick had had enough and sent Jeremy out for the Police whilst he waited to deal with whatever came back downstairs. When Jeremy came in the front door and told Rick that the police were on their way. The boy staggered down whether with fatigue or chemicals Rick wasn't concerned about and said, "You've sent for the Police haven't you?" By now there was only Rick, Jeremy and the boy in the hall. At the word Police everybody else decided it was time to make themselves scarce.

"Yeh," said Rick.

"Well I'll hide in here and you don't tell them where I am."

"Yeh. Okay." He went into the lounge.

The doorbell rang and a large Policeman stood in the doorway. "Trouble?"

"Yeh. He's in there."

Reaching college short tempered and needing sleep Rick looked at the notice board as he routinely did. There in the centre of the board so that it could not be missed was the announcement that there would be a fire drill for all of the university at ten forty that morning. Without really thinking about it he went off to his first lecture. After an hour of arguing for the existence of god he went for a coffee. It was crowded and he had difficulty finding a place to be alone. He didn't want to speak. He wanted to think. Dreaming about all sorts a bell sounded on and on. He became aware that people around him were leaving and he remembered the drill. He didn't move and became stranded sitting in the empty room where once it had been full and buzzing. It was quite perfect sitting alone with his thoughts knowing that no one could possibly disturb him. It might be improved if Helen were there but he wasn't sure...

"Come on now. All out."

Rick came back to a reality and looked up at the Vice Principal's face. He obviously had nothing better to do.

"Why?" Rick asked.

"Because it's the fire drill and once a year we have to see that we can evacuate the building efficiently."

"But you know that there's only me here. It has been a success."

"Come on now. Don't be difficult."

Reluctantly Rick got up and followed the ageing man who was nearing his retirement. They went down the stairs and reached the double fully glazed doors whilst the rest of the campus was outside waiting for them. Rick walked through the open door and to the delight of the student's waiting outside the older man walked straight into the windowed door and hit his head. A loud cheer went up and Rick raised his arms in a mock salute.

After the morning's excitement he decided to go to Helen's college that lunchtime and see if she were in the student bar there.

"Will you be late Helen?" asked her Mum earlier that morning.

They were barely speaking and Helen replied, "I don't know."

"Anything planned?"

"As I said, I don't know. I have to meet Rick at his college in the bar at lunchtime." She lied. She thought she might have to more often now.

"Will you have time to get there?"

"I'll have to make it."

"He has a girlfriend hasn't he?" She knew that she was sliding on thin ice.

"As I said the other day, yes. Fiancée I think. Anyway it's not that type of meeting. What is this the Spanish inquisition?"

After a morning full of typing errors and diverse thoughts Helen fled her college and went up see Rick. She arrived at a bar full of lunchtime drinkers. She could see little, certainly not the figure of Rick. She elbowed her way to the bar and bought an orange juice and stood nonchantly drinking it as though she were part of the furniture always there with the rest of the crowd. A voice sounded directly behind her, "Why, hello Helen. Looking for someone?" It was Stevi.

She turned "No. Yes. Rick."

"I haven't seen him since last Friday night. Have you?" Helen felt herself going hot. "Have you seen Rick this morning?" She spoke to a girl beside her.

"I think he was going into town. He seemed to be going in that direction when I saw him about twenty minutes ago."

"There we are then. Mystery solved." said Stevi. "Stood you up as he?"

"No it wasn't that type of meeting." Helen put down her glass and left the bar only just hearing Stevi ask what other sort of meetings there were.

She barely made the beginning of the afternoon session. A girl she hardly knew handed her a note. Her heart gave a leap, primary school or not. "A boy asked me to give you this. Don't worry I haven't read it. Could have done though. Its not in an envelope."

"Thanks." The waiting was unbearable as the teacher seem to drone on and on and all Helen wanted was the exercise to do then amongst the papers on the desk she could scan the note. At last she was able to spread the piece of paper.

"Must see you. Friday? Can you make it for the night? Meet you lunchtime at YOUR bar. Love Rick x."

Which lunchtime she thought. Friday lunchtime. Tomorrow lunchtime. She would wait for him every lunchtime until he turned up.

When Friday finally arrived Rick was waiting for her at the bar at her college.

"Want a drink?"

"Gin and tonic."

"No lectures this afternoon?" His penis was beginning to rouse itself as he thought of the potential for the rest of the day.

"Yes. Need a drink." It subsided.

"Are you doing anything tonight? Got this great new Cohen which I'd love to play to you."

She didn't care about the Cohen, whoever he was. 'Yeh. That sounds great.'

"Can you go to the bed sit and wait. I might be a bit caught up."

"With Tara."

"With Tara."

"I'll wait. But sort it. Do you want me to stay?"

"It could take all night for you to appreciate this record."

"It could." She finished her drink. "I'd better go. I'll see you later."

He was waiting for Tara when she arrived home from her shift. She was surprised to see him and pleased.

"Wait for me while I bath."

When she returned she was wearing only a shirt.

"I can't stay long. I have a Rag Week Disco to go to. You know raising funds so we can have some money in the bank for other events..."

"Well we can go together. I'll get dressed later."

"Aren't you tired?"

"Is there somebody else?"

"No of course not."

"Come here then. Afterwards I'll come with you."

He'd never found her so receiving as if she wanted to be completely at one with him. So much so that he could only turn his back on her after the sex.

"I have to go."

"Wait."

"By myself..."

"You're not coming back are you?"

"No."

"So. Little Miss Secretary won after all."

He got dressed. Leaving her expressionless, as she had known what to expect, in the bed he left closing the door behind him

When he got back to his bed sit he felt empty and fulfilled as though the past had left him and would never again be restored but never would need to be. He took the stairs to his room. He'd remembered to tell Jerry not to bring a friend home that night, not that he ever did. He wondered if it was all fantasy. Rick was in an excited state of anticipation. Two girls in one night, he was turning into a real Jimi Hendrix. He was faintly concerned to see that there was no light on in his room. Perhaps she was waiting for him between the sheets in the dark.

Helen had arrived at the front door of the house where Rick and his cronies lived. The building looked in complete darkness. She rang the bell but heard no sound. Perhaps it was broken. She banged on the door. There was no response. She stood back from the house and looked at it, taking in the full view as if she were about to do a drawing of the formidable building. Well she would have to wait it out she thought as long as he wasn't too long. She was cold. She decided to try a couple of more times and then go home. Perhaps it would be for the best. She hammered on the door for as long as she dared. She knew it was a big house and it was a Friday night but surely one of the students must be home. Faintly she saw a glimmer of light and then the light grew larger and larger like daybreak and footsteps approached and finally the door opened. It was Stevi the matriarch, who everyone appeared to be afraid of. She nodded to Helen to enter as though she were going into an illegal drinking den. She put her forefinger to her lips when Helen went to speak. She followed her into the kitchen and Stevi closed the door.

"He's upstairs with Tara. Sit down here. You wanna a glass of wine?"

Helen was confused. "I thought he was going to her place to finish it." And then realised that Stevi may not even know of this intention that night.

"I heard music earlier. Probably best if you keep out of the way, for a while, 'till she's gone. Unless you want to get your head knocked off." She laughed and raised her hands into fists. "You good at boxing?" No, no man is worth fighting over."

"Yeh." Lacking anything else to say. "Okay." She felt warm now so she took her coat off. And took a large swallow of the red wine.

Stevi looked at her slim figure and saw what Rick saw and Helen didn't. "You look like you needed that. You want a cigarette?"

"Well I do now. Wasn't expecting this." She paused in the trauma. "Here have one of mine."

"Go and have a look."

"No. I think I'll give that a miss."

"He asked you to marry you yet?"

"Helen felt taken aback by such a direct question. "What do you mean?"

"Our Rick," Stevi spoke with some affection," Falls in love in about two hours and gets engaged in about two days. None of them ever last." Stevi made it sound like a string of girls. Helen was only aware of Tara and the conquest she thought that she had made believing that he had been with Tara for two years or more. She wondered if for some reason Stevi was just being plain nasty and like to play with people's lives. Whether she was jealous. "It's a joke amongst a certain fraternity of the university. Don't tell him."

"No I won't and no he hasn't." She wondered if he'd ever been engaged to Stevi.

It was as if she were reading Helen's mind. "No, he's never even given me a kiss under the mistletoe. Well it's different." Helen looked puzzled as if she'd lost track of the conversation. What's different she thought. *"This* one might last then. Do you like him? Here let me fill you glass."

"Yes"

"Sorry you don't really know me and here I am asking you personal questions. Clement weather we're having for this time of the year don't you think? A cold snap I'd say. Should be warmer for Christmas."

"It's okay." She was wondering if Stevi was right in the head. Helen looked around the room and took in its lived in grubbiness but also its clean orderliness as though there were a guiding hand here, like a mother. Stevi watched her eyes moving.

"If I lived here permanently I'd decorate. But the residents here will be gone within six months or so from now. What's here probably won't even be a memory for some people. 59 Billing Road you'll ask them in ten years time when they're married in middle class suburbia and they won't want to remember. It will be too painful." As the one sided conversation went on Helen understood less and less and wondered if Stevi had drank a bottle of wine by herself before she arrived. "How old are you Helen?"

"Nearly eighteen."

"So seventeen. When's your birthday?"

"Next May."

"So nowhere near eighteen. A child." She laughed. "I'm eleven years older than you. Bet that sounds really old doesn't it?"

"No." Stevi looked at her as if to say you can tell the truth. "Well, yes."

"Don't worry I know what Rick and Jerry call me, Stalin's Grandmother." Helen tried to suppress a laugh, but it didn't really matter. "I should have been married by now, a part of the middle class suburbia as I call it. Here let me fill you glass. Have some more. The night is young and long and there is plenty where that came from." She poured. "I don't know what happened really. Well I do. I've got a sister five years younger than me. Or I should say I had. I hate her." She spoke with a vehemence that did not really belong to her or the occasion. "He thought it would be great fun, good for his ego, and all that crap, to bed the both of us. My sister knew what she was doing even though she was only fourteen. Well a great way to get one over the older sister isn't it? My flesh is better than yours, she was telling me." She took a swallow of the wine. "She hated me anyway. So let the fiancée screw her. At least he ran off and left the both of us. Neither of us has him now. She's married with a kid. Hate them all. You know what that flap of skin is called at the end of a blokes prick?" She went on before Helen could answer recalling her biology. "His brain. Wait." She raised a hand though Helen was silent. "I can hear someone coming downstairs."

"Helen?" but there was no reply as he entered the room. There was no one there, just the sound of the needle clicking away at the end of the end of an LP. He went over to the stereo and turned it off. He was alone. He sat on the bed and waited. It all comes round he thought. Was it some kind of game she was playing? The whole house was silent whereas he could normally hear Patti Smith, the latest craze amongst the girls. Some of them had even stopped shaving under their arms. It was as though he had been completely deserted. He listened to the sound of occasional traffic as a car passed. He daren't play a record. He might not hear the front door knock or the sound of her footsteps on the stairs. He felt very alone. After an hour he went downstairs for a coffee. He needed to put on a brave face, to show that he was intending to spend the evening at home by himself for a change. When he opened the kitchen door which wasn't usually closed Helen, sitting at the table with a glass of wine in front of her, looked up at him. Opposite her was Stevi. Between them was a nearly empty bottle.

Helen whispered almost mouthing at him, "Has she gone?"

"Who?" Rick smiled for the second time that night. Relief swept through him. "She's never been here. Not tonight anyway. She's part of the past. I forget the past."

"I thought…"

"Come on."

The next morning they rose at dawn and walked empty streets and through the park as though they were the only living people in the town. They watched the sun rise against a dark brown and the golden orb reflected off the newly fallen leaves, not dead but carrying on their existence to a new and greater depth. They stood and watched in absolute silence each knowing that there was nothing that they could say about the moments they were sharing. They returned along the streets, not touching as though they were just casual friends met to get the early morning milk. The pair returned to bed and made love slowly and more carefully and then slept until after noon.

Rick was awoken the following Tuesday to the sound of hammering on the front door for what seemed like an eternity. He could tell it was early by the grey morning gloom. He didn't care who it was and he was expecting no one. Alone in his bed he turned to the wall leaving the call to be answered by someone, if they could be bothered, closer to the door. Tough on whomever it was who had forgotten their key. When he finally got downstairs for his early morning lecture Stevi was in the kitchen sipping at a cup tea.

"I was up early for you."

"Yeh, morning to you as well."

"Did you not hear?"

"No. I just got up." He shook the kettle to see if it was full enough for boiling.

"Well it was for you."

As he filled the kettle the steam burned his hand. He winced with sharp pain. "Oh yeh who was it?" Though he now knew.

"Nursey wifey. On her way to work I think, or perhaps on her way home. Or going to a fancy dress or…"

"Yeh alright. Point taken. Get on with it." Rick was feeling irritated with the slow boil of the kettle. "What did she want? And she's not wifey any more."

"*Oh.* I am sorry."

"I knew you'd be pleased."

"I'm familiar with your present domestic arrangements. That's why it took two of us not to let her up to your room this morning. Thought you might be in bed with wifey secretary."

"And she's not my wifey either."

"What, you not asked her to marry you yet?"

"Well what did she want?" he asked feigning boredom.

"She thought you might not be looking after yourself properly so she brought you a pork pie round. Your favourite it seems. It's in the fridge."

"Oh good, breakfast."

Rebuffed that morning and feeling something that could only resemble hatred for the two girls who should have understood but would still not let her into his house. Tara had returned to her flat and sat alone. Looking at the walls she saw that Rick was there if she stayed around here. The posters. A man in dark glasses dragging on a cigarette. Everything about the place would remind her of Rick. She wondered where it was that she went wrong. She felt that she was to blame. They had been so good together. Even her parents, they were all expecting them to marry. They liked the idea of him as a future son-in-law, imagining the grandchildren. That was something she had taken for granted. Maybe it was something they'd all assumed. Maybe that was the key. She had taken Rick for granted and then a new model had come along. In his mind faster, younger and more exciting. She knew that she was lost. There could be no return. It was be that for the rest of her life. She would remember the time with Rick and that pain of nostalgia would cause her to ache even when she was loved again. On that day she determined never to love, never to give herself completely. There would always be a part of herself that she would hold back, which was for her alone. She had to get out and not just to work but also of the town, to start again. She would quit, work her notice and then another hospital could have her.

That lunchtime Rick went to the bar for an orange juice before the afternoon lecture. Helen came into the bar and took him by surprise, as he wasn't expecting her.

"What you doing here? We don't have a date do we?"

"No. Don't panic. My teacher is ill and so this afternoon's been cancelled. I thought we could find something to do."

"We could, but I have a seminar. Mind you its very subsidiary. Something about world religions. It won't catch on. And a really boring creep, Mr Fry, teaches it, he won't miss me. Come on let's go to the bed sit if that's what you had in mind."

"Well what else is there?

SIXTEEN

A few days later when Rick checked his address centre in the student's common room there was a note from Mr. Fry asking why he had missed his session on world religions the previous Tuesday. Rick replied that he had been unable to attend as he had been 'studying the contours of his girlfriend's body.' Adding 'that assuming you are human I'm sure you'll understand.'

When Mr. Fry received Rick's note he smiled inwardly to himself and stood up and feigning furiousness rushed to the vice principal's office, straight past a surprised Dr. Bonnet's secretary who, like St. Peter, held the keys as to who did or didn't see god.

"Vice-principal," he said in a rush of frenzied anxiety, "I am so sorry to disturb you as I know that you are a very busy man, but I have received the most offensive note from one of the students. And I do not think that this is trivial and I'm sure you won't either."

"You have? Now let me see. Sit down. Sit down. Calm yourself. You look in a state my man." Mr. Fry passed the note over. The vice-principal read, looking over the top of his half moon glasses. He tut tutted in disgust. "Who is this from Roger?" He asked even though he could see a name at the bottom of the note, scrawled. He felt that he should register his shock.

"Rick Sharpe, vice principal, as you can see."

"Is it indeed? Oh yes. I can see the name amongst the scribble now. It's a shame that he does not have more worthy matters on his mind. I will speak to the young man. Firmly. And now you Roger, you need a cup of tea. I have been meaning to talk to you about your future with us."

Making sure that he still appeared to be flustered he said, "That would be very pleasant sir."

Roger left the office sometime later and vice-principal Arthur Bonnet, who was nearing his retirement, swivelled, in his comfortable office armchair, so that he was looking out of his window across the well-kept green lawns of the campus. He watched the girl's arms crossed over their breast as though they were defending themselves from potential attack. He put his forefingers to his lips and thought and remembered his days at Oxford. He had received a first in the sciences (the only worthy subject he firmly believed) and should have moved onwards and upwards in his Oxford College. A don and who knows what. However, war broke out against Germany and put an end to all that, an end to his career. That's what these longhaired drug ridden layabouts needed with their music he didn't understand or want to. They had nothing to protest about. Higher grants...give them army pay for three years and a decent haircut. Turn them into correct citizens, worthy of contributing something useful to the nation. He'd joined the Air Force and became a pilot. He was really quite successful, proud to fight for his country and his monarch. Of course he'd fallen for a WAAF. Loved her to the ends of the world. Young people today think that they are the only ones to have discovered love. But as can happen even with the cleverest and most careful of men she became pregnant. That was something else they had too easy these days, the pill. He had to marry her of course, but he loved her anyway and wanted nothing else in the world. She gave birth as he was dropping bombs on Dresden. She and the boy died in childbirth. He spent months in a psychiatric hospital and had great difficulty resuming his career. He, for a while, taught in a grammar school in the Midlands finally getting a post as lecturer in a small teaching college. They gave him the post of vice-principal when the university opened. He was close to retirement. It was a reward. It would mean that the government would have to give him a good pension. But what would a lonely man spend that on? He had no grandchildren. He would live out his days thinking about what could have been. His wife still looked at him each day from his desk. He turned and looked at her. He only felt a burning anger. Now had come the time for some revenge. No matter how small and how petty. He called in his secretary to arrange an interview with Rick. She informed him that he, Dr. Bonnet, wasn't free until about five days time, next Tuesday.

"That's alright Judith." It would give the weekend for Rick to sweat as well. "Post him a note. Internal. Tell him that I have a concern with him missing lectures and that it may put his degree into jeopardy."

She nodded whilst at the same time writing shorthand.

"Let me see it before you send it out," he added, "I'd like to sign it."

She nodded assent again and briskly left the office.

Twenty minutes later he went home, as he was feeling slightly unwell. As he walked through his secretary's office he said as he always did, "Goodnight Judith and thank you."

"You wanted to sign the note to Mr. Sharpe, sir. It is ready and I can put it through internal post this evening."

"Oh yes. Thank you." He glanced through the note and satisfied with its content placed his squiggle.

Vice-principal Arthur Bonnet had been dead for some hours as Rick read and re-read the note hoping that the content might change on second, third and fourth reading. His immediate reaction was to dismiss it, but as his seminar progressed his mind kept coming back to the words 'degree in jeopardy'.

"Rick what about you?" His tutor asked.

"What about me what? Oh I'm sorry." His tutor let out a sigh. "My mind was somewhere else."

"I can see that. I shouldn't need to sound like a schoolteacher Rick but your finals aren't so far away."

That was just what Rick didn't need to hear.

Judith arrived as she normally did at 9pm prompt and thought it odd that Dr. Bonnet's car wasn't in his reserved parking space. By ten she was concerned enough to ring him at home. Getting no reply after forty-five minutes of trying she put her coat back on and drove to his house. A place she had only visited once for a pained evening of sherry one Christmas. She was the only guest, though whether others were supposed to turn up she never knew. But for two people working quite closely together they had run out of anything to say after ten minutes. She left with the dreadful excuse that her cat wasn't well. She didn't even possess a cat and for a few days had to report on the fictitious animal's progress to him. She was relieved to see his car in the drive and expected to be told that she was a 'silly girl' worrying over nothing and that he'd had a Doctor's appointment – I don't have to account for all of my movements do I Judith - as though he lived a wild life. She smiled at the thought. She rang his doorbell. There was no reply. The neighbour's hadn't seen him since the morning before so she rang the police from their house. After convincing them of her concern they broke in through the back door. A quick look downstairs yielded nothing. She remained where she was leaning against a kitchen chair whilst one of them went upstairs. As she waited her hands clasped against the wooden bar until her knuckles showed white she knew what it was that the policeman would say when he came back downstairs.

"Do want to sit down?"

"No." She shook her head as if it were the last thing she wanted to do.

"A cup of tea?" He looked around as if he were hoping would materialise.

"No. That's kind." She added as an afterthought. "But no thank you."

She'd been through this before. A well-meaning friend had once asked why she had never married. Even at nearly sixty she was still considered something of a beauty. The odd male student had embarrassed themselves by having the 'hots' for this late thirties Mrs. Robinson not realising that she was on the way to being the age of their grandmother.

"No," she told the friend, "I never married. There was only one man for me and he died."

"Oh. I'm sorry." The friends wished she'd never asked, and wanted the earth open up and hide her discomfiture. "I didn't realise."

"Well of course not or you wouldn't have asked. I've never really told anyone. Those who knew, like my parents, have long since passed away. He was a pilot in the Second World War. You know the type. You've seen them in a hundred films. Young, handsome, dashing, full of bravado. He even had the obligatory sports car!" She smiled at the pleasant thoughts, then her face became sad. "He died in The Battle of Britain. I knew that he had died when his Father turned up at home. You couldn't waste petrol then. For a moment I thought it was Douglas until I saw his Father get out of the car. His shoulders sagging as if the very life had been taken out of *him* and not his son."

The policeman came back downstairs and told his colleague that he had radioed for an ambulance. He turned to Judith. "I'm sorry."

"He was in RAF you know. He tried telling me about it one Christmas."

"Come on. Let's get you out of here and home."

That evening Rick was in a pub with Helen talking about the letter he had received. She was trying vainly to calm him down as he was completely pessimistically saying that it was the end. A student he barely knew came over to them.

"Hi Rick." Oh God, Rick thought. This is not the time for Rag Week pleasantries. "Have you heard the news?"

What now? "What news?"

"Arthur Bonnet." Does the whole world and his mother know that I'm about to be kicked out? "He's dead."

"What?"

"He's dead. Died in his sleep they say. Heart attack probably. Wonder who was in bed with him."

Incredulous Rick smiled and then laughed and then became hysterical. Laughing so much that tears were streaming down his face and his stomach ached.

The student and Helen just looked at him as if he were from another planet.

The following morning Roger Fry was appointed acting vice-principal and Rick tore up the note waiting to be summoned. He never was.

To celebrate they decided to have a real posh evening out as a couple. She had bragged all week to her parents and friends that Rick had booked them a table at the Imperial Hotel for dinner at eight that Saturday. She started dressing at four and met him at half past seven. They looked a handsome couple as they had a drink in a pub before going on for the meal. They felt like Hollywood stars as they climbed the steps to the hotel and Rick even opened the door for Helen. They walked across the foyer to the dining room as they went to enter the room they were stopped by the doorman who said, "I'm sorry you can't come in here without a tie."

"I don't own a tie," answered Rick.

"Well we can lend you one sir."

"So I could be a prize yob in a tie…"

"We do have standards to keep. And our clientele prefer it that way."

"Well fuck your clientele. Come on Helen. We'll go somewhere more welcoming."

But he was so self absorbed that he didn't see the look of disappointment cross her face, as she knew it would be another Chinese. And what would she tell her friends.

"I'm sorry sir, but I do hope that you will join us in the future."

Later she would remember and laugh about the evening when she and her husband went to a nightclub in New York that was supposedly frequented by Mick Jagger and Andy Warhol. They dressed up for the evening but when they arrived at the door they were stopped by a six foot ten gorilla, now they knew that they didn't look like Blondie and Sting but had no idea what was wrong until the bouncer said, "Sorry sir. You can't come in wearing a tie."

SEVENTEEN

On the evening of the Rag Ball, the highpoint of the week, Rick, Helen and his cronies were drinking in the guest's bar. Apart and not mixing with the general public Tara alone amongst the crowd watched. This should have been her evening, their night.

Rick had put the whole event over into hands of security officers. At their suggestion they were to allow in as many as they thought the hall would hold. This was way beyond the amount allowed for the event. If there was a fire it would be a total disaster but he wasn't thinking about that. This was to be the first Rag Ball in the history of the university that was to make money and a lot of money.

"Rick," someone touched his shoulder, "Your guest is here." He turned to see Richard Thompson standing at the door quite shyly. He was smaller than he had expected.

Rick walked over and shook his hand. "We share a name," he said for the want of something to say, "I'll take you to the room we've put aside as a sort of dressing room. Sorry but it's the changing rooms for the gym. Let me know if there's anything else you want..." The words gushed out in his nervousness.

"As long as the roadies have set up properly we should be ok. Not now there's no real chance of a sound check. I should have got here earlier, but for the traffic on the M1."

"Oh don't worry they'll love you."

"We hope."

They all laughed as people do when there's nothing really to laugh at.

As Rick left the 'dressing room' to return to the bar he was caught up by one of Richard's group. "Just to let you know man, he doesn't do encores. Doesn't play those games and doesn't like them."

They listened to the gig and Richard produced a set that could have only come from the gods. It didn't need any special effects or lights or sounds. It was simply perfect. They finished with the old Fairport classic 'Meet on the Ledge', a sad but strangely uplifting song. He bowed and left the stage to tumultuous and genuine applause. Rick followed him to the 'dressing' room.

"That was amazing Richard. I cannot describe how that felt. Won't you play another? They loved you." Rick was glowered at, but not by Richard.

"Yeh right. Come on." Richard spoke to his group who looked at him in amazement.

"Well there has to be a first time for anything," said Rick.

He and Helen watched as he took the stage and captured the audience for one last time. As the chords to 'Calvary Cross' opened Rick knew he was listening to history in the making; A song that would be archetypal, a recording that would have to be in everyone's collection that cared about music. The audience listened in stunned silence. Atmosphere layered upon atmosphere. Slowly one cigarette lighter was alight and soon the whole hall was ablaze with flickering lights as the music flowed and flowed and the lyrics rolled and rolled. They knew that they were listening to the greatest, probably the greatest moment of their concert lives as Richard and his band played for all they were worth. Rick knew he had succeeded. This would be remembered. Richard even looked him out to say goodbye after the circus had gone home saying what a great night it had been.

EIGHTEEN

Lesley was used to getting just what it was that she wanted. Ten years younger than her older sister and the surprise child of elderly parents she was the archetypal spoilt brat. All the family indulged her. She only had to ask and she got. A car is vital for getting to college. The buses are awful she told Daddy, 'I live miles from college,' and then she became one of the few students' in college with a car, a puce Beetle but 'It hasn't got a cassette player' as she told him on more than one occasion.

She couldn't have the student union president of the college as he was already married, though she did wonder if it might be worth the fun, so she decided to settle for next best male, the Rag Week chairman. Flaunting herself to him at a disco pretending to be drunk Helen had joked to Rick, "You could have her if you wanted," the inexperienced girl needed to know how much it was that he loved her and if at all.

Girls, it is said, like to marry someone who is like their father. Rick had heard of this but never really wondered whether the same applied to boys. Does the male look for someone who is just like his mother? If so then all Rick needed was someone who was bossy and domineering. In Lesley he had found the perfect match. And of course this gave him the security, which is what most people want and the belief that he had found a mummy. How many girls make their boyfriends a cake to show what a good homemaker they would be for them and their children. Marry me and everything will be as comfortable as warm chocolate gateau. He took Helen home once. His mother didn't like her. She probably saw the sensuous passion, the dark rhythm of he body, and was jealous. His Mother told him that she thought Helen was too young, loose and she didn't like the fact that she smoked. Rick had no answer to this against his mother, the woman who treated him akin to a boyfriend in the need and desire to remain young and in touch. Mother and son went to see 'Last Tango in Paris' together. And his mother made sure that everybody knew. Showing off about it. That really she was as young as he was. When he took Lesley home she was altogether a different proposition. Lesley recognized how to play the mother until she knew that she had won.

Later Rick thought that he was being very clever and desirable by having two girlfriends at the same time. Lesley played along with this game for a little while pretending not to know. Helen had absolutely no idea. Lesley got him to move back onto campus closer to her and more convenient for lectures she told him in his final important months. But he was within the trap she was weaving until he could no longer unpick it. Helen knew that Rick was losing his freedom but she didn't know why. Only that the room at the bed-sit had gone with the entire atmosphere that it had of careless living. All the students' had moved away as Stevi had predicted. Sometimes it had been so cold there that the only way to get warm was through the passion of holding each other so close under piles and piles of bedclothes. Maybe there had been a sign to read. In public, in the streets, with friends, in a bar or at a disco they never touched. He never reached out and held her hand. Never bought her flowers. It was as though he were afraid of her, or that their relationship never took off on being beyond sex or that he was the boss and she was the secretary. She was the only girl he never told he loved her or asked to marry him. She took him home once and he impressed her parents because he was studying theology and so must be moral. They had no fears of their daughter's honour being besmirched. He was able to answer questions on classical music on a television quiz so it followed that he was cultured, but he lost it all by announcing for some reason that he would never fight in a war and everybody who had ever done so needed their brains examining. Helen later told him that her father had spent his war in a Japanese war camp and had suffered dreadful hardships. So much so that he still had nightmares. 'My point exactly,' was all Rick told her. Now it was a clinical white painted room with a radiator where the atmosphere was warm and dry and the noises off were like sixth formers at a prep school.

"I can't come and stay here," she told him. "I can't come and stay here anymore. My mum and dad know that you've moved back now. They don't believe me anymore that I come to stay with one of the girls. They think I'll get up to all sorts that I'll later regret."

"Well you're going to the States aren't you?" He asked as if that were the answer to all their problems.

"No." She replied firmly.

"What are you going to do then?" He asked the question as if he already knew the answer and that was she wouldn't be around with him. It was a damp Sunday afternoon. The campus was as quiet as a graveyard. His window looked out across acres of green and then leafless trees, dead as though spring would never arrive again. From a grey sky it was drizzling a fine mist silently. But she thought it worth enquiring anyway.

"There's you and I."

"What do you mean?"

Helen paused and looked puzzled whilst the truth began to really take root. "Won't we be together?"

"Helen. You're barely eighteen." He sounded like a parent telling his 12-year-old child that they could not stay out after eight o'clock.

"Don't patronise me."

He thought of Lesley downstairs in a friend's room. Waiting. This was to be the afternoon that he would finish it with Helen. Lesley was a far more mature and sensible woman. A woman you could marry set up home with and have children. This girl was hardly more than a child.

He finally spoke again. "I'm not. I wouldn't do that. I just don't want to..."

"Fuck me anymore? Is that it?"

"No I just..." He searched around for words.

"You're arrogant..."

"I just think that we've reached the end of the road. You need to meet someone new."

"Doing me a favour now? Well you didn't do me many in the past. You were useless in bed. I never had an orgasm with you. You don't even know what a clitoris is."

"I think we should finish Helen. We can be friends."

"Oh the usual crap. How can you say that? I thought that we loved one another."

"I never said that."

"No. Neither did I. Perhaps I should have done." She paused and paced the room round in a circle trying to get out but not wanting to either. She came close to him and looked directly into his eyes. "You behave as if you owned the world just because you organised a rag event in a poxy college."

"Helen, try and calm down."

"Scared people will hear? Is that it? Calmness doesn't reign? What do you want? What do you want that I can't offer you? Well fuck you. I can screw who I like now. See if you like that."

"Helen I think that you should go."

She stopped and listened to the silence as if the whole college had been listening. She began to cry. "Oh no. Rick. I'm sorry. I'll do anything for you. I love you. Please forgive me. I beg you. I want you."

"You'll get over it."

She paused for some time as if forming an incantation. "I might Rick. But you won't. Not one day will pass when you don't think of me. But I'm never coming back."

She left the room sobbing. Lesley watched from the friend's downstairs until Helen had disappeared up the drive of the college and then went up to Rick's room. He was standing sombrely by the window. She went and held him. "You okay?" she said grinning over his shoulder out of the window at the fading figure.

Helen did not remember how she arrived home. Only that it involved walking streets that she barely recognised and seeing them through tears. Helen reached her front door and banged on it. She thought that she didn't want to see anyone but the effort of searching through he handbag for keys seemed too great an effort. She just wanted to be inside, maybe with her mother, maybe alone, on her bed. A neighbour passed and shouted cheerily "Hallo Helen. What you doing?" as he always had since she could toddle. She could only pretend that she hadn't heard. "No-one in? You can always wait at ours." She turned briefly and held up a key and he saw her streaked face, "You alright love?" She let out a sob and went into the house. Later the neighbour would not forgive himself for not insisting that she wait at his house instead of going to the shops for cigarettes. 'I shouldn't have walked on. I should have done more. I should have made her come to us.'

Helen stood in the empty house waiting for the silence. She needed a drink. Looking across at the polished surface of wood in the sterile room she saw a bottle of whisky. Dad had had that bottle of whisky, for she didn't know how long. It looked as if one perhaps two drinks had been taken from it and that was probably when someone was down with a cold and couldn't sleep. Rick had wanted a drink from it when he was here just two weeks ago. Just two weeks ago. Her parents were away on some excursion with the church that she used to go to and they wouldn't be back until late. They'd showered together and then wearing nothing but a red checked shirt she led him downstairs and they'd made love on the carpet in the living room. Right where she was standing. And the neighbours had walked past the house and had known nothing unless they had heard her passionate cries. She was a noisy lover. That had given her a kick. Rick's semen had stained her shirt and she vowed never to wash it again and had hidden it away. Then they had gone to her bed and done it again. She wanted to try every room in the house. But that had been pushing him to far so she had to settle for three. Now she filled a glass full of whisky and had gulped down the amber liquid burning her throat. She lit a cigarette. She never smoked at home. She didn't even know if her parents knew that she smoked. She didn't care. She'd fucked on the carpet. She poured another drink and staggered upstairs trying not to slosh it, the smoke from the cigarette between her lips making her squint. She sat at her table where she sometimes worked or occasionally wrote letters. A letter to Rick. She knew that once he read it everything between them would be understood and they could start again from where they had broken apart on this awful Sunday afternoon. She would tell him that she loved him as she should have done.

She read the letter through and through and noticed how she drank more whisky so the handwriting became more awful. Finally in a fit of anger once more she tore the papers up and let them fall about her as useless confetti. She hated it all. What was the point on doing anything? She'd given him everything. There was nothing more she could do. Did he think she enjoyed having a mouth full of semen? There was nothing so she might as well be nothing. Two years earlier a doctor for depression had given her diazepam. Let's see now if they'd make her happy. One tablet, a sip. Two tablets, a sip. Three tablets, a sip. This is taking too long and going nowhere. A handful and a swallow. There that's it. All gone.

A few hours later her parents came home. The house to them seemed eerily quiet. They had expected the TV to be on or music playing from their daughter's bedroom. There were no lights shining. She never went out on a Sunday night. That wasn't her habit. Not with college the next day.

Her father switched on the light in the living room and blinked at the sudden brightness. The first item to take his eye was the bottle of whisky half empty on the floor by the sofa. "If that boy, Mr Wonderful," he had an image of them both lying drunk in his daughter's bed.

"Shush." His wife held her hand up to quieten him. They could hear the loud purring of a cat. Or at least that was what it sounded like at first. Then the sound was more obviously of a person breathing through lungs that were obviously filled with phlegm.

She ran up the stairs closely followed by her husband terrified at what she was about to find. By the lamp of her daughter's bedroom she saw the girl lying flat on her back. Mouth open. Tiny pills were all over the bedding and the floor.

A glass broken as it had hit the bedside table. The lamp toppled. A magazine with a smiling young woman on the front and the headline, 'Keep your Man Ten Top tips How To' and 'Lose Weight Fast'. Die. The mother saw all this as if she were looking at a photograph and had an eternity to stand back and watch.

"Get an ambulance. Get an ambulance." He went to the telephone in their bedroom as she turned her to her side and asked, "Helen Helen Helen," needing her reply.

"I can't remember the number," she heard him shout sobbing, "What's the fucking number?" recognising that in twenty years of marriage she'd never heard him use foul language.

A few evenings after Rick had ended his relationship with Helen he went down to the university bar. It was surprisingly empty for eight o'clock, maybe because it was a Tuesday he mused. He bought a pint of Watneys took a sip and wiped his moustache on the back of his hand taking his drink over to a table. As he was wondering whether to go and buy a packet of crisps Fiona came into the area. She saw him and said, "You."

"Me," he answered smiling benignly.

"I've been looking for you." She came over to him and stood almost towering over him.

"Fiona. Look. I'd buy you a drink. But I'm a bit short."

"I wouldn't take a drink off you if I were dying of thirst."

"Oh I see. Teensy weensy bit upset about Helen are we?"

"Of course, but not only that."

He put his glass down. "Go on."

"I know all about the Wales trip."

"Every detail. Goodness I hope you weren't too shocked. Anyway you seem to get about a bit yourself. Malcolm's looking for a girlfriend I hear. He's pretty desperate so you could be in for a chance."

She tried to ignore the snide comments. "Any of us could have gone to Wales. I've seen the letter. You could have passed the letter round and asked for volunteers. We were all working hard, harder than you anyway. You just wanted a free trip away. Not even free. We paid your train fare and hotel bill."

"So?"

"You never reported back with anything useful."

"So? You wanted the free holiday?"

"I would have put it to a lot more use."

"Great."

"Well, what I mean is, what else have you got away with?" She felt on unsure ground now and he knew it.

"Implying what? I don't like the way this conversation is going. I understand you are upset. But help me with the rest. Are you upset because I dumped your friend or because I wasn't screwing you?"

"Oh, fuck you Rick." She reddened.

"This is not Watergate Fiona. Have you heard of that beyond the walls of your squat? We made more money than last year. And Helen, don't forget, showed you the letter?" He waited for a reply but none was forthcoming. "So she knew all about it. I seem to remember that she enjoyed it as well. Tell anybody who's interested Fiona. Make your friend look an idiot. Then you can be idiots together."

"You don't know do you Rick?"

"Know? I know plenty. That's why I'm at university and you're at some poxy college."

"No. You don't know."

He picked up his glass and went to lean on the bar. When he turned round she was gone. He shrugged and bought another drink and a packet of peanuts.

NINETEEN

Lesley stayed put in college to finish her course whilst Rick went off to Devon to teach. He started to enlighten pupils in his care at the local comprehensive on his twenty-second birthday. He didn't mind. He would probably have to put up with that for the rest of his teaching career. He didn't remember celebrating his eighteenth or twenty-first birthday and one of them was supposed to be special.

He was lodging with a female maths teacher from his school in a city about twenty kilometres away from his place of work. She and her family lived in a big three storey terraced house close to the main streets of the city. The house was very like his student house, in substance. Her husband was weird. He once asked Rick if he wanted to go out for a beer one evening. So Rick sat for the whole night waiting for the call. It finally came about half an hour before closing time. And this was his norm. Go to the pub and drink four or five pints in less than thirty minutes. The whole act caused Rick to vomit in the gents and he never went with him again.

He didn't like living with the family. He was too beholden to them. Too like living with mummy. Though he could watch the town's football matches from his bedroom window.

Rick was pleased when he moved and lived for a while with another male teacher and in a grand house overlooking the estuary. A prime minister had lived their once and kept pigs. One Sunday the owner of the house came to tell him off for feeding the pigs but he never fed the pigs any day. They were smelly and a city man wasn't interested in the country though he particularly loved the sea. He'd had fond imaginings of wandering the beach in his hippy gear and living off the shellfish, something never realised because he quickly found out that a lot of the town recognised him through their children and they would have laughed. He wasn't local. In fact he was never local, even years later though his grandfather had been born close to where he now taught.

On a Friday evening he went on a pub crawl with his colleagues. A lot of staff were appointed each year to the largest comprehensive in the country so it followed that a number of them were fresh to teaching. They started at the dingy cider bar overlooking the beach where the grockles sat and sunned themselves. It was a good place to get the alcohol flowing and it was full of the most interesting local characters. One evening Rick had been in the bar and one of these men had come in with piles of money to spend and bought drinks all round. Only an hour before he had murdered the local bookie and robbed him of the day's takings. Rick had played darts with him that evening. The murderer didn't behave like he'd just taken another human's life. Maybe he just felt that at last he was getting his rewards for a lifetime of drudgery. The police picked him up that evening, because when he heard about the murder in the small town the landlord of the pub became suspicious. Rick looked over at the darts board where he had stood with the killer that night, it reminded him of another occasion in the bar where he was chatting to a couple of local fishermen and they told him how during the Second World War that had seen a German pilot parachute from his plane. They had motored over to him in the sea and made for rescuing him. When he was close enough to the side they held him under the water until the pilot drowned. They didn't consider that murder. It was an act of war, they declared.

"Come on Rick. Drink up. Rick! Wake up!" He looked up from the bar at his friend's smiling face. "Com on mate. You were miles away. We're waiting."

The group moved on and on, louder and louder until it turned into a real crawl. Finally at closing time they decided to go to the town's only nightclub, 'SmokeyJoes'. Rick really just wanted to go home and to bed. He'd had enough. But he didn't want to be the killjoy. The one that they laughed at in the staffroom on Monday.

The club lived up to its name. It was ill lit, smoky and humid with stale sweat. Soul music pounded out a bass. When they went in they doubled the clientele to about twenty people. When the pubs finally locked their doors more joined and the place began to get something like atmosphere but it was not like university. This was pretending.

Rick stood watching holding a pint of tepid lager in one hand and a cigarette in the other when an attractive looking girl staggered over to him. She was dressed as if she'd fallen out of the screen of the Woodstock film.

"Don't I know you?" she asked him.

He had never set eyes on her in his life. He would have remembered if he had and could only answer her, "I don't think so."

"Wouldn't you like to."

"What?"

"Get to know me."

"I haven't really had the opportunity to think about it."

"Here get me a drink. I'll hold yours." At that point she started to giggle uncontrollably.

"Okay. What do you want?"

"You choose."

So he went and got her a gin and tonic as he used to buy Helen. He asked for ice and lemon but of course that was beyond them. He took it back and they swapped drinks. She had smoked his cigarette in his absence.

"Do you dance?"

"No. Never." He lied

"Can you take me home then. I want to go home."

Rick appreciated the excuse to get out of there but had to say, "I don't have a car."

"Say let's walk."

So they walked. I'm Rick he introduced himself and she told him she was Marcia. She hung onto his arm.

"My house is pretty empty tonight. I get frightened. Can I go to yours?"

He knew the route that this was going but decided to go there anyway.

"Yeh course. Let's get a taxi."

So they went back to his large flat overlooking the estuary. It was pitch black after the lights of the taxi had gone and Rick had to hold her very close as he fumbled for the light so that they could see there way down the steps to the kitchen door, the entrance to the flat. She smelt of patchouli and it took him right back to his university and Stevi's room. They went into the kitchen. Rick assumed that his flatmate was back and asleep. It was after one in the morning. And he wasn't one of the boys but a thirty year old head of the geography department.

"You want a coffee?"

"My mum usually makes me cocoa. You got any?"

"Yeh. I love it."

"I'll have to use your loo." And off she went.

"Left and you can't miss it," he said to the retreating figure.

Rick made two mugs of cocoa and took them into the living room. Marcia was not to be seen. He put them down and pushed the door carefully open in the bathroom. She wasn't there. He had a pee and cleaned his teeth. When he went back into the lounge he noticed that the bedroom door was ajar. Taking the mugs he shoved the door with his foot. It opened further revealing Marcia lying naked on the bed. Rick thought that she looked lovely.

"Oh goody," she said, "I can get into bed and have my cocoa. Come in. And close the door behind you."

For sex Marcia was more demanding than any woman he had ever known. Her love making was selfish until she was charitable and it was breaking light when they finally slept.

Rick awoke his arm entwined around her and edged closer for more.

"Oh God." She suddenly sat up. "Is that the time. I've got to go." She leapt from the bed and fell into her clothes. He asked if he would see her again. "Not like that," was her reply, "You've had your fill." Then she was gone from the room and the last he heard of her was the door to the flat slamming hard.

Rick pulled on his underwear and staggered into the kitchen for a mug of sweet tea. His flatmate Alan was there.

"What…"

"Yeh." Alan nodded as if saying you may well ask. "What do you think you're up to?"

Rick thought that he was joking then realised that he sounded quite serious.

"She came home with me. It happens you know." Rick tried to sound piqued.

"Do you know who she is?"

"Marcia. Well that's what she told me."

"You don't do you. I teach her for Geography Rick. Do you know how old she is?"

"No. She's not…" Rick felt sick.

"Lucky for you mate, this time. But she's not long past sixteen. And you don't screw your pupils, at least not like that. We teach in a big school. You better hope she doesn't say too much or it will be bye bye teaching career, and not a word yourself. This is not bragging time. It won't go beyond this room. And if she does we'll just lie our asses off. I'll back you."

"Thanks mate. I owe you one."

"And don't do it again, at least not with schoolgirls. We all fancy them, but we control ourselves, cold showers and a vegetable diet. Come on. Cheer up. I'm sure it was a night to remember."

"Forget more likely." Rick went back to his bed and pulled the covers over his head.

Rick expected the worst when he arrived at school on Monday morning. He had kept a low profile for the rest of the fateful weekend. Staying in the flat for the whole of the time. Even forgoing his usual Sunday lunchtime trip to the pub, which he loved. Nobody could contact him there was no phone. If any person had wanted to see him it would have meant a walk out to his place. That rarely happened as no soul was going to make the effort to walk all the way out there just to find that Rick wasn't at home.

As he was looking at the relief timetable a friend commented that he had been missed the day before. "Not like you Rick."

"Still had a hangover."

"Ah, I see. A lost weekend." If only.

Weeks passed. He didn't see Marcia about the school. He never had before the Friday they slept together so there was no reason to now.

One Tuesday morning when he checked the mail in his pigeonhole there was a letter from the headteacher. Rick rarely saw him, let alone received a letter from him. Mr. Thorpe, the head, hadn't interviewed him for his post. The school was too big for that. He was some distant administrative boss who people talked about but didn't see, rather like god.

The letter asked to see him that coming Thursday at 1045am. Cover would be provided for his lesson, so it looked like it was serious but Rick tried to think that it was probably about nothing and that the other first year teachers' had also received similar invitations. When he asked, none of them had.

"What you been up to then?" one of them shouted across the staffroom. Rick and his flatmate's Alan's eyes met briefly and both of them knew what it was about.

"Nothing." He already felt like he was defending himself. "That is I shall find out on Wednesday. I'll let you all know. Promotion I expect."

They jeered at that.

Try as he might Rick could not put the meeting out of his mind. But it was very difficult. It was like re-living the whole event with Dr.Bonnet again. Except that this time it was more serious. Perhaps he had come to haunt him, the past had at last caught up with him. He couldn't expect Mr Thorpe to conveniently die though. He taught badly, slept fitfully, ate poorly. Mr Thorpe hadn't spoken to Alan. He knew nothing. Perhaps there wasn't anything to worry about, but he knew he was kidding himself.

On Thursday Rick's first two lessons finally ended and he made his way across to the head's office up flights of stairs in a house separate from the school buildings. He knocked on the secretary's door and entered without waiting for a come in. Her smiling face greeted him, which made him feel a little more at ease, as he knew that she knew what this was all about. Mrs Thorogood was a lovely and approachable woman for someone so removed from the ordinary clerical staff. She had every excuse for airs and graces but had none.

"Hello Rick," she said. He was taken aback because she knew his name. "Go straight in. He's expecting you."

He opened the door to the inner sanctum and went into the head's office for the first and last time. It was very old fashioned with dark oak furniture and dull curtains rather like the head's office at his old grammar school. But that wasn't so very long ago. Maybe he had inherited it this way.

"Sit down Rick." Mr Thorpe wasn't smiling. He sat down. Maybe he wasn't a smiley man. This was his way. "Do you know of a Marcia Whittle? One of our students."

So it was about that. "Er, no. Though to be honest, I'm not good on names and I may teach her. I seem to teach a lot of children." Rick smiled. Good so far.

"You won't come across her in you normal course of duties. She's in the sixth form. And she's not doing Religious Studies anyway." He paused and reflected. "Not really the type." He fiddled with a pen on his desk. "I'm sorry to have to ask you this Rick. But she has made a rather unsavoury accusation against you."

Rick did his best to look aghast and hurt and replied, "What? I've never come across this girl. What has she said?"

"That she spent the night at your flat a few weeks ago. One Friday."

"The night?" Rick asked as if he wanted to know what that could possibly mean.

"Well she says that you didn't sleep on the sofa and her in your bed but that you slept together and all that that entails."

"No. For whatever reason she's lying. I am engaged. We plan to marry in the summer. If this girl was able to give me a specific date it may have even been that my fiancée, Lesley, was staying that weekend." That thought hadn't occurred to him until that moment and he felt pleased with himself, as it was a good defence.

"Good. That's the answer I hoped to hear, expected to hear from one of my young and professional staff. You teach religion so you know all about morals and the importance of telling the truth. You're a good looking lad my secretary tells me and I expect this girl has seen you about the school and wanted to take her revenge by picking on someone susceptible."

"Revenge?"

"Yes. You wouldn't know but she's always been a handful and I had to expel her on Monday for inappropriate behaviour with a fifth form boy in a stock cupboard whilst a lesson was going on."

"Oh. I see."

"This will all blow over. Our stand will be that you didn't even know the girl. You are careful aren't you?"

"Careful?" Rick thought that he was speaking about contraception, which he hadn't been with Marcia. That hadn't occurred to him. She may be pregnant. Still from the sounds of it the baby could be anybody's.

"Yes. Never be alone with any of our girls, of any age. They could say anything and on occasions do. As we've had in this case." He stopped and looked at Rick to make sure that his words of advice had sunk in. "Coffee?"

"Oh yes."

Mr Thorpe went and popped his head round the door of his office.

"Coffee please Mrs Thorogood. And I expect our young teacher would like some shortbread. I know I would."

When he got home after school that afternoon Alan asked if it had all gone okay.
"Yes. How did you know for certain that's what it was?"

"He tried to get me off my guard I think as I was going to my first class this morning. In the corridor. Asked me if you ever had female company staying overnight. I said no. He wanted to know if I could be sure. I told him very sure. Our bedrooms are adjacent and I can hear everything."

"You can't can you?"

"Sure can mate."

"Oh no. I owe you one. Forget eating here. I'll buy you a pint and we'll have fish and chips. My treat."

TWENTY

Rick and Lesley married a few months later. The night before his wedding he had lain awake all night. Or at least it felt like that. The stars were even appearing on the ceiling of his bedroom. As the gloom gave into some kind of light he knew it was time to leave his bed, to wash and dress. Down stairs in the kitchen he waited for the kettle to boil longing for a cup of tea. He didn't have a hangover, as his Mother hadn't allowed any of them to drink too much the night before. The dog moved around him knowing that there might be a walk in this somewhere. One of his master's was already dressed. As Rick stood sipping his scolding tea he heard the toilet flush and footsteps on the stairs. The top step always creaked giving the game away. Many times he had silently entered the house and made it to the top of the stairs before his mother shouted 'is that you Rick?' who else was she expecting he thought. His Father entered the room, bare chested, though the day was already warm enough.

"You alright boy?"

"Yes fine. Couldn't sleep. Want a cup of tea?"

"No. I'll wait until the teasmade. Don't want to wake your mother."

"Might take the dog for a walk. Be peaceful this time of the morning."

"Okay. Don't run off!" He went back upstairs laughing.

Rick put on his jacket and attached the dog's lead, which began to get into a frenzy of excitement. Rick shushed him as he began to bark and left the house. He walked down the street. Most of the curtains were still drawn and it was if the whole world had died. There was only the lonely cat and the noise of the seagulls. Why did they want to be here so far from the sea? At the end of the street the hill overlooked the city where smoke rose from an industrial chimney sweeping across the buildings. He patted the dog's head and rubbed him behind the ears as he loved and Rick watched and thought. He felt as though he had lived on this hill for more than a lifetime.

Rick had been born in that house back up the road in the room next to the one that he hadn't slept in last night. He stroked the dogs behind his ears that looked at him plaintively as if to say 'Why aren't we walking?'

"Wait awhile," Rick said out loud to the dog that seemed to understand by settling down. "Good idea," and Jonathan joined him on the damp morning grass, "If I get wet it doesn't matter. I have to change."

Rick's father had paced nervously downstairs in the living room. He thought you only did this kind of thing in the films. But this was real. He had been the same at the first two births. He lit another cigarette. He'd promised to stop after the birth of this one. But tonight he couldn't.

Up stairs the midwife was saying to the doctor that she wouldn't have normally called him out but she felt worried about this one.

"You were quite right Mrs. Bullock, but I reckon that we'll be okay."

"I would have preferred her to have had it at the hospital."

"They all will one day Mrs. Bullock. But she won't be having anymore anyway." They spoke in hushed tones as if they were attending a religious act. "You will work there, in the hospital, not in the home."

"Ah, here he comes doctor. A boy Mrs. Sharpe." Her voice rose with the necessary excitement that attends a birth. But Mrs. Sharpe wasn't hearing. There followed a rush of blood and then another body.

"Did you know she was having twins?"

"I had no idea."

"She should never have had this pregnancy at home." He picked up the corpse. "He's dead. Wrap him up. There's no need to tell anyone. We'll dispose of him when we get to the hospital."

"As you say doctor."

"We need an ambulance and quickly. She needs a transfusion. That's our priority. Is there a telephone here?"

"No."

"There never is in these council houses."

Mrs. Bullock went quickly from the room and he heard her shouting. Mr. Sharpe realising that the baby had been born shot up the stairs hearing the panic in her voice.

"Run and get an ambulance. Quickly. Your wife is alright but we must get her to the infirmary."

He heard her last words as he bolted out into the night. It was teeming with rain in a sudden September storm. He was breathless as he reached the box. There was someone using it. Why is someone using it on a night like this he wanted to scream? He pulled open the door, "My wife. She needs an ambulance." The youth seeing the distress and panic in the man's face like something that he'd never seen before replaced the receiver without any explanation and picked it up again to dial nine nine nine.

"There you are mate," he said handing the telephone to Mr. Sharpe, "You tell 'em."

Back at the house the doctor and midwife were coping as well as they could. Waiting. Neither giving away any sign of panic. Mrs. Bullock cleaned the boy up and wrapped him in the ready and waiting blankets.

"He's very healthy," the doctor spoke as if saying well at least one of them will live. "I think it would be better if he wasn't in here. We'll take him along to the hospital."

She took the baby to the bedroom next door. There a boy of about five years old lay wide-awake. "Look," she said, "A new brother." The little boy sat up to stare incredulous. "Would you like him in bed with you? Just for a few minutes?" The boy nodded slowly and carefully. "I'll put him in here." She placed the baby beneath the bedclothes. "Now look after him won't you." The serious face nodded again and lay down gazing lovingly at the baby's closed newly born eyes.

Mr. Sharpe ran home and once in the house straight up the stairs and into his and his wife's bedroom.

"Is the ambulance on its way?" asked the doctor as the midwife was attempting to usher Mr. Sharpe from the room.

"Yes." He looked at this wife. She lay drained like a corpse. "Is she?" He couldn't finish the sentence.

"No. But she needs a blood transfusion." On cue they heard the ambulance. "Try and keep out of the way now Mr. Sharpe. That really is the best way that you can help."

"Your new son is in the other room," went on the midwife.

He left the room and went into his older son's bedroom. Already the baby had found his thumb and was sucking vigorously and they both made a beautiful memory. He picked the baby boy up and held him in his arms as the cortege passed the room on its way to the ambulance. Bringing up the rear was Mrs. Bullock. "I'll take him now." He followed them downstairs and out into the street.

The noise of the siren had brought half the population of the street out and the rest looking from behind curtains. He watched helplessly as the doors of the ambulance closed in finality and he knew that it might be the last time he saw his wife alive.

"What is it Bill?" asked a well-meaning neighbour.

"I don't know," he managed to reply. Grown men, he believed, didn't cry but he felt the tears beginning to roll. "The baby."

"Is there anything I can do?" He looked at the neighbour. He worked as a travelling salesman and was one of the few people on the estate with a car.

"Take me to the hospital."

"I'll sit in with the children," said his wife, "But you put dry clothes on. You'll catch your death." Her hand went to her mouth but it was too late.

They arrived at the hospital about a half an hour later. A priest was sitting by his wife's bed as a nurse took him in telling him that his wife was very sick. He took a look at the priest and asked vehemently, "What's he doing here?"

"Your wife is a Catholic."

"And," the priest carried on the sentence, "The Catholic church wants her to enter heaven full of grace, spending as little time in purgatory so that she knows the glory of Jesus and his angels and saints this night."

"Get out. Get out." He spoke in a hiss that was full of hate, "Or you will be aware of hell long before I am."

"I..." and stopped as he saw the fear in the man's eyes.

"Get out."

The priest went straight to the hospital chapel where he knelt and prayed with strength that this woman should not die but that God should give this man a miracle. Maybe that was what caused her to live, just the unshakeable need and selfishness of his father, when she would have been more comfortable dying.

Rick got up and walked down the hill towards the city farms. They were now covered in another modern housing estate. Once they had seemed like and eternity away from his home when he went to play there with Billy in an afternoon that was one huge adventure.

He stopped and paused for a moment. The afternoons with his mother used to be as it was now that morning. There used to be a strange kind of atmospheric silence, which gave a surround of eeriness. There were no phones to ring. Daytime television wasn't even a twinkle in the eye of the programme planner. Only 'Listen with Mother' on the radio and that had long past. Just the wait now for his brother and sister to come home from school and then the even longer wait for children's television to start. Sometimes the house was full of little girls though who had come to learn tap from his mother. He didn't like that. He was the special one.

Now there was a name to conjure with Wally Prickhead. That wasn't his real name but it summed up his character, how he was, though he never had that image of himself. He loved to arrange community events on the local council estate. It was all sort of an overspill from the Second World War when troupes went around to secret locations entertaining the pack of soldiers. He did this with a brand of religious zeal making sure that the whole event would reflect favourably on himself. One evening involved his mother's dancing class, a few jokes and a song or two and of course the raffle. As luck would have it Wally won the raffle and it was, to the eight year old Rick, a huge teddy bear. Now old Prickhead could have re-raffled it but no. He put on his most solemn voice standing there on the community hall stage as though he were addressing crowds at the last night of the proms and said, "Well I didn't expect to win this," laugh, go on Wally let us win it, "And I have no use for it. In fact," looking directly into the teddy's face, "I'm a bit too old for this," he allowed himself a smile while the audience laughed again with bated breath, "But as some of you know I'm a regular visitor to the children's ward at the hospital," in fact none of them did – good old Wally keeping his light under a bushel, "And I know a very ill little girl who is going to love him when I visit her tomorrow." He left the stage to thunderous applause, Rick clapping like a mad thing, managing to show the whole world what a saint he really was. But that was what adults were like really selfishly revolving everything themselves. He had a daughter, Rick remembered, who was a slapper. She got pregnant when she was fifteen.

There was a different afternoon though – his mother scrubbed him (he hated it even more when they arrived at the bus stop and she noticed the remains of dinner round his mouth and she spat on a handkerchief and rubbed at his face) and dressed him up and took him up to the school further up the hill, at the top in fact. She was to put his name down, that was what she told him. He didn't understand what that meant. Put his name down what? But he did when his mother took him to the school a few months later and left him with a lot of other children and a teacher. He was one of the few children that was not crying as their mothers and childhood disappeared forever. Rick remembered that they wrote their names on a piece of card so that the teacher would know who they were. He wished that his name been short like his friend Glyn Pope. Richard Sharpe was just, well too much for a little boy.

But there was another time as well when he was very young. How old he did not know. No other children were in the house so he must have been preschool, unless he was home from school poorly but it didn't feel like that. If you were poorly then you were kept in bed regardless. The time was during the day. He remembers it as a damp grey morning. Quite suddenly his father was at home and his mother was crying. They, his mother and father, held one another as if both were in great need but he was completely shut out. He wasn't included and nobody explained why.

In fact Rick's mother had gone round to the neighbour with the telephone so that she wouldn't have to walk up the hill to the box, which would have meant taking Rick with her. She could leave Rick for a minute or two. He was intent on his model cars. She needed her husband and he would have to come home from work. She would telephone from there. The doctor had gone. She was pregnant. Five months gone and she'd told nobody. Not her husband. Not her mother. Now the doctor had told her that it would be dangerous for her to have another baby.

"You should have told me earlier Mrs Sharpe. After last time."

"What will you do?"

"It will have to be a termination," he said grimly, "And soon." He took her hand kindly as she began to cry. "There'll be nothing to worry about. You will be safer this way, for you and your family. I'll try and get you into hospital this afternoon. Can you get your husband?" She nodded. "I'll be in touch with you later on."

His grandmother arrived later in the day and looked after them for a week or so.

Rick liked junior school where he was called Rick and one of the stars. He'd had a girlfriend at the school as well. A family from India had moved into the street. They were the first foreign people that most of its inhabitants had ever seen on his street. Out of their earshot his brother had sang,

'I'm gonna tell you how it's gonna be
Too many wogs in this country
And I'll tell you what they eat
Kit-eKat and Pal dog meat '

to the tune of a Buddy Holly song and his mother had complained about the smell of their cooking. "Eat that muck they call food," his father had said, "And it will poison you," as he cut with relish into another spam fritter.

The Indian family had a daughter named Sunni who was in Rick's class. They had passed surreptitious notes and she had become his first girlfriend. Not that they ever made any physical contact. But they and other children played together. A lot of the prejudice was bluff with some fear.

Rick didn't tell anyone about his girlfriend. He was afraid of his family's reaction. His brother would have laughed at him. But he thought her beautiful with her skin like the suntan that they spent hours trying to get in the summer rain. It never occurred to him either that his brother might have been jealous.

One evening at dusk they were out playing in the street. The latest craze was skipping with a long piece of elastic around two pairs of legs and one person jumped in and out and landed on the elastic in various sequences. Sunni and another girl had been holding the elastic and Rick had been doing the acrobatics when all at once a motorbike and sidecar roared around the corner of the street. Rick and the girl had raced from the game to the pavement, leaving Sunni tangled up in the elastic. She hadn't really stood a chance they said. She died as soon as her head hit the hard concrete surface her family was told later.

A police constable had come to his house later for his explanation of the events to see if it matched the driver's. His father had sat in with him and had had a very serious face but was enjoying the contact with officialdom.

"Well, I think that's about the lot," the policeman had said folding up his notebook and putting it away in his top pocket, "Nobody's to blame, I think we'll find." He looked directly at Rick, "Don't play in the road." Rick nodded emphatically. And to his father had said "At least it was only a paki this time." The policeman and his father had laughed.

They said nothing about her at school at all. It was as though she had never existed. Rick cried when he was alone for a long time after. A while later the Indian family moved somewhere else. Rick could never forgive her though. She had left so suddenly. He ached for the time back when they were playing in the street and he could have pulled her with him from the path of the motorbike.

In his mother's room was an old fashioned oak dressing table that looked as though she inherited from someone who didn't really want it anymore. Amongst all the pots of make-up and other cheap jewellery, which he liked to pick up and trail through his fingers like water, stood a small unused new looking teddy bear. One day he asked his mother if he could have it.

"No." She spoke kindly but firmly.

"Why?" He felt as though he shouldn't ask. That it told a tale, a secret that he wasn't to know about.

"Your Dad bought it for another baby."

"Another baby? What baby?"

"Jonathan." He thought she had said. "Leave it," Moving from the room and expecting him to follow, "It doesn't matter now."

In the long summer school holidays the three children took a turn in staying with their grandparents. He loved it. It wasn't the country full of adventures and ginger beer but he could watch television all evening and even see Coronation Street. His grandma he remembered was a superb cook. She taught him how to make chips properly. She told him stories about the war and ghosts that she had seen. At nine o'clock in the evening she made supper, a treat that never happened at home. They lived in a terraced house with a long entrance passageway and an outside toilet that froze in the winter. Once a man we-ed in the passageway while he was drunk coming home from the pub and it was if the third world war had broken out as Grandma went for him with a broom. Rick couldn't laugh. He felt embarrassed. The room he slept in had a high double bed that almost needed a chair to climb into. As well as religious statues and crosses on the wall there was a painting of the Virgin Mary whose sad eyes followed him wherever he went in the room. He was afraid of it when the moon caught her shining blue eyes. She reminded him of Sunni. In the morning he would wake feeling warm and terribly comfortable as the smell of woodbine drifted from the kitchen below and he knew that breakfast was waiting for him.

Rick's family also went to the seaside in the summer. Two weeks in a caravan at Norfolk. Rick's Father parked the car outside the caravan, turned the engine occasionally to make sure that the battery hadn't gone flat but the family didn't get back in it again until it was time to go home. So come rain or shine, and it was often rain he remembered, their days were breakfast, beach, pub, beach, tea, pub, fish and chips, bed, the same routine without fail. Over the years the schedule never altered. His memories were marred by the tetchy times spent of five people stuck in a caravan listening to the sound of rain falling without rhythm on the roof waiting for opening time. It began his dream though of having a cottage in the countryside.

A hard rain nearly fell on the world in October 1962 when Rick was just nine. He became so frightened that the world was going to end in a nuclear holocaust that he feigned illness. In the morning when he came round from a sleepless night he told his mother "I don't feel well."

"What's wrong?"

He was astute enough to know that an all over pain was difficult to assess so he replied in a feeble voice, "All over. I ache all over."

It was still the days when a poorly person meant a day in bed. She took his temperature and fortunately for him found it slightly raised. He probably looked ill from the lack of sleep. He lay in bed until October 28th 1962 too scared to eat properly straining to hear the news on the hour. Nobody ever said anything about the crisis but the radio stayed switched on all day when it was usually turned off after Workers Playtime and she turned the sound up and stopped whatever she was doing when the serious voice of the newscaster sounded. At the end he heard the world's collective sigh of relief and returned to school.

At times, about twice a year they would visit a large cemetery outside of the town. It seemed miles away. When Richard was adult he realised it was very close. The family went to put flowers on the grave of his father's brother who had died when he was only twenty- two. It was a family outing. Taken only in sunshine, so there was nothing sad about it. It was quite adventurous to play hide and seek amongst the gravestones. There wasn't anything reverent about it. The most exciting part was to catch a Midland Red bus back into the town or out to the Flying Horse pub. These buses were the buses of long journeys to exciting places. They went to Oadby, Quornby, Coalville and other far of villages that were on the unknown outskirts of the city. Then as dusk fell they would take a bus back home and the night would be warm and still and bizarre beneath the orange streetlights. If his parents had known how he loved travelling on that big red bus they might have taken him more often, but probably not. When his grandma died he took his own children out to the cemetery where uncle Joe was. It wasn't even very far by the slow moving hearse and uncle's grave had gone. It had been moved to make way for the expansion of the crematorium and behind the burning building as the hearse circled were newly dug plots each marked with a wooden cross like a First World War battlefield.

Rick laughed out loud as he recalled two more significant events of his early life making the dog start. The first was his brother taking him to see The Rolling Stones for his tenth birthday. The concert was in a cinema with masses of support bands like Charlie And Inez Foxx with Mockingbird and then the moment, the Stones themselves. They had arrived in a battered car to the back of the Odeon and they had all ran round to watch. In the concert he never heard a thing above the perpetual frenzied screams other than the word 'walkin', which must have been the song 'Walking The Dog.' That's what he was doing now. He chuckled some more and felt pleased that there was no one there to see him.

Like the rest of the young nation he saw 'A Hard Day's Night'. He didn't remember whom he went with but he could take anyone back to the seat he sat in staring entranced at the screen. It was a Saturday afternoon. He was eleven. He would go to the grammar school in a month. It was a time of change. It was raining outside, but he didn't know that. As the helicopter left the ground at the end of the film carrying the four god's he watched rapt. After the lights had come up he went into the foyer of the cinema along with a mass of people, seeing the queue to get in, them wanting to get out of the afternoon drizzle, whilst he was to return to a council house on an estate amongst many other council houses amongst many other council estates he felt the tears begin to fill his eyes as he realised that the kind of life he wanted belonged only in the womb of the darkness of the cinema where fantasy was played out. It was like that many years later when he realised that God did not exist as he had heard the wrong Beatle was shot dead.

Rick carried on walking and singing 'If I Fell' the dog trotting happily by his side as if it were enjoying the song.

Everyone, it was said, could remember precisely where he or she was when Kennedy was shot. For Rick it was a Friday afternoon. He heard the news and from his father's serious face recognised that something very significant had happened. But life carried on he still went to his swimming club that night.

Music had always played a great part in his life. When Rick was twelve or thirteen he went to the fun fair and spun on the waltzers at a tremendous speed listening to the most amazing six minutes of music that he had ever heard in his short life. "What forty-five was that?" he asked his brother as they got off the ride, Bob Dylan 'Like A Rolling Stone' was the reply. He'd never looked back then and quite soon it was the loneliness of the scratched copy he'd bought for fifty pence of Leonard Cohen loving all the girls of his fantasies in the morning and then Nashville Skyline the most perfect twenty nine minutes of music ever made

He'd passed his eleven plus. Wrote an essay about Route 66. When he did the maths the teacher stood over him and shook her head as she passed so he put the calculation right. Maybe he had cheated. From the moment he passed he and Billy's paths parted. Although Billy only lived three doors away he only saw him once again. It was as though he had ceased to exist. Billy went to a different school, a place for illiterates and delinquents, the local secondary modern. The only worse fate could be the new County Comprehensive where according to the local newspaper deeds happened that would have put their satanic majesties to shame.

Billy turned up unexpectedly one Thursday night when Rick was twelve and had been at his new school for a year.

"You wanna come to speedway?" Billy asked. "I got free tickets and my mate can't go."

Without realising that he was second choice in this game Rick went to beg his parents to allow him out.

"Please! Billy's got free tickets. It's only near where Dad works. I can walk there and back. And I'll be with Billy."

"Straight back mind. As soon as it finishes." As if he were likely to go onto an all night party with the riders and their girlfriends.

"Yes. Yes. I can go Billy." He ran from the room pulling on his coat though he wouldn't need it against the warm summer night.

He had laid on his bed on hot summer nights too much for under the covers and listened to the revs and roars of the bikes and had wanted to know what went on behind those high white walls. His father wasn't the kind of dad to have taken him. But now he was about to find out.

They went into the stadium and very soon Billy left him and met up with his own mates and they even talked to one of the riders. The 'mates' looked over at Rick as though going to the Grammar school meant that he had an infectious disease. Rick soon grew bored with the wheelies, the roar, and the chasing round and round the track, the thrills and spills that he had expected didn't exist for him. Only the sweet smell of oil and exhaust remained with him. He left without telling Billy and never spoke to him again. He got home. His parents had gone out. His brother and sister had just started watching a film on BBC2.

"You should see this," his sister had said without taking her eyes from the screen, "It'll do you more good than little boys and their toy motorbikes."

"Why. What's it about?" He felt he was about to defend the speedway.

"A man who plays chess with death."

"Either shut up and go away or watch it," said his brother.

So he sat and watched as the film played out to its final dramatic dance.

As he went to bed she said, "It's about time you started reading some good books as well."

The next day he started reading 'The Outsider' by Camus that she gave him.

Rick looked over at where the stadium had been. It had long been knocked down and the land sold to developers for a new estate. Just as his father's factory was an empty ghost shell. He had grown up that night and found his favourite film and book but the smell of the speedway was still in his nostrils remembering the past. The dog tugged to carry on with his walk.

Rick hated the grammar school. The system. The uniform. He had to wear a cap until he was fourteen. The teachers steeped in a tradition that belonged to the nineteenth century. He just couldn't care. Neither did his parents. The older children had fled and were well onto being teachers themselves. If you weren't clever enough to be a doctor then do the next best thing his mother had drilled into them "Be a teacher, you don't want to be like your father working in a factory." Though he had quite a nice life this past few years drinking home brewed beer all day on his redundancy money and the dole.

Rick excelled at swimming and never lost a race until he chose to do so when he was seventeen years old lacking the desire then for the prestige achieved by competition. He scraped together four GCEs, which just took him into the sixth form where he studied English, History and Religion. He didn't mind this. He was learning about what he really wanted to learn about and could live the Tudors, loved Luke's Gospel taught by the ascetic worldly wise teacher but English contained books, the fantasy for a dreamer. Yes, the incredibly boring ones by the minor 18th century writers, but there was also Hamlet At times he felt that he was Hamlet wanting to be. Or Joyce. How Rick also loved the girl with seaweed on her thigh. He was Yeats and the hardly controlled passion for Maud Gonne. T.S. Eliot. Rick had felt like a pair of ragged claws scuttling across the floors of silent seas how often human voices woke him and he had drowned. He could be just like Benjamin in The Graduate. A film he watched countless times. He'd always reckoned that he'd passed his

English because he knew nothing about The Professor, little about Major Barbara and Chaucer, but the examiner recognised genuine passion for some of the texts he was reading. He'd passed his 'A' levels and went to study Religion at a local University became a teacher, spent a year teaching which was where he was today.

But there had been Mary on the way in the sixth form. For the study of 20th century literature they shared their English classes with the girls of the same named school. It was the first time that some of the boys had come into such close proximity with girls and the anticipation was feverish. For their lessons they had a 'just out of' university teacher. He'd recommended 'Last Exit To Brooklyn' on his reading list and when it had been passed onto Rick it was confiscated by one of the ancients. They would have loved to be a fly on the wall of the staff room when they argued about that one.

In the first class with the opposite sex there were twenty of them, ten boys ten girls. The teacher referred to them as students and he was their tutor. They arrived to find the chairs placed in a circle no doubt put there by now exhausted first years one of the wags quipped. They had sat down. Ten boys seated together. Ten girls seated together. The boy next to the girl had moved his seat about ten centimetres from hers. The teacher Mr. Gauch laughed.

"Shall we sit in alphabetical order?" he asked them.

That meant they had to communicate to find out each other's names. After sitting like shy children on a beach when their parents had told them just go and say hello to another equally embarrassed child and another ten minutes moving about Mr. Gauch felt like this was going to take forever he stopped them.

"Are we going to do this before we die?" One or two tittered. "What's up?"

"We can't decide whether to use first or last names..."

"We're called by our first and the boys their last."

"First names," said Mr. Gauch, "Let's be polite."

So Rick found himself sitting opposite Mary who was to carry their baby.

After that first lesson, they could sit where they liked and Rick timed it so that Mary went in first and he followed and sat by her.

"Come here often?" he asked her

"Well, twice a week." She didn't see the humour, as she wouldn't on many occasions afterwards. "Why?"

"Nothing. It's okay."

Rick felt like the whole room was looking at him for beginning a conversation with the opposite sex. Who was this quite handsome idiot she thought. At the end of the lesson as they were leaving she said, "I see now."

"See what?"

"It was a joke. Supposed to be funny."

"Well I hope you've been thinking about more than that for the last hour."

"T.S. Eliot. Too much for me."

"You will be like a patient anaesthetised upon a table."

"What?"

"Never mind. Something else for you to think about."

She went from the room.

Later, his friend John who was studying sciences said, "I hear you tried to anaesthetise Mary. Kindly leave that to me. I'm the one who's going to be a doctor."

"Oh John. I'm sorry. I didn't realise she is your girlfriend. Have I put my foot in it? You won't punch me out will you, a duel at dawn. Name your weapon."

"I might. No, she's not my girlfriend. She's my sister."

"Your sister. How can you have a sister in the same year?"

"Because my dear man, I'm so clever that I was moved up a year."

"How come I've never seen her when I came to you house?"

"Dunno. Probably up in her bedroom doing whatever girls do in their bedrooms."

"You kept her hidden."

"Put in a word for you, shall I?"

So it went from there. Soon they were an item reading but not accepting 'Love's lost as soon as it's won.' Mr. Gauch would embarrass them by referring to them as 'our own Yeats and Maud Gonne' but they loved it really. She was like a poem herself, a pre-Raphaelite beauty. She had auburn hair down to her waist. Her face was too perfectly formed for mere mortals. It was all too idyllic for Rick to understand.

They were both virgins. But they were sensible virgins. As soon as the petting became heavy petting and then serious petting she went on the pill. After their 'A' levels they went to different universities promising undying love and faithfulness. She went to Oxford, he to his Midlands University. At his university there were more willing girls than he had dreamed of and he only visited her once. She came to him, but she had lost him on his first night. He made excuses and they drifted until they were no longer an inseparable pair. When he went home for Christmas he saw John at the pub. After the initial chat John said "You and Mary..."

"Yeah. Are no longer."

"I had high hopes for you two. I'd hoped you'd be my brother in law."

"Yeah. But you move on."

"I haven't. I still love Ruth. I shall marry her."

"Yeah okay. Maybe..."

"You're still immature."

Rick took a careless sip of his beer. "Blimey. That's a bit pompous."

They laughed politely, but knew that they'd moved on as well and wouldn't be brothers.

Rick went to New Year's Eve party and amongst the revellers was Mary. She believed that the way to get and keep Rick was by making herself available for sex. For Rick it was easier than chatting someone else up. They copulated. Afterwards she admitted that she wasn't on the pill anymore. He went home and his mother was watching a film on the television with Spencer Tracy arm wrestling another man.

Rick knew that Mary was pregnant. It was just another way to catch the fly.

He ignored her letters. He told friends in the halls of residence that he was never at home to anyone called Mary. He never answered the phone. She married a few months later. His parents told him that over the last three years she had been to the house occasionally with 'a lovely baby boy'.

A few weeks ago he had sent her a typed addressed personal envelope that he tried to make look official and had asked her whether he had a son. He had received the reply the day before. He took the letter from his pocket and re-read it: -

Rick, When you finished with me in December 1972 I was absolutely heartbroken. Then I found out I was pregnant a few weeks later (well that could not have come as much of a surprise he had thought when he first read the letter) *and didn't have anyone to talk to. I decided that as you didn't want me any more and I needed to finish my degree, as I was only eighteen I decided to have an abortion. My parents were very supportive and paid for me to go down to London, but I shall never forget the guilt and trauma of that experience. A few weeks later I met Graham.* (He stopped and thought. Graham, he remembered then the tall lanky creep in English who liked Genesis and lived in two houses knocked together. He'd never liked him.) *He was so adoring and swept me off my feet, it was just what I needed at the time. Then I became pregnant a couple of months later. Graham was wonderful and really wanted the baby,* (Two babies together, Rick shook his head in disbelief) *so we decided to get married, which did just six weeks before Roger was born.*

Graham is still with me, (well it has only been three years) *and although we have had some bad times because of what happened we are still together and I feel sure that we will stay together. He is my soul mate and understands where I have come from.*

I do not have any bitterness towards you about what happened and I will always remember how I loved you then. These sorts of feelings never go away.

I hope you can forgive me for not having your baby, but he/she is still in my memory and is therefore not totally destroyed. (I doubt the foetus feels that way.)

I also hope you can be happy over the coming years. Be happy in your marriage and have lots of children. I would like to think that we could both look back with love at the times we shared. I know it has helped make me into the person I am today.

Rick took the paper and tore it into tiny pieces and threw it into the gentle breeze where it settled to the ground like confetti. He turned and started moving towards home. Sunni, Ali, Mary, Tara, Helen. Dead babies. Helen had I done my time with you? Is today the right action that I am taking? When the day passes that I do not think of you then I shall know that I have completely forgotten you. When he was young he'd had a kaleidoscope and he would hold it to the light to watch the colours fall into patterns and then fall out again. He'd asked his mother once who she loved most, him or his father. His father of course was her reply. He had wanted to be the only one in her life. He went up the path to the front door and turned the key in the lock and went in.

"Is that you boy?" his Father shouted the same ridiculous question. "We thought that you weren't coming back!"

"Can't run off on your wedding day," said his podgy mother as she came down the stairs. "Come on," she said excitedly, "We've got a lot to do."

TWENTY-ONE

The wedding was a family affair with relatives that you never see, or for that matter, want to see again. An occasion where everybody tells themselves and one another that they are having a wonderful time forgetting that two out of three marriages end in divorce. His grandmother had said to his mother that Lesley would have him running round after her within weeks. Why didn't she tell him before the great day? Would he have believed her? Within six months he realised that he had married the wrong person and maybe she felt the same. He had never asked her. He heard a joke once: 'Question. How are woman cured of their sexual appetites? Answer. 'By eating wedding cake'. It was true in his case until she wanted children and then they were at it like the proverbial bonking rabbits. Getting pregnant was for her a way of getting out of going to work. It never occurred to him to offer to look after the children while she worked or for that matter for her to ask. It was just that she didn't look after the children. He got up to them in the night after a day at work. He spent all his weekends with them. He was even left on his own in half terms while she went and spent them with her mother. He did not resent the children, not at all. But he did begrudge the fact that she seemed to get away with doing very little and making it look as though she did everything. He never felt completely comfortable with this situation but just took it as his way of life, what was to be.

After they had been married about eight or nine months Lesley announced she was going to visit her mother. "In the February half term so that you can have a week with your mates." She made it sound like doing him a favour. Rick was quite happy with that and looked forward to the time alone. Someone commented that it seemed a bit odd that she would want to go and visit her mother by herself reasonably early in their marriage.

"I don't mind," he supposed, "Whatever she wants."

When Lesley arrived at her Mother's she thought it was wonderful. It was as if she had never married and she was at home again, the only child, the besotted offspring.

After a couple of days Lesley's mother thought to ask after Rick.

"Oh he's okay. Enjoying a few days freedom I expect."

"It's just that you haven't rung him. He hasn't called you either."

"I told him not to." Her mother looked quite taken aback at the aggression in her reply. "We don't have to live in each other's pockets you know."

"No. Quite right. But well…"

"What?"

"Well you've not been married a year. I wouldn't have wanted to be away from your Dad. I don't even like it now." She saw tears well up in her daughter's eyes. "What is it? Come on nothing can be that bad."

"Oh it can."

"You're not pregnant are you?"

"No no," Lesley waved her hand as if dismissing a servant and was quiet for some moments. "I wish."

"What do you wish?"

"Oh its nothing, just the time of the year. It's always miserable after Christmas. You do all that hard work and then its flat."

"You can say that again."

Lesley went over to the window and looked out at the garden in its lowest ebb of winter as if the tide had gone out and it would never return. It was how she felt. "It wasn't like I expected it to be."

"Well marriage isn't a bed of roses." Though she was surprised and worried to hear her daughter speak this way and alarm bells began to ring. "It'll just be the first flush of marriage over, you know the honeymoon over. You both have to teach. You have to go out to work. You have a different life now."

"It's not that. It's Rick. He's boring."

"Boring?" and said to herself, "Here we go."

"Well at university he was a laugh. He had a lot going for him you know like with that Rag Week thing. Now all he wants to do is go to the pub, listen to music, buy a takeaway, Sunday roast on a Sunday just like his mum made and the excitement of our week is the supermarket and laundrette on a Friday."

"Do you want me to buy you a washing machine?"

"What instead of a husband. Might be more fun." They were both laughing now.

"Give it more time. Try and talk to him. You've got to talk. Make him aware of what you're thinking."

"Yeh. Don't worry mum. It's just the way I feel at the moment."

But she knew she wasn't missing him and didn't care whether she went back or not.

PART TWO

ONE

Today Rick was thirteen again. Though he believed in reality he had been thirteen for some months. The feelings of first love again which had been the pain of so long ago. That time he had been pushed by a friend into a girl looking at birthday cards in the department store, Woolworth's. That shop was now long gone. And her memory hadn't stayed with him. He'd forgotten the craving that he'd had for his first love even though she had given him his first real lovers kiss out in the summer evening that had made his stomach churn with delight. It was a kind of summer of youth, where the remembered days were of endless sunshine and the pavements burned. The Beatles dared to make a record that was seven minutes long and the radio station had to play it because it was the 'Fab Four'.

Rick and his girl 'snogged' on a park bench and drank milky coffee in a cafe making sure that she was home by ten. Then two days later they had parted and he was left only with the pain of McArthur Park. Why hadn't they swapped addresses? They knew they were children. Between the ages of 13 and 39 he had never again been in love, women usually loved him. This completely suited his vanity. His heart had been totally hardened after it had been broken when he was fifteen. That was years before but he had never recovered. Afterwards to distance himself from love was the only way to cope. The cause of his attitude to women had been Alyson. She was slim and attractive though not particularly pretty. She just had the warm rhythm in her soul that made her desirable. She went to what the stupid boys believed to be the sexiest school in town. A school can't be sexy. They knew that really, but it was an all girls' school and there the girl's had the reputation of being nymphomaniacs.

He was a swimmer then and determined not to drown. He picked her up and she dropped him like the tennis ball she liked to racquet. Very middle class she was the daughter of a vet and she wanted rebel against the image of what her father expected of her. Rick lived in a council house. She thought he was like something out of DH Lawrence. She finally she went off with his best friend who lived in a terrace house with an outside toilet but probably didn't marry him. Even now he remembers one night holding her close in his bed whilst John and Yoko toured the best hotels of Europe. With his first love he was naked. They were both naked. He touched her. She held his penis. In his embarrassment he stopped her. Years later he still wondered why? It might have been the perfect orgasm. He had no idea how to make her have an orgasm. He'd never heard of the clitoris.

The lesson he'd learnt though was never to be bounced, caught and dropped again.

A single woman had moved in across the road. The house nearly opposite, she had two young children, a boy and a girl. Only just school age he thought. But he wasn't very interested. He hardly noticed her. Lesley, his wife, had remarked, 'She seems nice'. He didn't reply. It was possible, he knew, to become friends with the neighbours and then spend the next fifty years wishing you hadn't. So, as the saying goes, he kept himself to himself. He was even beginning to keep a distance from Lesley.

One morning, as he was about to leave for work, he saw Lesley chatting to the 'new' neighbour. Rick paid little attention to them both laughing, probably at nothing, as people do when they first meet.

That evening as he was bringing through the meal he'd cooked, whilst Lesley rested from the day's exertions, she said, "She seemed very nice."

"Who?"

"The new woman, Christine, across the road. She seemed very sweet."

Disinterested Rick replied "Oh yes. First name terms already is it. Swapping recipes soon. Mind you in your case that would be a bit pointless as you've forgotten where the kitchen is."

"Why don't you like anybody? Why don't you try?"

"I like you," he lied, "I like the children. I like the dog." Wagging her tail she came across to him hoping to food. "I like the cat." The cat looked down from the top of the fridge in disdain as if to say I have no interest in you. "I like the hamsters."

"You like drinking..."

"It's Monday. I'm not allowed a drink until Tuesday and then not until Saturday. And only then because we're eating out with tedious people or because boring tedious people are eating with us."

During this conversation Liam and Hannah concentrated on their meals staring intently at the fish fingers and beans as though it were a gourmet delight sensing an argument.

"We aren't the same are we?"

"That's right. Well done. I'm male you're female."

"I loathe your sarcasm."

"I think that I'm rather funny."

Lesley picked up her meal and stomped off to watch a soap. That's real life he thought. He played a CD loud to irritate her.

Across the road the situation hadn't been so very different before Steve disappeared. Their relationship had been lost but Christine didn't watch soaps whilst she was eating she just didn't eat or sometimes nibbled at what the little boy on occasions left. She couldn't bear eating with Steve, his mouth always open and the slapping noises he made. Bed often hadn't provided any solace either with his long neck straining above her head, his skinny effeminate body; the selfishness that was going on inside her. The last time sex had been satisfying was when she'd conned him that she was still on the pill and his orgasm was perfect for her because she knew that she'd become pregnant again.

It had got to the stage then, after the birth of the baby girl, she'd put the child to bed and then she would feign tiredness and would go soon after wards herself leaving Steve to his wine and cigarettes. When at last she heard his steps on the stairs she would pretend to sleep with the sick pit in her stomach, as Steve would masturbate squirting his spunk over the sheets she would have to wash.

It was a different birth from the first with the boy. Anna was as perfect as a child's doll on Christmas morning. Before the birth of her boy, Ben, her husband Steve had punched Christine whilst in the bath. The pain of the birth had started then and for a while after the birth she had rejected Ben. She wasn't afraid that he wouldn't grow up normal because of the attack, but frightened that he would grow up to be like his father. Christine's love was only for her children. She emphatically believed that she would never want any affection from any man again.

Lesley said, "It must be difficult for her with those two children and one so tiny."

"Yes. Very interesting."

"I was thinking of someone else."

Rick raised his arms in mock amazement. "You thinking of someone else!"

She ignored the comment. "I mean that it must be difficult for her to get one ready for school and the little one for the childminder. She works you know. A teacher."

"Oh God we could start a school down here."

"And I bet that little one keeps her up at night."

"Well that's something you never knew about."

"I did my share." She waited for him to agree. "I've sent a card over from us welcoming her to the avenue."

"Oh God you are magnanimous. I wouldn't know her if I fell over her corpse in the street. And she wouldn't know me."

"I thought it would be nice and the right thing to do."

"I hate the word nice and why does everything you do have to be the right thing."

It was Tuesday so he poured himself another cider before he made the evening meal.

But Christine saw Rick as that 'funny man' across the road, like somebody she'd met once but she couldn't place him. Appearing in the morning with his big black battered old briefcase and disappearing at night as though the whole thing was being played in reverse. She just thought him odd. She wasn't intrigued, though in moments she wondered why he never looked right or left or made any kind of gesture of recognition to any of his neighbours. She wondered if he was lonely. Rather like herself.

TWO

As they'd had a party the year before Lesley decided to make a tradition of it when they came back from holiday and invite them again. At this all 'their friends' could get together and swap news about all the 'jolly' happenings away. It was a "nice way to start term and finish the holiday on a high note," Lesley said. And she hoped that many of them would remember that it was her birthday around that date as well and bring presents with them. She'd invite half of the town. The occasion was going to be the first time that he met Christine.

The day of the gathering started in earnest with fixing up a string of bright lights. The event would be outdoors as the weather promised to be a fine September evening. Tesco provided quiches and baguettes, and the wine shop glasses. Rick was given the task of providing music from his vast collection as long as it wasn't Jazz or Blues. He was a good host after a few glasses of wine just as Lesley enjoyed flitting and flirting from guest to guest, taking pleasure from being the centre of attention.

Christine was invited to the party. A friend and her mother both told her to go – 'get yourself out more'. So she went but only for a short time she decided. Having checked that the babysitter knew to call her should the smallest incident arise. She stood in her neighbour's garden feeling most alone. Lesley flapped over to her and asked if she was enjoying herself.

"Wonderful," came the lie from Christine's lips.

Rick came over to give her more wine and as he poured she covered the glass with her hand and the liquid splashed down her dress.

"Oh. I'm sorry."

"It's okay. I wasn't going to stay long, so I'll go now and get out of this."

"You're coming back?"

"No. But thank you for a nice time. A most memorable night."

"I'm sorry. Again."

"It doesn't matter."

"Don't tell Lesley I poured wine all over you."

She laughed. "It'll be our secret."

She went home, paid off the babysitter and sat looking at the wall she thought that she should change her dress and get ready for bed. She wished she had someone to make a cup of tea for her. She thought about Steve. Thinking about Steve was something that she did less and less these days. She believed that even the children would forget all about him one day. He would have never spilt wine over her. He was too cool for that. She knew that the first time she saw him. That was when she decided she would marry him and he would be the father of her children. Many years later she knew that she had been the black widow spider ensnaring and 'killing' him after he had vanished. She didn't know why; she was wondering what there was to attraction for people, for herself even. Was it all just physical attraction, pure sex? Or was there some emotional piece to it? Or chemistry? Possibly it was all a combination of the lot. Maybe the only way was the wild years of uncommitted relationships and lived out sex drive before you were committed to move on to a degree and, if that was what you wanted, eventually marriage.

Christine went hundreds of miles away from home to go to university. Her choice. She had worked hard to escape and gained brilliant 'A' level passes. Any 'A' level was good. Her parents hadn't always been aware of the benefits of a sound education. Christine could be a free spirit. Independent of her parents and background. Little in her upbringing though would have prepared her for the life she could choose to lead. She wasn't aware but her parents; close relatives and neighbours were her role models. School had given her the academic side to life. Nowhere though was there any depth. No one had explored with her the routes; if you take this path this may happen. So she ended up taking the way she knew, the one she was experienced with. She wasn't aware of, or prepared take, the other roads with different destinations. Education just became the sideline. She could see no further than the walls of her bedsit and boyfriend. They would develop into a house, husband and work and all the responsibilities that entailed.

But with Steve they were heady days and the first flush of being in love was so complete as only new lovers know. Days became irrelevant as they happened. In a joint diary they recorded such meteoric events as to whether they ate beef burgers, had breakfast in bed or out of it, got up incredibly late, did a psychology test in a magazine, went to see the Tempest and so on. Their song became Lou Reed's 'Perfect Day' because every day was perfect as well as for remembering the day that they had visited the zoo and everything had been flawless. A moment in caught in time. The song was like a photograph. They remembered where they were at a special place and time. They enjoyed all that students' take delight in and noted these. Christine bought a handbag for two pounds, Steve a new pair of jeans in the hippest of shops that was playing the new Riders of the Purple Sage record so he had to have them. They smoked and got a little high and then went for a drink with friends. They noted beautiful sunsets and watched it drinking a bottle of wine before they went to a party smoking too many cigarettes and not arriving home until 3.30am. The day after they were pleased to wake up for The Archers radio programme and Steve served Christine breakfast in bed. They took a long walk and returned home in the rain, cold, wet, hungry and thirsty and spent the rest of the day in bed eating cheese on toast and drinking tea, laughing. And so life went on, seemingly adventurous but also very normal. They did smoke the joints, did the parties but lived like an old married couple. There were times when she was afraid of him. His temper would flare up. She could see no reason for this. Not her, the pressure of his degree work or their friends. She never spoke to anyone about it. She just put down any inclinations towards violence as a mix up or misunderstanding as she *knew* that they really loved one another.

Christine was terrified at the prospect of her parents visiting her and they seemed to spend about a fortnight cleaning their own bed sit and finding them totally suitable and clean lodgings for the few days they would spend with them before taking her back home for the holidays. Her parents arrived and it appeared to go well, even though on their first walk through the town they met, what her mother would have considered to have been, every scruffy student and squatter that Christine and Steve ever knew. She felt the visit went on too long and once the novelty of the first couple of days has passed it ended in argument. Christine's mother put far too much emphasis on what a person looked like, the material, the quality and their surroundings rather than their intellectual attributes or even whether there were a nice person or not. She was horrified to think that her daughter's friends were scruffs and squatters who no doubt took plenty of drugs and never did any real work and would only have the completely negative effect on her daughter who would with no doubt end up a drug addict like her them and then probably dead. She didn't know what she was going to say to her neighbours and relatives about her daughter's life other than to tell a lie. 'Thank goodness,' she thought, 'That she had a son with a proper job and who had joined the golf club and would not disgrace them.' When it finally came to taking Christine home for the holidays at the end of their visit everything ended in tears and argument and they drove home without speaking. There was only a tense nervous silence; except for Christine holding back the tears with occasional muffled sobs. For Christine it was totally unnatural to be leaving the man she loved. She was grown up and yet suddenly she was made to feel like a child again. She was supposed to be grateful for all that her parents did for her. When she got 'home' she was then faced with the worst horror of all. Her room, her territory, had been completely gutted. She felt as if it belonged to somebody else. The essence that was Christine had disappeared. Even a simple, almost childish thing, like her 'prize' poster of Yes's Steve Howe was nowhere to be found.

"I expect that's in the dustbin a long time ago. We thought you were past all that," said her Dad.

Her room was newly decorated, new carpet and furniture but with it had gone her sense of belonging to the family, her home.

It had become a hotel room. She decided upon walking through the doorway, murmuring the right noises about how lovely it was, that she would never come home again.

The next academic year was spent seriously saving money. Steve even got a job. Their aim was Paris for as much as the summer as possible. Christine even thought that she might be able to get a job there, but that proved to be a naive dream. It seemed no time at all when they were on the Rue Monmartre drinking wine and sharing real bread, the baguette. The whole of Paris was theirs even if they couldn't afford to eat out and pay to go up the Eiffel Tower. But they could look and most of the art galleries were free. They could walk the whole of the Rivoli. Starting with the grand shop of Samaritane, where she could look and appreciate the beauty of the place the structure and art nouveau.

"When you look at some of these places," Steve said, "You wonder who really knows how to live. We've no idea in England."

Then past quaint Les Halles and the supreme majesty of the Louvre, through the gardens of Champ Elysees where the heat was as intense as in the desert on through to the Arc de Triomphe circled by traffic and the world's crowds. Sunday was spent at the huge market at Porte de Cligancourt where they enjoyed snacks cooked on an open fire, watching dubious jewellery and sophisticated antiques. This was where Christine bought her first Maxime Le Forestier record, 'because he has a lovely face'. It was all about just being there and twenty. Life was like Paris full of the whole mixture of being. It had been all there for the taking. A few weeks after they returned to England they married. Both sets of parents were against her walking up the aisle to Lou Reed's 'Perfect Day' and the vicar wasn't very keen either, but she left the church to the song. Now, she was wondering if everything since was only a descent, even her.

THREE

Completely out of character for Rick he said that he wanted to invite Christine for a meal. "We've Maurelian etc and those other two iumps on Saturday. Add Christine. Make a change to listen to a bit of different less talk. Somewhat surprised Lesley agreed. Christine wished she'd never accepted the invitation. She thought the dinner party a disaster. Of the others there was Sue, one of the party. She was infatuated with Rick. She thought him rather gorgeous in a dashing type of way. Unfortunately for Sue the feelings weren't reciprocated. The other couple Maurelian and Dorian believed themselves to be a cut above the rest. They were like someone upon whom tasting the French cheese 'Chevre' cries out, 'this is just demanding red wine'. Some simply felt that they were arrogant as well as pompous. Christine was in complete agreement with the 'some'.

Lesley had discovered a new recipe for the evening, a peculiar tasting cold chicken. Rick never cooked for these evenings though he would have loved to do so.

With a mouthful of chicken Maurelian said, "You teach at Woodstock then Christine."

Before she could reply, Dorian interceded with "Our boys go there."

Christine then realised who the boys were. Overbearing loathsome children that she recoiled from teaching. On meeting the parents it told her a lot about the offspring.

"How are they getting on?" Dorian went on, believing that the boys were the most important item in Christine's mind on a Saturday night.

Christine hadn't the courage to say that this wasn't a reports evening. She was saved when one of the other men informed them all that he was a governor at the school. It was from seeing him around the school that made him familiar.

"That's why education is in the state it's in with governor's like that!" Rick said with a childish grin.

Lesley glowered at him and there were feeble attempts at laughter and Christine felt it was time to leave. But she couldn't leave yet. She willed Anna to wake so that the sitter would have to call her as she had emphatically instructed.

There was silence. The atmosphere was as brittle as broken glass.

"Is your husband looking after the little one tonight? What is she called, Anna? Said Dorian in a feeble attempt to bring the conversation back on track.

"No. We're separated. And yes."

"Oh I'm sorry." The woman wished for a huge black hole to come and swallow her up. The steely silence pervaded.

"It's quite a long story. But not one I'm inclined top tell." Christine fingered the stem of her glass. There were murmurs of assent and agreement as each guest thought what a bummer of an evening this was turning into. But Christine remembered the whole film in a second or two then.

Steve had hated the journey down to the south of Brittany. They had gone via Cherbourg and that peninsula seemed to take forever. He'd believed that he knew the best way rather than checking with the AA or even buying an up to date road map and the only signs in France seemed to point to the nearest crêperie. And of course Christine had insisted that they stop for lunch 'as the children would need the food and the break to run around'. As a mother and even more so as a wife she was in his opinion pretty useless. Steve had to constantly remind her to entertain the children or peel him an orange. When they finally arrived and he'd erected the tent he knew then that he'd done his bit. He'd organised the holiday. They were here, rest relaxation and three weeks of French finest wines. It wouldn't be on his conscience now to let Christine look after the children and take her share of the burden.

By the next day their site was beginning to look like home, comfortable and lived in. Christine had gone off with Anna in tow to do the washing up after a late breakfast of croissants and coffee. Steve was walking around looking busy and English testing the tension in the guy ropes and Ben was following him on his bike. They were next to a French family and the Monsieur with whom Steve had enjoyed a few glasses of vino the night before asked him if he knew the way to the beach.

"No. But I'm sure we can find out at the site office."

"No my pot. I know. Shall I show you?"

"Oh yes. Ben!" Ben was miles away in a cycle rally full of noises and did not immediately respond. "Ben. Do you want to go to the beach?" He came back to reality at the rhetorical question.

"And your wife?"

"Oh she'll be ages yet. Polishes the dishes."

When Christine returned carrying the bowl of dishes with Anna, their site looked deserted. Where is everyone she thought? She went into the tent and as soon as she saw that Ben's beach toys had disappeared she said to Anna, "They might have waited for us. Why didn't he wait for me?"

Anna toddled after, "Where's Daddy?" she asked.

After an hour or so Steve returned.

"I'm in here."

Full of bravado Steve said to Ben, "Doesn't sound too jolly."

Tent walls are thin and although the campers in earshot tried hard not to listen their voices were broadcast everywhere and they understood even if English wasn't their language.

"Why didn't you wait for me? Why didn't you wait for your daughter? She would have liked to have gone to the beach!"

"I thought that you'd be ages."

"It doesn't take ages to wash up."

"Jean Pierre looked ready to go."

"Oh Jean Pierre now is it. Well bloody well marry him then!"

"I didn't know where you were..."

"You could have found out. Look! Ask someone. I expect Mrs. Jean Pierre knows where the washing up is done!

"I never thought."

"You won't have to think tonight! Well you're bloody well going to find out where to wash up because you're going to be washing up!"

"I drove a long way yesterday..."

"And if you think that means that you're going to do bugger all for next three weeks think again."

Steve came out of the tent and with forced jollity and said to Ben, 'Come on. Let's go for a bike ride.'

"Penny for your thoughts," said Rick. "Can I get you another glass of wine?"

Coming back to a reality she looked at him for a moment. "No I'd better be going. Anna's very little and I don't like to leave her too long on the first times out for me."

Inwardly some of the guests breathed a sigh of relief.

"Are you sure you won't stay for dessert. I could put you some out now."

"No, I'll go. Thank you for the invitation."

"Do you want me to see you across the road?"

"It's alright. It *is* only across the road." Maurelian and Dorian caught one another's eye in an instant.

Like Christine, Rick was out of bed before nine the following morning. He knew that he would have to clear up the place. Thank Christ for dishwashers he thought. He made tea and took one to Hannah who as Ben across the road was watching TV.

"Do you want anything Liam?"

"No."

"I'll get you some breakfast when I've cleared away."

"Good night Dad?"

"Yes. Fab." Rick laughed.

Later he took Lesley some tea. She wanted waking for the socially necessity of visiting church on a Sunday morning so that she could be seen. She had converted quite recently.

"Great evening Lesley. Really enjoyed it."

"No it wasn't."

"Why invite people then? Especially such odd people."

"It's you that's odd. They have no idea how to react to such a weirdo. Christine must wonder who she's moved next to."

"Opposite. I live opposite her. Great evening though, best yet."

"Bastard."

He had dreamt. He dreamt that he was in a room with Lesley. He said that a friend of his would be along soon and was that ok. It was Jeremy from his old college days. Yes that would be nice said Lesley. He went away to get a knife. He made sure that the knife was very sharp. When he returned to the room where he was to meet Jeremy it was full of Lesley's friends drinking tea and nobody knew anything about Jeremy. He told them to be careful of his knife, as it was very sharp. He went out of the room carefully so as not to harm anyone. He went into another room that was one of the rooms at his mother's house. He was very thirsty and he wanted to a cup of tea. He also needed the bathroom. He looked down at his penis and he had cut it off; but it wasn't bleeding nor hurting only stinging a bit. He held it back onto his body to get it back together again. He woke up. It was morning. It was daylight. His bladder was full. Lesley was still sleeping. So he went to have a bath to try and wash the night away. He lay there dreaming. Lying watching waiting for voices to disappear. Where are you? Sunny outside, wishing he was out there alone flying as a seagull white and grey against the foam instead real crisis's need to be faced head bent as he left the bath he saw how bald he really was.

FOUR

Christine began to receive the invitations to dinner. She should have been flattered that her company was wanted. But she liked the time to herself when the children had gone to bed. She felt uncomfortable leaving them with a babysitter. She grew angry with herself for not refusing the invites. The three met again through an invite from Maurelian and Dorian. Maurelian and Dorian felt that they may be missing out and wanted to make sure that they were part of the same social circle so made regular invites. Their perception of themselves was that they felt they were liked, even though at Maurelian's fortieth birthday party over a hundred people were invited but less than twenty turned up. Rick taught at the same school as Maurelian where very few staff expressed a preference and he'd only had a negative view of Maurelian from the students where he was thoroughly disliked by most.

Because of their pretensions the dinner party was very formal. Sip a sherry to begin, brandy and coffee to end and drink the most discerning wines between. Maurelian's father was French so he felt that this made him the universal expert on etiquette as well as the world's finest wines.

Clutching a sherry each they moved into the dining room to look at a painting Maurelian had had commissioned of the local coastline. Whilst appreciating the mess, Rick saw to his horror that name cards had been laid out and that he would be next to Dorian. He moved the cards about so that he and Christine were together.

Maurelian was appalled as only a doting Father can be, "Jacques spent a long time doing those on the computer."

"Fine."

"It means that we're not sitting next to people that we haven't had supper with in a while", he went on.

"Supper? You mean like cocoa and a cheese sandwich?"

Dorian's face came through the kitchen hatch like a jack in a box, "Anything the matter?"

"He's moving the place names about instead of looking at the painting."

"I have looked and a five year old could do better. Ask Christine."

"Jacques spent a long time doing those on the computer."

"Put them back," said Lesley.

"No. I don't want to sit by..."

Lesley interrupted him before he could go any further. "Leave him Maurelian. You know what he's like. He won't say a word all evening."

They left the room leaving Rick to his cards. He moved them about a bit and then picked up Maurelian's and looked closely at it. He took a pen from the side and scrubbed a few letters from the name. He went and joined the others again. When they all returned Maurelian tried to joke, "Now we shall all have to look for our names again, wont we Rick?"

"Oh yeh, you certainly will. Will *you* find yours I ask myself?"

"Rick. That's a bit weak. Even from you," said Maurelian as he picked up his card.

"What is it?" asked Dorian. "Oh yes. Very funny, Mauran." They all attempted a feeble laugh whilst Rick was in hysteria pathetically laughing at his own joke.

For Rick there might have been no one else there all that night. He drank ate giggled and flirted with Christine and drank becoming more crazed as the evening progressed. Upon completion of the final course Maurelian moved them all into the other room for coffee, brandy and Trivial Pursuits. Rick pointed out that they'd been playing that all evening.

"That is," said Dorian the perfect hostess, "Unless anyone would like anything else to eat?"

"Well," Rick leaned over to the fruit bowl and picking up a banana said, "I'd rather like one of these. What about you Christine?"

He then went into laughter, again explicable only to himself. There were tears and a cramped stomach as though he were in great pain. The rest looked on as if watching something that they could not touch and definitely not understand.

In his madness only Rick knew the game to be truly trivial. It was for Maurelian and Dorian the most wonderful opportunity to show of their fluency in Spanish, as the only version they claimed they could get due to its popularity was the

Spanish version. Why couldn't they be normal *and* get the English one Rick thought. The two vied for reading each question out in Spanish and then translating it. Only Christine out of the guests knew Spanish but because she had nothing to prove she wasn't saying anything.

Rick hated the game at the best of times, even in English, because one either knew the answer or didn't. There wasn't a particular skill involved. He felt left out as well. Maurelian was vying with Lesley for who had the greater general knowledge. Dorian was trying to compete with Christine pretending not to notice where her husband's affections lay that evening.

The telephone beeped. "Sorry Christine it's your babysitter,' said Dorian pulling a wretched face as though she were totally responsible as she returned to the room holding the handset whilst Maurelian was eagerly holding a card and saying, "Shall we get on now?"

"It's Anna," said Christine "She's woken and won't go back to sleep."

Rick saw it as a way to escape. "It's okay. I'll walk Christine round and go home. It'll relieve our babysitter as well." He looked at Lesley who nodded. "Save money." Which she would like even more.

As they left Rick said to Dorian, "Thank you for a wonderful evening. Can't remember when I've enjoyed an evening more. Only sorry to be missing the game." They hardly spoke as they walked home. Neither seemed to have any interest now in the other. Christine had been a useful diversion at the dinner table. Each only wanted to be at their own home.

Christine went indoors also thankful to be away though she did wish that she had someone at home waiting for her, someone to share her bed that wasn't a child. She hadn't enjoyed the evening particularly. Maurelian, Dorian and Lesley were just so full of themselves but at least that meant she hadn't had to start or keep a conversation going. She'd barely got a word in edgeways and walking home with Rick she'd decided not to even try. It became obvious why he'd agreed to see her home. He was simply ignorant. He had behaved as though she meant something to him and then became insular as if she weren't there. She wondered why anyone bothered with him. It was rapidly becoming obvious why Lesley didn't try too hard. Why nobody did.

When she got indoors Anna was settling but Christine didn't feel like going to bed. She paid the cash and said goodbye to the babysitter. She checked on Anna, who was now of course, sound asleep. As she went back downstairs she thought she heard a noise from the kitchen diner. A light from that room cast a beam as if there were someone in there waiting for her. She felt afraid to go on and stopped half down or half up the stairs. To go down would be to descend into madness and nightmares to go up was calmness and peace. But sometimes you had to go down to go up again, she knew that. So she went down slowly, step by step moving inexorably towards that light. She could smell smoke and heard the sound of liquid being poured into a glass. She turned the corner and into the room. She knew what she would see. Steve becoming aware of her presence turned and looked. He had the tarot pack laid out as if he were giving a reading. He twisted the next card and it was the skeleton for dramatic change. A sardonic smile spread over his face and his eyes shone. "Christine," he whispered barely audibly, "The point is."

"The point is what?" she found herself saying.

"The point is."

She woke on the sofa with a start. On the television was a Spanish film, obscure late night viewing. She sat up, not remembering falling asleep. She thought now that she obviously ought to go to bed. Anna might wake again and the toil of dragging herself from sleep would be like pulling herself out of a hole. She made herself tea. Looking at the table there was a glass there with some coke left in it and cards spread where the babysitter had been playing with Ben. She thought the girl had been lighting joss sticks as well. Perhaps she had been smoking and wanted to get rid of the smell. She would talk to her about it next time she was here. She sat down again to the film. Spanish. Why hadn't she told them that she could speak Spanish and understood the questions on the cards? Why had she pretended to be as ignorant as the rest? She replayed the scene in her mind. 'Oh Christine,' a surprised Dorian would have exclaimed, 'I didn't know that you could speak Spanish.' Rick might have liked that and laughed with her on the way home. She thought about the dream. There were times when she would have liked Steve back. Smoke, sticky wine glasses hadn't mattered once.

Rick sat watching a home-movie he'd shot on 8mm camera that he'd been given for his twenty-first birthday. It was of Helen in Wales when they'd been there for the Rag Week conference. It was Aberdovey by the sea. He had bought two book of poetry by R.S. Thomas. He preferred the one for children as it spoke more directly to him. Helen looked self-consciously at the camera and then walked across the screen the sea pounding in white horses behind her. He wanted to climb into the screen to join her there. But he was behind the camera just as now he was behind the projector viewing something that happened in the past. For a moment she stares directly at him in his living room across all the years and it was as if they were together again. He glances towards the window as he hears a car turn into the short drive. When he looks back at the wall it is a white light and the reel is flapping. The moment is lost forever. He gets up to put the projector away to make Lesley a mug of weak tea.

Now we speak coolly, politely to each other as strangers or little known visitors to a house. Your coldness is tangible all around for me to touch unlike you. You said you loved me while drinking wine and playing cards with friends not bothering to look up when I entered but then I turned from you. I couldn't bear to feel your skin bare against mine.

Dorian and Maurelian cleaned the rooms completely that night so that in the morning there would be nothing to do. Though tasteful, the rooms would look as clinical as they always were.

Maurelian went to bed feeling randy. It was Lesley who had that effect on him. He turned over and squeezed Dorian's sagging breasts after stroking his hands on her dough like stomach. She bent towards him and he knew he was in luck. She felt loving. She imagined an actor's slim body that she'd seen on a film recently, his bright eyes and youthful laugh so little fore play was needed. Maurelian mounted her as he imagined Lesley stripping for him. As Maurelian exploded inside her she came. A mutual orgasm rarely happened to them.

"Oh Maurelian," she murmured like a seventeen year old discovering sex, "That was wonderful."

"I love you Dorian."

FIVE

It wasn't until lunch break the following Monday that Christine had the opportunity to pass even a few words with her closest friend Louise. School was so busy.

"Weekend okay?"

"Oh yes. *Great*." Christine answered with more than a hint of sarcasm.

"You went with that new couple you'd met. In your road, didn't you?"

"With the fatuous parents of a couple of our delightful children" answered Christine.

"Nice new friends for you?" Said with a hint of tongue in cheek.

"Well, I enjoyed that as much as a parents' evening. Let's put it that way. In fact I enjoy a parents evening more. At least I know why I'm there!"

"Oh. I'm sure it was all right. It couldn't have been that bad."

"Well it was awful. I don't know why I went. It got me out on a Saturday night I suppose. At least Anna had the sense to wake so I could go back home and rescue the babysitter. It was a bore."

"Oh. Not like you to be so forthright!" Louise answered smiling benevolently.

"That Lesley is totally full of herself as well. Verbal diarrhoea. But," in an attempt to salvage something from the evening, "Rick was okay. Just about, and I *mean* just about. He has my sympathies." She didn't want to give anyone any ideas. And Louise wasn't interested in pursuing it. "Dry sense of humour anyway. When he chooses to speak. And like me he doesn't suffer fools."

"Could you stand all of them for a meal? I suppose you have to return the favour. It's a problem but you're a bit obliged."

"I'm having a house warming, all my real university friends, and you. They'll have to put up with that."

A couple of weeks passed and whilst Lesley was having a lie down an envelope popped through the door. Rick left the fish fingers cooking and retrieved it from the floor. Opening it he saw an invitation to a party from Christine. He quite fancied a party. He could lose himself there standing in the kitchen drinking. Drinking wine, he sang to himself as he shook the chips in their hot fat about, 'you always find me in the kitchen at parties'.

Lesley staggered down the stairs demanding tea and picked up the invitation.

"Oh that's nice," she said.

"I'll try to anaesthetise myself when I'm there."

"With the amount you drink you'll succeed."

Rick put the chips onto the plates and fried the eggs. Lesley took hers into the front room. He cooked his egg last. That way he always got the one that broke and nobody else could complain. He sat down with the children, pleased that Lesley was out of the way so that they could all make a chip butty.

"I didn't know her name is Christine," he told the children.

The phone began to ring just as Rick was about to take the first bite into his sandwich. It rang and rang.

"Don't worry anybody. Stay where you are. I'll get it." He got up and went to the machine.

From the lounge Lesley heard him say 'Paul!' in surprise and then she took more notice of the conversation and less of the soap opera and attempted to guess the other half of the conversation from the half that she was hearing at the same wishing that it was she who had answered the phone. But she'd had a hard day and all she'd wanted to do was eat and watch the television. "That's amazing you don't sound as if you're in Canada." She turned down the sound on the television. "You're not in Canada. You're at your mother's, with the children?

Where's Lucy? Oh, I see. Yes of course you can. Yes I'll do that. Don't you worry about a thing. Everything will be fine. I've written the time down. See you then."

Rick put down the receiver and went back to his tea humming as he went along the hall. He was not going to report straight back to Lesley. Let her stew.

After a few minutes she could bear it no longer. "What did he want?"

"The tomato sauce, but we've run out. Have to get some more because I like it as well."

"No, not Liam, on the phone. Paul?" She was trying hard to fit in with his humour or she'd never find out what was going on.

"The phone? Did the phone ring?" He looked at Hannah and Liam who were grinning but hoping that the humour didn't overspill into argument as it often did. "Hang on. I'll come and tell you." He stuffed three chips coated in egg and brown sauce into his mouth and went into the front room and sat down. "That was Paul." He choked through the words swallowing at the same time. "On the blower from his mother's. He's coming down on Saturday to stay for a few days."

"What by himself?"

"No." Paul was married to an extremely intelligent but unstable woman. Lesley did not want her in the house for more than a few minutes. "No. They've split up. He couldn't stand the extreme mood changes anymore. He's left Lucy and will be bringing the children with him. I think that he's already got a job here." Paul was a laboratory technician. "And he wants to use our place as a take off point looking for a flat for him and the kids."

"Why couldn't he go to Elizabeth's? I don't want to be looking after his children while he's out at work for too long."

Well you don't spend much time looking after ours thought Rick. "I think we know why, don't we."

"Oh yes. The wife swapping."

"Ssh. Little pitchers have big ears." They looked at each other as if the very idea disgusted them. But they hadn't had anything resembling sex for about four months and each wondered way somewhere in the back of their minds what they would do if they were offered the opportunity. "I'm going to get him and the kids from the coach station on Saturday morning. Unless you want to go?"

"No. You go. How long will he be staying?"

"No idea. I would imagine that he'd want to get out from under our feet as quickly as possible. I just don't know."

On Saturday Rick collected them and brought them back to the house. They were tired after their long journey and Paul didn't really want to talk and the children just stared at the television all afternoon. Paul didn't want to go to the party with them so they cancelled their babysitter and left him to it and went over to Christine's.

The party was like getting into the Tardis and going back to the seventies. If it were only that easy Rick thought. There were cushions spread on the floor, candles and joss sticks. It was the first time that he had been into Christine's house. She hadn't been there long but even so absolutely nothing had been done to it unless one happened to love loud sixties wallpaper and swirling carpets that made Rick feel as though he'd already drunk too much. As well as the other guests the music was also strange. Lesley would have never allowed the sounds of Grateful Dead at their dinner parties. The kitchen was a slum in comparison to Lesley's, which had been newly fitted in time for their end of holiday party. This not only put Rick off drinking in there but also eating though he hated eating in front of strangers. However Lesley guided him to the table to make sure that the wine had something to soak into.

Shocked to the core Rick exclaimed in an overloud voice "There's no meat!"

"It was easier..."

"And cheaper no doubt," said a lanky male who looked as though he should have still been at school.

A longhaired huge faced friend of Christine's continued, "Most of the people here are vegetarians. Whilst at university together we rarely ate meat." He sounded momentous.

"Actually," said a skinny female with greasy hair, "Dryden and I are vegans." She spoke as if Dryden were her pet dog.

"Ah," Rick said, "Mind you I always, thought that vegans had green faces with big ears and were on Star Trek." Nobody laughed.

Rick followed Lesley and they sat down on the floor. He leaned over and whispered in her ear, "She looks to me as though she could do with a good meal as well as a good rogering." Away from the rest even Lesley smiled in agreement.

After quite a sort time Lesley was bored. The people at the party weren't her kind of friends. They didn't want to play court to her. They weren't impressed by the blonde hair and the Laura Ashley clothes or that she did her own watercolours. She'd tried that tack with one of the women who had responded by asking her if she had ever exhibited. When Lesley replied "No," it seemed like the ultimate failing.

"My husband Gerald is exhibiting his happenings in mud next week. Cardiff? Would you like to come? I can see if I can get you an invitation even though it's short notice."

Lesley had wondered off by herself after that. Christine's cronies had found out that Rick had interviewed Bob Marley so he was on the celebrity trip. It would be Richard Thompson next and who knows what memories that would lead to. She got him alone for a moment and told him that she was going home.

"You stay." And when she saw his amazed face she said, "No, I really mean it. I can see you're enjoying yourself. I really don't mind. It's okay. And maybe Paul will want to talk."

She went back over the road. Paul was Staring fairly blankly at the television screen as his children had done earlier. He was wearing Rick's dressing gown.

"Hope you don't mind me wearing this. I had a bath and but I hadn't unpacked yet."

"That's okay. Fancy a coffee?"

"Yeh. That would be nice." She went into the kitchen. He followed her. "I just want to say thanks and all that. You know."

"I know. Don't worry. I told Rick to stay. I don't think he'll be home for ages. He seemed to be having a good time. I haven't had a good time for such a long time."

"No. Nor have I." He moved closer to her. She reached forward and pulled him even closer by the gown. She put her hand inside and felt for his stiffening penis.

"Hm. I can see why Elizabeth liked you. You're quite a big boy aren't you? Come on, coffee can wait. I'll lock the door, but we won't be long, I've been waiting for this."

While Rick the children where at school Paul and Lesley had days of frenzied copulation.

After quite a few weeks Paul got his own place and moved out. They were all quite relieved on both sides, as the house had been full with two families in it. Lesley assumed that Paul would still be around during the day for sex and told him so.

"But, it's more difficult now."

"Why?" she asked, "Why should it be more difficult?"

"Well, now you've got some work in school I can't just keep popping over to see you. You know people will start to talk. It won't be easy."

"Like it wasn't with Elizabeth? Didn't seem to bother you then." He ignored that comment as though she hadn't spoken. "But you'll see what you can do?"

"Of course. Of course. I will see you." He kissed her lightly on the cheek and was gone. She thought of talking to Elizabeth about it and then decided against it.

A couple of weeks later on a Saturday morning as Rick was washing up the breakfast things the doorbell rang. He heard Hannah, who had been expecting a friend and had rushed to the door, invite Paul in. Both Rick and Paul shouted hello at virtually the same time. Rick went to meet him and Paul looked very pleased with himself. By his side was a female, quite a lot younger than Paul and very pretty.

He said, "This is Rick. Who's been a great friend over the past few weeks. A tower of strength." They all laughed feeling a bit embarrassed. "No true. Rick. Joanna."

"Ah visions of Joanna." Nobody seemed to recognise the allusion. "Good to meet you." He went to the foot of the stairs. "Lesley – Lesley, Paul's here. He's got someone for you to meet.

A surprise!" There was no reply so he went up to their bedroom. "Did you hear me?"

"Yes. I heard you. I'm just about to get into the bath."

He went back down stairs. "She's just about to have a bath. She won't be long. Want a coffee."

"No, we won't hang around holding your morning up."

"Oh, it's alright I expect Lesley's got a few little jobs lined up for my weekend."

"We're having a party in a few weeks if you're up to it."

"We will. Engagement is it?"

"No," said Joanna smiling, "Not yet."

They left.

After they'd gone he went back upstairs to Lesley who was still sitting on the bed.

"I've just seen enough of him," was all she said.

After committing adultery once it was easy for Lesley to do so again. She arranged for Hannah to spend a night with a friend and for Rick to take Liam to the cinema.

"That will be useful," she told Rick, "As I've asked Julian to come round and talk me through some new curriculum."

Rick knew that she was completely neurotic about teaching and being caught out not knowing something rather than just getting on with the job.

"Carry on like this and you'll be headmistress. Get it, head mistress." She laughed politely so as not to irritate him. Julian arrived before Liam and Rick left.

"What are you going to see?" he asked Liam in a friendly way.

"ET," answered Liam excited about the cinema and enjoying the fact that one of his teachers was in his house. It made him feel important.

"You'll enjoy that."

Not half as much as I plan to enjoy myself thought Lesley.

SIX

Rick had the idea of inviting their friends for a meal. "We'll make it the night before Christmas Eve. I'll cook it as though it's going to be a Sunday roast. Lamb, mint sauce, Yorkshire pudding the lot. It'll make a change from all that clever stuff everybody tries to think up."

Lesley demurred, though she had to remind him that Dorian was a vegetarian. "Don't worry. I'll make her something." He smiled. "I could add some poison," he mused to himself.

"Oh lucky Dorian."

It was a huge success. Maurelian particularly enjoyed himself, as he wasn't allowed roast potatoes at home.

"This is the first one I've been given permission to eat for years."

"And I allowed you to sit where you liked."

Everyone enjoyed themselves so much that they decided that Rick probably wasn't such a bad chap after all.

After the meal they sat around a real fire with a Christmas tree and soft jazz in the background. They all felt very contented.

"I thought we'd give Trivial Pursuits a miss tonight. Lesley and I only have the Arabic version and Lesley's Arabic isn't too good."

Again everyone showed good humour towards him. Rick felt like he was making history.

"Going to France again next year Maurelian?"

"Yes. Take the caravan over."

Perhaps it was the wine, the warmth but Christine heard a voice in her head. "We thought about going to France in the summer didn't we Christine?" That was Steve's voice. It was the ghost from the past again to haunt her. It was going to be a much better campsite for them than last year. It was almost literally on the beach with a swimming pool for the children, a playground, bar, small restaurant, disco, shop and so on. He said he would even help with the washing up and perhaps Christine could have driving lessons when they got back to England.

Christine hated the place from the moment they drew up to reception and saw the closely packed caravans and tents with the hum of the people. She knew she would rather have the emptiness and tranquillity of the previous year's site. There, they had had all the space around them as if in their own garden.

"This looks good," said Steve positively and optimistically as they drove slowly and carefully to their allotted patch, "The children will enjoy the pool and the playthings."

"And I wonder who is going to constantly make sure that they don't drown?"

"And the beach is very close..."

"And no doubt as crowded as Blackpool on a Bank Holiday."

"And there's a little shop..."

Little when we're being talked down to and yet big for sex. I'm always the underdog, under bitch, was what she wanted to say.

The thoughtful and caring French owners of this site believed that nationals would like to spend a holiday with their own kind. So they were put into the British corner, the Germans in another, the French in another and so on. They found their space. To Christine's horror she saw a Volvo Estate parked to one side of them. She had an aversion to people with Volvos. In her experience it meant lots of children and bossy women with loud voices.

"Looks like we'll have people to talk to as well," said Steve.

"My French is perfect," she replied.

Her worst nightmare was realised when a women came across for a natter. It was like a welcoming committee. Within minutes Christine knew all the facilities of the site as well as the women's name, Maureen, and her husband's, Maurice, and their children's, Jason, Natalie, Timothy, Loren and little Erica.

Finally Maureen said, "It's a good idea putting all the Brits together. Don't you think? My Maurice does. He won't speak the language and why should we anyway? We're all Europe now so let's make English the language! It's great to have someone to talk to. I expect he'll take... what did you say your husband was called?"

"Steven."

"Stevie, that's right, over to the bar at lunchtime to meet the lads. Does he play darts your Stevie? Expect he'll like a kick around later anyway."

Christine went over to Steve who was busy with the construction of the tent and whispered as loudly as she dared, "Put it all back. I hate it here. I want to go back to other site. The one we went to last year."

"Christine we haven't been here five minutes. Give it a chance. Besides we'd look silly. And they probably won't have spaces there."

"Of course they will. It was half empty last year. Just do it!"

"Can we go to the pool with the other children?" asked Ben.

In the mid evening after she'd got Anna to sleep Christine climbed into her the double sleeping bag. It was too early to sleep but it was her only escape. Steve came back from the shower. It was also too early to pretend to be asleep.

"Hi," she said, 'Good shower?"

"Yes. Felling a bit happier now?"

She lied. "Yes. I still preferred the other site. But Anna and Ben like the pool and playground."

"You're under covers early."

"I was just lying down waiting for you." Almost as soon as she said she regretted the words.

Steve undressed and she looked in revulsion at his bulging erect penis. He slipped into the bag beside her.

"Steve. I'm not on the pill anymore."

"I'll pull out before I come." She loathed that.

He stroked her breasts. Her nipples remained flaccid and he knew.

"Christine I love you."

"Steve I can't."

"You don't love me. Do you?"

"Of course I do. I'm just not in the mood. It's been a tiring day. Anyway people might hear."

"If you loved me it wouldn't matter. It didn't matter once."

"I'm sorry." she buried herself into the bag.

Steve slid out. He went into the corner of the tent and began to cry. She hated this. "You don't love me," he began to moan.

'I do.'

"You've had the children you wanted. I've given you the children." I wanted a lot more she thought. "And now I'm useless."

"Steve." She went to comfort him. "I do love you. Come on."

He got up dressed went to the car and drove away the lights very bright against the dusk. Christine stood at the tent watching. Relieved. She never saw him again.

He drove all night. Perhaps round in circles he didn't know. Finally he ended up at the sea again. He thought he was perhaps near Brest. The coast was brown and grey and rugged like the north coast of Cornwall. He stopped the car and in a field. Nearby a horse stood up as if it were waiting only for him to arrive. The animal looked over at him. It seemed to join the sky and the field together and at once he felt that he was part of the whole world. The sea rolled grey and brown inwards and onwards. There may be the beginnings of a blue day. A day of harmony and light. He wanted whatever he had done wrong to stop. He wanted to go back to the bed-sit in the university town. He wanted to be a child again. But he knew that it was over. His demons had finally caught up with him and he was not a person that anyone could live with. They could only live without. He thought I am as a sailor; marooned out at sea alone. The sea is rough. I may drown. The sea I fear is me. That part of me that I don't understand. The needs I can't control. The rejection. I will become part of it overcome my fear. In a desert there is a fire burning, stars sparkling, and people waiting under a tree. I approach and am welcomed as I sit, a guest.

Two days later she left the tent and all the equipment. Caught a train and the ferry back to England.

"Yes." A present day voice brought her back to the day's surroundings.

"We haven't done anything about it yet."

"You must book the ferry soon," put in Dorian bossily. "Where are you two going?" she asked looking at Lesley.

"Across the river. I could book the ferry to there," replied Rick.

"I haven't thought about it yet," put in Lesley.

"Why don't we all go to France? Together," said Maurelian full of bonhomie.

"Hm," went Rick.

"You sound doubtful."

"We don't have to stay together," said Maurelian, "We can meet up for a few days, go our separate ways and then meet again..."

"I think that it would be wonderful." Lesley enthused. She knew then that she wouldn't have to spend the holiday alone with Rick.

"Right," said Maurelian, "In the New Year you and me will get the ferry and dates organised."

"I want to do it," said a petulant Dorian.

"I don't care as long as I get there." Rick raised his glass in a toast.

"Nor do I. It would be good for me and the children to go with someone," said Christine.

So the plans were made and they were still talking about the summer at three in the morning when they called it a night.

As they left the house saying their farewell greetings the cold air gave them the feeling of Christmas excitement and the warmth of the summer to come. The milkman eager to finish his round, his float lights shining in the dark still and quite silent night, delivered their milk. He happily they wished him Merry Christmas. It was bizarre Rick thought as one day was ending so another was beginning.

"That was a lovely evening and your meal was a great success."

"Well I thought that something ordinary would be very different."

"Yes. I'm ever so excited about the summer now. A holiday with friends."

"Yeh. Maybe you're right."

SEVEN

The telephone rang at Jonathan's house and his father went to answer it.

"Mr. Sharpe?" a man's voice said.

"Yes," he replied and then instantly went to put the phone down because he didn't want to buy double glazing but the man's voice went on, "Mr. Newstead. You may remember me. I'm..."

"Lesley's father."

"Yes that's right," as if he were talking to a child who had successfully remembered it's three times table, "I could do with having a chat with you."

"Have you heard from Jonathan?"

"No. I'm sorry."

"'Right." He sighed with disappointment. "Do you want to come here, or shall I come to you?"

"No, better if we meet in a bar. Have you got a Grand Hotel in your town? I'm sure you have."

"Yes. In the High street."

"I'll meet you there in two hours time. Can you bring any letters or postcards that you've had from him."

"What's this about?"

"I'll explain later. Probably better if you don't mention this Mrs. Sharpe, don't want to raise any unnecessary hopes. Say you've got to meet a friend or something."

William Sharpe put the phone down when his wife opened the back door and shouted, "Who was that on the phone?"

"Eric. He wants to meet up later for a drink."

"Oh, that'll be nice. I'll get changed and we'll have these chops tonight. I haven't had a natter with Mu for ages. Not a proper one anyway. I saw her in town last week but she was running for her bus."

"No. She won't be there. She's gone to stay with her girl for a few days. I think Eric is feeling a bit lonely."

"They haven't got a daughter."

"He must have said son."

"Not a lot of difference." She fussed with her shopping lifting the bags onto the side of the kitchen cabinet. "She didn't say anything about it last week."

"Because she was running for her bus. Perhaps it was all last minute."

"Yes because he was to have a sex change." She smiled at her own joke. "Are you alright?"

"Fine fine."

"You look as if you've had a bit of a shock. You sure? Might do you good to get out by yourself."

" What have you bought?"

"Just food. Nothing exciting."

"Here let me give you a hand to put it away."

EIGHT

In July a week or two before the families went away Rick and Lesley were due at Maurelian's and Dorian's for dinner.

Rick said to Christine in morning as they got into their respective cars, "Shall we walk together to Maurelian's on Saturday?"

"Saturday?"

Christine hadn't been invited. They knew that they were not totally 'in' though neither would they admit it. They played one pair of friends against the other and then they felt in control when someone was missing the delights of their company on a Saturday night.

As usual it was formality to its extreme with the pompous pair on the following Saturday. As they sat sipping sherry and nibbling Rick enquired "Just the four of us then?"

"No we're expecting Louise and Alexander. I don't think that you've met them."

Rick hated the whole act of meeting people for the first time, talking through the formalities, shaking hands, pretending that you liked them and were interested in them their jobs and their children. I'm a stoma nurse he often dared himself to say.

The doorbell rang and his nerves began. He knew that the acting would have to begin. Lesley knew that he found this difficult. It was the one thing that she had sympathy with him for and would often help. In his first term at college he had almost become anorexic because he avoided lunch in the canteen and with it anyone potentially joining his table.

"Hi, come in," a jovial Dorian cried as though the new arrivals were people she'd always wanted to have met.

"Sorry we're late. Babysitter and settling children and all that."

Rick stood up as the door to the lounge opened. Ready for the play to begin. A rather tall man entered followed by a woman. She was slim vivacious, auburn hair.

"Alexander and Louise," said Dorian. "Have you met?"

Lesley spoke for him. "Weren't you at Philip and Elizabeth's Christmas thing? And at Christine's house warming, some time ago now?"

"Yes I teach with Christine. She has spoken about you."

"Anyone for a sherry? First course is about ready I think."

In thoughtful silence Rick was saying oh God, show me there is a God. Please make Jacques who puts the names out boy girl boy girl...put me next to Louise. I'll do anything except move the names. That would be too obvious. He stared straight ahead.

"Are you alright?" asked Lesley, "It's just that you haven't spoken." She hissed "Be friendly."

He tried to raise a smile. "Just a bit hot."

"Come through now." Dorian ordered.

Rick went after everybody else so that at least he could see where the empty chair was. Heart pounding and stomach on fire he momentarily stood at the door. Maurelian was at the head of the table with Dorian on his left so that she was near to the serving hatch. Opposite her was Lesley with Alexander next to her, opposite Alexander was Louise, which left him a space at the other end of the table next to his infatuation.

"We don't seem to be quite boy girl boy girl...."

"We weren't going to bother with names but Jacques likes to do them on the computer."

They were the only family with a computer and they liked to make sure that all knew. "And we know how much you like them Rick. Unless you'd like us all to change places?"

"Oh don't encourage him."

"No I'm fine as I am."

Rick was sitting by Louise. She spoke to him and she talked back when he spoke. He held a conversation. Nothing else existed. Twice, was it accidental or was she flirting, their legs touched. He realised now that infidelity was not a sin. He didn't necessarily have to remain faithful to a woman he didn't like for the rest of his life because of outside pressures. When they went through to the lounge for brandy and coffee the talk got round to how they first met their respective partners. They relived the heady scented days of falling in love. Lesley loved to give the impression that she was wooed rather than that she had thrown herself at Rick. Rick, for his part, let her live out this fantasy, a scene that she had seen in a film once. It was easier that way. She believed it now. And it meant that he didn't have to contribute anything to the legend.

"And," Lesley went on enjoying not only the sound of her own voice but the rapt new audience in Alex and Louise, "When he asked me to marry him," she looked at *him,* "I didn't answer straight away. Oh no. I made him wait." She paused for the chuckles, which usually came at this point and were on this occasion politely supplied even though Maurelian was thinking how many more times will Lesley tell this story. They all looked at Rick who felt like a hamster on a wheel. "I drove in my car, a Beetle. 883 EXN, I even remember the registration! White it was. I had the Beach Boys on the tape and I just drove. In the end I realised that I'd ended up at Robin Hood's Bay..."

"Where's that?" asked Maurelian as though it were a vital part of the tale.

"Near Scarborough." Lesley was slightly miffed now that she'd lost the flow and wanted to quickly get it back on track. "The cliffs were deserted. I drove close to the edge. I was looking out across the sea at the sunset. I got up onto the roof and just sat cross legged and thought." Rick always found this part difficult to imagine. The thought of the rather plump figure of his wife, who was sitting here in this room, being capable of climbing anywhere. He suppressed a laugh and didn't speak. He'd heard it all before, wishing she'd just driven off the edge.

She went on, "I just watched the sunset and the Beach Boys were singing." 'Wouldn't it be nice?' And I decided. Yes." She said the word as if she might have said no, but obviously she didn't or they wouldn't be here now.

Why didn't you say no, Rick thought, why?

On the way home he said, 'That Alex fellow was nice wasn't he?'

"I thought you hated the word nice. You hardly spoke to him."

"Could invite them to dinner."

"Why?"

"A change is good. Needed."

House horrendous. Disorder. Everything everywhere. And life is limping along as I struggle to cope if only you were there for me. In the eye of the storm there is darkness stillness ready to anaesthetise to put me out of misery.

NINE

Jonathan entered the village of St Aurelien in France. He knew he would spend the rest of his life there. It was the most beautiful place he had ever visited, and as time went past it became lovelier. He was in the deepest part of France, the real France not even the part where a French person may holiday let alone the English tourist. It was a very rural place where farming and some wine making was the main trade. It boasted a church, boulangerie, food shop and bar. There was of course the Mairie and he was introduced to the mayor soon after his arrival, as he had to have his 'permission' to remain in the country. A short fat man with a large head handed over Jonathan's papers and identity card welcoming him to the country and the village, "The finest place in Europe, indeed in the world!" and they raised a glass of wine to that.

Stephi had a large house in the village of only six hundred people. She lived there with her husband and two adolescent sons. Jonathan would have his own room. He shared everything else with them as a member of the family.

"You must act like you are part of the family. We want to treat you like that," she told him.

He took quickly to village life. He enjoyed his time in school. He wasn't paid well but not a great deal of responsible teaching was expected from him. He had small groups of students to which he mainly spoke English and told them about English life and culture. It was rather like holding a conversation all day. He had the advantage of having been trained as a teacher so discipline problems were unknown in the groups that would normally take advantage of an inexperienced assistant.

Over dinner, one evening towards the end of November, Jonathan asked who lived in the small house opposite them.

"Why are you wanting to leave us?"

"No." He smiled at the fact that they might care. "It's just that I never see any lights on or anyone coming in or out and I believe I know everyone by sight now."

"Well they know you. You were the talk of the village for a while. Not now though."

"It's empty," said Marc, one of the boys.

"Haunted!" said the other with an eerie effect to his voice.

"It belonged to a M. Biardeau. She died only last year."

"Oh, well if it were empty and nobody wanted it..."

"You could live there," shouted one of the boys sounding as excited as if he were about to buy it him self, "And you could still come here to eat."

Jonathan smiled at that. "Well it's a thought."

And a thought that would please M. Maulin as it would show that Jonathan was keen on staying, Stephi decided to tell her in the morning. "Maybe it's for sale or rent. See if you can find out," She said to her husband who was always given jobs like that to do.

Jonathan moved into the house opposite just before Christmas. The price was so cheap that he could actually afford a deposit and mortgage on his salary. The house came with a little furniture, a bed and a very old but working cooker. However he felt that he had fulfilled a childhood dream of living in a cottage in the countryside.

Stephi wanted him to eat with them on Christmas Eve but he felt that he had taken everything from them and he had gained so much in his short time in France.

"But you can't be alone at Christmas."

"I'm only across the road. It is important to me that I spend my first Christmas in my house. My own home."

"Okay okay. I understand. But you must come for lunch and drinks on Christmas day. We are having friends over. There will be plenty of people here. Come on. You will enjoy it. Also you won't get your Christmas present..."

"Well, you won't get yours either if I don't turn up."

Jonathan's house was still and silent on Christmas day. He thought about all the times that this old house had seen. How many days like these, a years worth? And each one was unique. He woke early on Christmas Day. It seemed very strange not to be sharing it with any one. He had a book and a cd for himself, which he had vowed not to open or listen to until that morning.

He sat drinking coffee looking out at the completely still countryside watching the stars disappear one by one. The sun rose glowing red to yellow. It gave some warmth to the icy earth and the few animals dotted around. He felt completely content.

At one o'clock he went over the road to his friend's house. There were already plenty of people present. He kissed his hostess and wished her a Happy Christmas.

"Here," she said, "Let me introduce you to a few people." She walked off and he followed. "I think I know who you would like. Now where is she? Helene," she exclaimed, "You must meet Jonathan. Helene Jonathan, Jonathan Helene," she looked from one to the other, "You can both speak? Good. I'll leave you to it then."

They spent the afternoon. He learnt that she was an estate agent and that she had seen him when he came into the office to buy his house. She was a year his junior. She got to know all that he chose to tell her. Finally she said that she had to go as her mother was 'making impatient eyes' at her.

"Can I take you out for dinner tomorrow," he asked.

"Well, yes. But I was going to come and cook for you. Six o'clock, at your house? Is that okay? By the way it is the custom of French people to kiss when they meet and depart. You've done neither so far. You may now."

He kissed her as was the tradition but needed so much more.

"Till tomorrow then."

After she'd gone Stephi asked him, "Did you like your Christmas present?"

"That was devious, underhand and scheming."

"Yes and you'd better go and clean your house up."

Helene arrived promptly to a clean house at six o'clock. He had even changed the sheets on the bed. Though perhaps it was too soon for that, forever the optimist. She looked; words failed him, as she struggled through the door with two bags. He was too rooted to help.

"What have you got there? Enough to feed an army?"

"I had to assume that you had nothing in the kitchen. Not even wine."

"Well I have. Would you like a glass?"

"Yes. And then go and find something to do."

"I could help you."

"No."

"I could be with you. Keep you company."

"No. I cook alone. Go."

He sat in his front room by the fire trying to read. The smells of food, which came from the kitchen, were beautiful, full of an aroma, which only the French are able to produce. At last she called him. "You need a new cooker," she told him as he went into his kitchen. "This meal may not be up to my usual standard." The table was laid and ready. There was chevre chaud for starter, pork marinated in cider. "The pig was from my uncle," she told him. With French beans, blet and violette potatoes followed by a selection of cheeses including comte which he adored (how did she know this) and crème brûlé to finish.

Finally she asked "Coffee?"

"I'll get it. Why don't you go into the front room now next to the fire? I'll bring it in. I have some brandy somewhere."

She sat on the sofa with her legs curled up beneath her. He sat down in a chair towards the side of her after he had put the drinks down. They drank in silence savouring the moments of complete peace watching the darting movements of the hot flames.

"That was perfect," Jonathan told her.

"Thank you. You're very kind." She looked directly at him. "Are you tired?" she asked.

"No." He was puzzled and sad that the evening should be ending. "Do you have to go?"

She stood up. "Well only to bed." She took him by the hand and led him up the stairs, "This way?"

"Thank God I put clean sheets on," he thought.

Later she sat astride him a blanket wrapped around her to keep out the cold.

"Helene that was..."

"Don't start that nonsense. I've plenty of lovers. I'm a proper French woman. You are only the next in a long line of willing males."

He couldn't say anything. Disappointment filled his body. It was pay back time he guessed.

"Your face," she said, "It's a picture." She got off the bed still wrapped in the blanket leaving him naked and feeling vulnerable and cold. He assumed she was going to get dressed and leave. She went to her bag and took something from it. "Here you are, for you. A late Christmas present."

Puzzled. He tore off the wrapping and looked at the gift. "Thank you. A CD. Francis Cabrel," Trying to sound like he knew the singer and all of his work.

"Do you have a cd player in this room?" She looked around.

"Yes."

"Play track five," she ordered and then laughed at what she had sounded like. They both lay down together to listen. 'Je t'aimais, je t'aime, je t'aimerai'

They both spoke. "I have loved you I love you I will love you."

"You are the only one."

"Will you be my wife Helene?"

"Yes, but you will have to ask my father first. He is very traditional. But he will say yes as I will tell my mother I want to marry you and he always does as he is told. You to will have to get used to that."

"I'll cope."

"Always show me that you love me."

Grey mist hung like gloom over the trees, but with such promise of beauty, sun bursts through the clouds as my sleeper soon wakes and holds me.

TEN

The following day Rick was preparing dinner and dreaming of Louise listening to Leonard Cohen loving her in the morning. The front door burst open and Maurelian rushed in full of self importance. He always felt that he didn't need to knock. Rick jumped back quickly into a type of reality.

"The ferry, the St. Clementin, is on fire!"

"Well I shouldn't worry we're not on it!"

Maurelian was usually impatient at the best of times, now he was in frenzy. Lesley came rushing down the stairs almost two at a time from where she'd been preparing for school after a lengthy lie in bed for most of the morning.

"The St. Clementin's on fire!" shouting again. Maurelian hoping for a different reaction this time.

"The St. Clementin's on fire?!" exclaimed Lesley.

"Well why don't you both go and put it out?" Rick was giggling. Lesley and Maurelian stood now not quite knowing what to.

"That's the boat we're getting in a few weeks Rick."

"The Handsworths are on that one now going to France, don't you realise!" Lesley dramatically cried.

"Well that's good news anyway. Let's hope that they go down with it." They both studiously ignored him.

"How do you know?"

"It's on ceefax." He liked to show off that he had ceefax as well as a computer.

"I've told Christine and she said to go over there to see what can be sorted. Dorian's already with her." Sensing some drama was about to be enacted the children followed.

Rick calmly carried on with dinner, thoughts of those eyes. The mouth. Of slowly undressing her and kissing her all over. He felt a bulge in his trousers.

Later after dealing with his frustration he ambled across the road as unconcerned as possible. He felt that this was a much cooler way to be. They were all there now as well as the children.

"The St. Clementin is on fire. The Handsworths are on it!" Rick shouted at them and then starting laughing. Dorian looked at him with a scorn that said he was mad.

"Oh leave him. He thinks he's funny."

Maurelian was speaking hurriedly, impatiently and importantly on the telephone. He gestured to them to be quiet raising an arm, pleased as well that it wasn't his phone bill he was running up. Everything was so hushed and serious that Rick had to turn away and put a fist into his mouth.

Finally Maurelian put down the 'phone. "I think I've got it sorted." He sounded triumphant.

Rich exploded with laughter. "But are the Handsworths alright?" The rest had sat waiting for Maurelian's speech with serious and sensitive anticipation. He giggled away. He went into the kitchen.

Ten minutes later Lesley came in to the room and closed the door. "That was bloody rude."

"Sorry I feel a bit silly today."

"If Maurelian hadn't been watching TV then we wouldn't have known about the St. Clementin. As it is Maurelian was one of the first people to contact The Poitou Ferries. The St. Clementin is likely to be out of action for months. It could have ruined our holiday. It could have been impossible to get another ferry with the two caravans. As it is, he's managed it." Well what a hero Rick thought. He wanted to organise it and he loves every minute of it. "We go from Poole to Cherbourg now." This meant nothing to him.

"Thanks Maurelian," he said as Maurelian came into the kitchen bristling with self importance.

"I expect you'd like a drink after that would you Maurelian?" Christine shouted from the adjoining room.

"Any excuse!" She brought him a glass of wine and Lesley, Maurelian and Christine went to join the others leaving Rick alone in the kitchen. After a minute or two Christine came back into the room.

"I think they're being over dramatic as well," she said. "What are you doing?"

"Washing up. My penance. I didn't know that you taught with Louise?"

"You didn't ask."

"I met her last night."

"Oh?"

He looked at her and raised his eyebrows instinctively, embarrassed.

She put a hand on his arm. "She leaves at the end of this term. Got a headship up North. Newcastle. Didn't you know?"

"No."

"It can be difficult at times. I realise that."

One day when you asked me to hold you tight. You said you'd been lonely for a long time. I wanted to wrap you in my arms forever envelop you.

ELEVEN

When on holiday Rick always kept a diary of the events as they went along. He preferred reading it later rather than looking at the photographs. It was the one time when he actually had the time to write. Time not only to record the daily happenings but also his thoughts. Lesley promised never to read it and he almost believed her, which meant that he was nearly honest in his writings. He would for example never mention Louise. He could not say that he was longing to be back home in England, to work some way of seeing her again before she left for good. Rick was aware of the subconscious thoughts that might come out. Maybe one day he would just sit and write and write for days and days on end without stopping and seeing what it was he was producing. He could then sit back and read the full truth.

They all arrived after a very long and boring journey. Cherbourg wasn't a very convenient place to arrive at in France since they were aiming for the southern part of Brittany.

Travelling down to Brittany they insisted on stopping again for yet another picnic. It was no wonder that their children were so fat. Consequently it was quite late by the time they arrived at the campsite.

Once Rick had unhitched their caravan Lesley and Christine went off to the local supermarche for food and drink before it closed for the weekend. Hannah was old enough to be useful with the caravan and so stayed behind. They had a good first evening totally content with salad, cheese, cold meat and wine and any edginess felt began to ebb away.

Dorian and Maurelian had disappeared down the road a few kilometres to stay with friends. Others knew it by sponging on the goodwill of others for a few free meals and nights.

Lesley hadn't enjoyed the journey either. She had wanted Rick to speak to her when she could hardly keep her eyes open but he wouldn't. He really didn't have anything to say to her. She didn't like him to drive in England and she believed it took an expert in France. 'She had people to talk to. He could be as quiet as he liked,' she thought.

Rick was writing his diary the Monday when Maurelian and Dorian arrived. Their site already looked like home with the elder children and Ben riding around on their bikes, Anna who was still too young for a bike running round after them. Maurelian remarked on the contented atmosphere as though he were paying them a compliment. Christine had gone off to do the washing up after their breakfast of coffee, tea and croissants. Rick was keeping an eye on Anna whilst reading.

"We're off to the Le Clerc," Dorian said, "Want to come?"

"Oh I need to," answered Lesley. "Rick said that he didn't want to."

"Well you keep an eye on the children then. Christine is washing up."

"Fine. I'll manage that."

"You shouldn't sit like that," Dorian told Rick.

"Oh why? Shall I stand on my head?"

"I mean without a shirt on..."

"Why? Do you fancy me then?" He moved to cuddle her.

Dorian managed a smile whilst putting a distance between herself and Rick. "If you stay in the sun all day you'll get skin cancer."

"No she's right. We don't go down to the beach until about four o'clock!" announced Maurelian.

"With any luck just when we're returning." They'd given up trying to find any humour.

Rick wrote *'In silence. Sometimes I find too many people overbearing. The talk about spoons, knives, big plates, and the little ones are a disturbance. It seemed to take forever to get here due to the ferry from Plymouth being cancelled. So the drive from Cherbourg to Letty (Treffigiat) took about seven hours. I'm sure that that there must have been a quicker way but still I hadn't taken any part in the organisation of this holiday so I'm maybe the last person to criticise. The campsite is wonderful because it is so quiet, quite empty, well organised and clean. Last night I just slept and slept and dreamt and dreamt. I awoke once because it was cold so I spent some time looking at the stars.'* He paused and decided to call the diary *'Looking at Stars'*. He continued *'The sky was clear and I was able to trace a satellite moving across it.*

The weather is very hot here and they've all gone off to the Le Clerc to do some shopping. It's nice to be alone. I certainly won't miss Dorian when our ways part. I found her quite rude this morning and I don't think that I would get way with it. Still it cheered me up no end knowing that I'm in for a good bout of skin cancer by sitting in the sun all day.'

He closed the book and his eyes until the sound of cars and human voices woke him. They all piled out full of chatter.

Christine appeared, washing bowl full of dried and clean dishes, just as Dorian and her cronies arrived back from the shops.

"Well we'd better go," said Dorian. "See you later on the beach?"

"Sorry Christine, they wanted to go. Was there anything you needed? I can take you later if you like," said Lesley.

"Don't worry I was here to keep her company."

Christine tried to look cheerful. It seemed she was only good for washing up.

After the meal that night Rick pushed out his legs in font of him in contentment and looked at the dirty dishes waiting for Hannah to gather them together and wash them for two francs a meal.

Whilst Liam and Hannah were absent Maurelian and Dorian arrived.

"We're off the day after tomorrow." They informed them. "We've friends in the Dordogne we're staying with." Inviting themselves again no doubt Rick thought. "And Jacques," 'Oh no the dreadful son, what's he thought of now? He definitely won't be going on a diet. It will have to do with food,' thought Rick, "Has had a wonderful idea. He wants us all to get together for pizzas and desserts." Lesley thought that it was a magnificent idea. "Dorian is going to make some pizza's at the house…"

"You'll help won't you Rick?" He could hardly say no.

"And Jacques has written a list of the desserts he likes for the rest of you to buy! Brilliant eh?"

The following morning he wrote; *'I awoke again in the night and looked at the stars - I may not always love you but as long as there are stars above you - I saw a shooting star. Liam tells me that on the 16/17th of August we should be able to see lots of them. We'll be at home then!!! Yesterday it occurred to me on the beach what Dorian is. She is a more intelligent version of my niece. Anyone who has ever met my niece will know precisely what it is I mean, perhaps even sympathise. She talks incessantly about all subjects and believes she know all that there is to know. What I think may make Dorian different is that her voice is incredibly dominant and she will interrupt and talk over people. Certainly she gives the world the impression of being intelligent but where this intelligence/knowledge (if she has any) comes from I don't know as she rarely listens. Perhaps she is well read, perhaps insecure. I nearly had a stroke when Lesley told me that I was to go and make pizzas with her, still c'est la vie. It was good on the beach yesterday afternoon with the three families together though the younger children were a bit tetchy. I floated between waking and sleeping and had a lovely swim in the sea. Its coolness was so refreshing on my sunburn. I suppose*

Dorian was right about the sun, though I haven't got cancer - yet.'

Whilst Rick was making pizzas with Dorian later that day Lesley and Christine went off to play tennis. Rick hadn't played since he'd accidentally hit Lesley in the mouth with the racquet some years earlier and had been banned by her like a recalcitrant footballer. The ladies played a few sets then Lesley asked her if she felt like a walk. Christine was a bit surprised because she thought the idea odd but agreed. They went down the empty lanes towards the sea.

"You and Rick seem happy. I wish my marriage had been as comfortable."

"Rick and I argued yesterday."

"Yes Lesley," touching her arm, "But over a minor thing. We'd had such a long journey. We hardly spoke at all. We went stale."

"It happens in marriage...Rick and I are not what we seem. I don't think that he's happy. I'm not happy. All our friends are happy. I'm not." Christine wondered if she wanted to hear this conversation. "I've grown out of love." Lesley went on.

"Oh." She looked at her watch for something to do. "I think you both love one another. There are bound to be ups and downs when you've been together for a long time and know each other well. Try and make a new start here."

"That's what I'd like. But because I just know what he's like. I can tell, my women's intuition." They both smiled trying to hide the embarrassment of what was being said and where the conversation might be going ."He loves you. I wish I could be loved."

Christine felt an uneasy trepidation that bordered on excitement. "I think we'd better get back. I could do with a shower. I think you have the wrong impression. Rick and I have never even looked at one another in any way..."

"Well, you are welcome to him."

"No I don't think of him that way." She needed to make it clear. "I never will. I'm sure it will all work out well in the end."

"I don't think it will. In fact I know it won't. He's down to his last few months in our marriage if he carries on the way that he does." Lesley stopped and turned and looked at her. "You'll keep this to yourself."

"Why?"

"I want to handle the children in my own way. I'd prefer that. Okay?"

"Yes. Okay. I know nothing."

'I don't want your cast offs,' thought Christine. 'If I wanted a man in my life then it would be through my own choosing and it would be the ideal person for my children and myself equally. It would not be someone who was born out of necessity or worse still, lust. I am quite content. I am complete.' These were words that she should have said to Lesley as they made their way back to the campsite

Maurelian and Dorian arrived with the pizzas.

"First of all," Dorian announced as if a momentous event were about to take place, "We'll play a team game. Jacques wants to play rounders and we think it's a great idea."

Lesley who loved this kind of physical activity thought so too and heartily agreed, "It'll give us a good appetite," she went on with enthusiasm, "I'll organise the teams!"

"No. It's okay," said Jacques, "I've already done that." Lesley's face fell as she was intending to be one of the captains. "I'm captain of the boys and mum's captain for the girls."

After the game the evening went very well and all seemed to have been forgotten and in honour of them leaving the following day Maurelian and Dorian brought along a very special bottle of wine, Pinot. They wouldn't be all back together again until they returned to England. Ceremoniously Maurelian uncorked the bottle and poured each adult a glass and very pompously proposed, "To us. A good holiday and a safe journey home."

Dorian simply sighed in physical pleasure. "Oh that is good, a wonderful wine, so crisp and clean without being overbearing and just leaving the right after taste. A perfect accompaniment to fish. Don't you all agree?"

There were nods of agreement

"Actually Dorian," said Rick (why can't you just agree for once thought Lesley) "I don't think that this is any better than the litre of ten Franc wine I drank last night."

Furiously she retorted. "Well you just don't have any palate."

"Mind you the pizzas are nice. Though that's probably because I helped make them."

Rick smiled, more so when Maurelian added, "He could be right you know Dorian." She was now aghast. "This is not the best example of a Pinot."

She felt a complete fool and everyone present knew. It quickly dawned on Maurelian that he would be in for a rocket when they got back to their caravan.

"No bonks for you tonight Maurelian," said Rick successfully lightning the atmosphere.

"Nor for you" added Lesley.

Bon, that was his name now, caught a plane to America from Heathrow. His daughter checked his passport and said it was okay. After New York he went to the mid-west and then caught a bus to the small town of Little Hibbing. He had to see Helena again. He stayed the night in a small motel called Bates and spent the hours of darkness drinking whisky and rye. After a breakfast of waffles he asked the bellboy if he knew Helena.

"I isn't heard of nobody called Helena sir, not round these parts. You could try the County Library."

"The County Library?"

"Yes sir. They keeps a register of everyone who lives here."

Bon walked the dusty street, quite surprised at how empty it was for the time in the morning. A lady waved at him from a diner called Tom's, and Bon saluted back. The lady raised a hand to stop him and mouthed through the reflection, "The County Library's straight ahead."

"How did you know I was looking?"

"Well everybody ends up there sometime or another."

Bon went into the library, which was empty except for a lady behind the counter dusting a book.

"Can I be of help to you sir?" she asked him.

"I'm looking for Helena."

"I don't know of her. But if she's here her name will be in my book." She took a huge tome from under the counter. "Now then let's see. F,G,H...yes here we are, Harriet, Helena." She showed him the page and her name glowed with gold. "And an address as well. You'll find it three blocks down and two across. I know of it now. It has a rocking chair on the front porch. A very cute house. Don't know any Helena though. A lovely old couple live there."

Bon walked down the deserted hot morning blocks. A spaniel ran up tail wagging furiously like he knew him. At last he spied the house and hoped beyond hope that she would give him a drink. He was very thirsty. A very old man was sitting on the rocking chair slowly moving the rest of his life like the pendulum of a clock. As he approached the house the man shouted, "Mother."

Bon stopped and looked and waited at the sound of tiny footsteps and the screen door opened.

"What is it Henry?"

"A messenger."

"At this time of day?" The old woman looked at Bon. "What can we be doing for you?"

"I came to see Helena. Does she live here?"

"No young man. She don't."

"What does he want?" ranted on the old man.

"Helena. But she don't live here."

"Do you know her?"

"Oh yes. She's our daughter."

"Can you tell me how I can find her?"

"Oh yes. She's in town visiting. It's my birthday. Always visits on celebration days."

At that he heard a voice. "Who is it Mother?" Helena's voice. No mistake. She was dressed head to foot in a gabardine hunters mac.

"You expecting rain?"

"Is that you Bon?"

"It sure is." For some reason he had developed an American accent like John Wayne while she sounded as though she had just completed finishing school.

"I can't see you. I have to stay with my Mother. It's her birthday."

"What about a stroll in the mid morning sunshine?"

Helena looked at her mother who imperceptibly nodded. "Okay. Just around the block."

They started to walk.

"Aren't you hot," he asked her, "I'm hot."

"Well you have to be prepared for every eventuality."

"You cursed me. Can I have you back?"

"No," she said, "For I am already married." She paused for the effect to sink in. "To the Lord." At that the cloak fell from her revealing a full nun's habit. "See," she went on, "Stigmata." She held up her hands from which blood was flowing from her palms. She turned to him and opened her mouth. Her face to one of terror, her eyes blazing, her teeth savage, "I am a bride of Christ," she hissed. All at once a torrent of blood erupted from every orifice in her face.

He woke screaming.

"Not only are you a fucking pain in the day, but at night as well," said Lesley unsympathetically. "Shut the fuck up. You'll wake the whole campsite."

TWELVE

Jonathan's father washed, shaved and dressed as if he were about to go to a wedding.

"If I didn't know you better I'd say that you had a fancy woman."

He smiled enjoying the compliment, kissed his wife, left the house and walked up the street to catch the bus. As the vehicle wended its way through the estate, past houses and factories and car showrooms, and the huge bakery, that fed most of the town, he saw all that he had seen for the past forty-five years at all times from early in the day on his way to work to quite late at night after pub throwing out time. It made him think of how he had past all this and taken it for granted that it was there and always would be there and how nothing ever changes, well at least not in a lifetime. They travelled past the park. Jonathan had liked to sit upstairs on the bus to see what he could catch sight of over the wall. A child always perceives more and distinguishes something different even when nothing seems to have changed. How long had Thomas Wolsey laid there in the middle of the ruined monastery, four hundred years? It just looked the same flat oblong piece of stone with the inscription. He died, perhaps, of a broken heart because he was unable to change centuries of what he believed in, what was right, what was established. Jonathan's father sometimes felt like that. You were born. You grew up. You did your best. You couldn't do anymore. You married and had children. You did as well as you could for them. You couldn't do anymore. No-one asked anymore of you. You didn't run away at the first hurdle. You stayed and fought your ground. Everything had a course to run along like a rail track and it caused chaos if the engine wanted to go in a different direction. He boiled inside when he thought of what Rick had done to him, them, how they had to explain him away. Well it was as if he were dead, he'd decided that long ago.

Mr. Sharpe got off the bus in the town and walked to the Grand Hotel. He liked to go there with Jonathan's mother if it was a special occasion like their wedding anniversary. But they hadn't been there for along time. The streets were crowded as if only the shop assistants worked these days. He looked in the windows of shops at the displays without really seeing them and briefly through an alley into a market that always seemed so alive. They used to enjoy shopping together but they hadn't been together for pleasure for a long time. Perhaps it was time to put everything behind them. Perhaps they should try again. He turned into the hotel entrance and took the steps with a slight jog as he'd seen important people on the news do when they had nothing to say to the waiting press. The porter stopped him. He wondered if he was about to be refused entry. He had a tie on.

"Mr. Sharpe?" enquired the man.

"Er, yes," he answered in surprise. He'd never been greeted before. He did feel significant now.

"Mr. Newstead is waiting for you. This way sir. Follow me please."

"Thanks." He wondered whether he should tip the man and felt in his pocket for loose change. This is all a bit formal he thought.

"Lesley's father stood as he approached and extending his hand in what seemed to be a warm handshake said, "Good of you to make it Bill. No troubles I hope. You're both well?"

"Yes." Though he wasn't quite sure what he was saying yes to.

"You can wait in the car now Michael. I like to have a drink," he said with a wink and a smile at Mr. Sharpe, "So I got a driver to bring me over." He sat down. "You've time for a coffee and a look round," he called to the receding figure. "Come on Bill. You sit your self down. Now what can I get you. A whisky? Two whiskies please," he said to the hovering waiter.

"No. I'd rather have a pint of bitter. Thanks all the same."

"A chaser with it?" Mr. Sharpe shook his head. "You heard the man," and the waiter left them.

They passed pleasantries until the waiter brought their drinks and they were alone. Mr. Sharpe took in the plush surroundings and rather enjoyed the feeling that he was drinking with someone who had plenty of money and probably influence to go with it. They were social circles that he would have enjoyed living in.

Finally he asked, "Did you receive any letters from Jonathan, Bill?"

"Yes. Didn't you?"

"Lesley destroyed anything of his. He hurt her bad. Destroyed her hopes, self confidence and pride in herself." He sighed as if taking the weight of Lesley's sorrows on his own shoulders.

"I'm sorry. I'm sorry for her, for you and your wife..."

"And yourselves Bill. We've all been hurt."

"Mr. Sharpe sat for a moment as a token of silence also wishing that he knew Mr. Newstead's name so that he could sound as familiar and chummy. But it was too late now. "Ah you're right there. Broke his Grandpa's heart."

Both men sat looking miserable.

"Can I have a look at the letters then? Want another drink?" He signalled to the waiter. "Same again lad. Make mine a double."

"Well what I have is what I could find. I'm sure that the missus has more somewhere. But you said not to say anything."

"One is more than I have. And you were quite right about Mrs Sharpe. Mum's the word." He put a finger to the side of his nose and winked again.

"Why?"

He ignored the question. "Let's have a look." He took the proffered mail. He quickly read and dismissed the cards. Tells us which region he is in."

"Are you going to bring him back and make him marry Lesley."

"Now there's a thought." He paused as if considering that option carefully. "No Bill. You can take a horse, you know the rest." He held up an envelope eyebrows raised questioning, "Mind?"

"Go ahead."

"Here we are. He tells us where he lives. I expect you'll want to put this back?" Mr. Sharpe nodded. "I'll write it down. He took a small book from an inside pocket.

"What are you doing?"

"Bill, you said that he broke is grandpa's heart. He hurt us all. I can't think of him living the life of Riley in some foul French village with the wops pulling the birds while we, well we will never get over it." He pulled a clean white handkerchief from a pocket and wiped his nose as if he were crying. "I'll pay him a visit. Or at least Michael will. Very discreet I assure you." He turned round and looked at the door as pre-arranged and Michael who was standing there waved him over. "Sorry Bill. Looks like I've got to rush. Something must have come up." He put his hand on Mr. Sharpe's forearm holding it tightly and said quite firmly. "You'll forget all about this won't you."

He stood up and left without shaking hands or looking back. Mr Sharpe wondered what he had done. He left the rest of his drink. It was sour. He felt tainted and dirty as though he were some part of an unpleasant plot. He looked around him at the furnishings and they didn't seem as plush as they had only half an hour ago. The men and women drinking and eating looked as if they had walked out of a Bacon painting. He felt sick. He didn't know what to do. He left the room ignoring the man who said "Good afternoon," in farewell and wandered the town for an hour before he got on a bus home. He had intended to take some flowers home but forgot.

He got in the door hung his coat up and accepted the offer of a cup of tea. He often had a lot to say when he had been with Eric, as Eric liked to gossip as a tabloid paper would and his stories if tall were always good for a laugh. But Mrs. Sharpe noticed that he was quiet, to quiet for someone who had just spent a 'jolly lunchtime' in the pub with a mate.

"How was Eric?" she asked.

"Oh, fine."

"What did you talk about?"

"This and that. You know."

"Well obviously not or I wouldn't bother asking. And Mu?"

"He didn't say."

"You sat there for two or three hours and he never said anything about his wife or what she was doing and why she was visiting her daughter."

"No."

There he'd even forgotten that. She decided to leave it and maybe he would come round later. Something was not quite right though.

Just before they went to bed they always walked the dog together. That night Mrs. Sharpe didn't go making the excuse of a tiring day. As soon as she heard the gate close she went to the phone and rang Eric and Mu's number. It was Mu who answered the call.

"I've been meaning to give you a ring," she said sounding quite surprised probably because it was late in the evening.

"Yes. We must get together." While talking and listening Mrs Sharpe was almost unconsciously feeling the jacket that Bill had worn out that day. "I'll have to be quick as Bill's out walking the dog." She found herself going through his pockets then. "Bill's got a special birthday coming up."

"Sixty five."

"Yes that's right." She stopped for a moment and looked at what she held in her hand that she had taken from his pocket, all the mail that they had received from Jonathan.

"Still there."

"Yes sorry. I thought I heard him back. Any way I'd want to get him something special." She put the envelopes back where she had found them. "Can you ask Eric, and yourself of course, to see if you can dig around to see what he would really like that's special."

"Of course. Now I know he was onto Eric, cause Eric said…"

"When?"

"Weeks ago."

"Not today then."

"Not today. Eric had a day in the garden."

"And you were there?"

"Yes. Why?"

"I'll have to go. I've just heard the gate. Nothing to Bill."

She put the phone down sharply leaving Mu bewildered. "Eric?" she shouted

THIRTEEN

The next day Rick wrote *'At the end of an excellent evening I sat with the children. Christine was trying to get Anna off to sleep by lying with her. Lesley is prostrate on a bed inside the caravan sulking and sighing about how alone she was. We watched the stars, as they appeared one by one. Hannah saw three in a row but Liam couldn't see any at all. Other stars appeared popping out one by one. Liam asked if he could see a planet and I showed him Venus above a cloud. Perhaps because the sky is so vast and the stars so beautiful the three of us talked religion. Perhaps all religions are one. Perhaps they are all nonsense. Perhaps we take ourselves so seriously against infinity and think that we are so important. I wanted to explain this to the children and to tell them that you have to look if you want to see all the stars, but Lesley appeared at the door and upon seeing a glow worm took them off to show off to show to the children. I couldn't help but think of the phrase 'I think therefore*

I am' and whether it's only a neurosis of the human being that thinks so therefore worries about dying. The glow worm in its beauty does not think about dying. There's a lesson to be learnt. She's back now and I've just been told off for enjoying myself, writing. I do sympathise. Perhaps I am obtuse.'

'Fuck. I hate this place,' thought Christine, 'I just want to be at home.' They were in the final few days of their holiday in Northern Brittany. She had woken to the sound of rain against the canvas that morning and after trying to keep two bored and fractious children entertained all day it was now evening. She'd been invited to the caravan to play cards and had told Rick and Lesley that she would come over once the children were sound asleep; but she felt that she couldn't. She sat in the dim light of the tent halfway through her second bottle of wine feeling ill.

The last day of their holiday was very hot as though the weather had wanted to send them off home on a high. It was a day at the beach and then a last supper at the local restaurant. Lesley was way down towards the water's edge playing tennis with Liam. Hannah was staring abstractedly into rock pools. Christine looked from her book at Rick. He was a very different specimen from the way Steve had been. A bigger build and covered in hair. He had caught the sun well other than he would be very white round the middle without his trunks. She turned onto her front the sunning warming her. The conversation with Lesley came back to her.

On the ferry he wrote: *'We're on our way home now. I can't see the French coastline anymore. The weather is poor and the boat is swaying a lot. We spent the last night in Le Mao eating after a hot day on the beach. I was allowed a night cap looking at the stars, reminded me of nearly three and half weeks previously that seemed so recent and yet a time ago. I have now mixed feelings about going home. Sometimes infatuation recedes into the background, but perhaps it all comes round again. I don't know whether I want it to. It's not knowing what to think'.* When came back from buying himself a drink Lesley had added *'How profound. There I've committed sacrilege in your book too. Shame I can't touch you as easily as this paper.'*

FOURTEEN

A day or two after Rick and his family arrived back in England his mother telephoned him. After she had thanked him for his postcard they passed the usual holiday chitchat. They were to spend their holiday at the Blackpool Illuminations, the yearly pilgrimage. It never failed to fascinate it seemed. Just as she was about to put the 'phone down she told him that his Grandpa was dying and probably wouldn't see the week out. If she wasn't involved directly she assumed no interest for others. "She thought she'd better tell him she said, "so that he could arrange to have time off school for the funeral. That is if he wanted to go."

He put the 'phone back and went and sat down. Lesley was watching a lunchtime magazine programme about the Midlands. A town with some very old buildings came onto the screen. "There's my old school." She exclaimed. "Quick children come and look." They all sat staring at the television. "Did I ever take you Rick?" She looked across at him. "What's up now? Fallen out with your mother again. Or is your miserable face just an excuse for a drink."

"My grandpa's dying."

"Well he's an old man. What is he, eighty-five, eighty-six? It happens. Fact of life."

"I wish you were eighty-seven then."

"Do you. I just wish that you were dead."

He sat and looked at the silence.

On one cold afternoon in October when the trees were naked the telephone rang. As Jonathan talked into the mouthpiece Helene could see and hear that whatever was going on it was serious. As he put the phone down she touched his arm and asked.

"My grandpa. He's dying. He's asking to see me. I shall have to go."

"Of course you will. Don't you worry about a thing here."

Within twenty-four hours he was at the hospital by his grandpa's side. The doctor had told Jonathan that his grandpa was a very sick man and that he only had a very short time to live.

"He probably doesn't even know that you are here," the woman said, "But he may and that is a comfort to both of you."

Jonathan sat by the old man's bed holding his hand and talking continuously. Finally he knew that he had to leave or he would be stuck in England for five days. He did not want to meet his family. He would not even be welcome at the funeral. He kissed him on the forehead for the last and first time and left for his home, wife and family.

Rick arrived at the hospital twenty minutes later.

"I think you're only just in time. He's a very sick man. You know that he's going to die don't you?"

Rick nodded. "Yes." He sat down. A nurse stood on the other side of the bed as if waiting for him to die. All at once grandpa opened his eyes and spoke.

"Jonathan!" He said.

"No. It's Rick."

His final breath's came in laboured gasps as Rick leant over the old man and whispered into his ear all the words of love that he could think of so that his death was as beautiful and momentous as birth.

While he was dying Christine was on a train travelling north. She didn't take the children home to her parents as often as she should. It was a very long way. Six hours on the train. Not a weekend jaunt and sometime the holidays just had to be for her and the children and she needed just to completely relax after the stress of school and time spent as a single parent. But that October she decided that she would make the effort. Take the Christmas presents with her, which would be a terrific job out of the way, and maybe the change would do them all good. Possibly it would be just what she needed - someone else to look after the children. Perhaps she could shop by herself meet an old friend. Who knows, she thought, she might run into Jonathan again. She wondered if he ever made it to France.

The children were surprisingly good for such a long journey. Anna seemed content to sit and stare out of the window as long as there was drawing and eating thrown in as a distraction. Ben was beginning to act far beyond his years. He could be taking on the role of dominant male in the house Christine assumed. So he was determined to be no trouble. Reading he liked to give the impression was his passion, especially if it was about the Titanic. This all gave Christine plenty of time just to sit and do nothing. She was aware that if she had been at home she would have always been on the go, looking for what needed doing next.

She could just look at the scenery, the towns, villages and churches. She observed the way that the passengers changed in the carriage. One moment there would be a raven-haired youth with his hennaed haired girlfriend and the next time she looked and came back to a kind of reality they had been replaced by a chubby man with a plump wife and podgy children. The males wearing England t-shirts and sporting crew cuts and the females pierced slags, even the little girls. In front of them would be burgers, lager and fizzy drinks. An old couple, bickering slightly because he had spilt tea down his clean shirtfront.

Once in Newcastle and at her parent's house the joy lasted about an hour. They arrived there full of the excitement of seeing one another after such a long time when suddenly Anna turned a hue of green and a projectile of vomit of the lunch and chocolate eaten on the journey spread itself on the pristine sofa. Of course it didn't matter said her grandma when really it did. They cleared the mess up until really it looked as good as new but a rancid smell remained.

The following day they sent Christine into the city. "It would do you good," said her mother, "A bit of retail therapy."

Christine hadn't been off the metro and on the streets for more than twenty minutes when she was a sick as Anna had been the day before. She felt that people were looking at her as if she was some kind of drunken leper. She made it home and spent the rest of the day and night in bed with a bucket nearby.

Only Ben seemed unaffected and they waited but nothing came.

The following morning Christine woke late and felt better and made her way downstairs for a cup of tea. She could hear voices coming from the kitchen. She stopped to listen, she didn't know why. Later she wished she hadn't.

"Some stay this is turning out to be," she heard her father say.

"Childminders. Babysitters. That's all we are. And any minute I shall be cleaning up after little Ben. I was awake all night waiting for him to go. Poor lamb."

"Yeh," Christine could imagine her father shaking his head in despair, "If he had his Father here it would be better. I feel sorry for the lad not having a dad. When I think of all that I did with mine. Fishing." He stopped as if he couldn't think of anything else.

"Where do you think *she* went wrong?" added her mother.

Unable to listen to anymore of this Christine burst into the kitchen.

"Me, went wrong?" She asked looking at them both in turn shaking with anger. "Me went wrong. It might not have been him then?"

"No. I was just saying," she was unaware of how much her daughter had heard, "Me and your dad were just saying that you and the children must miss Steve."

"No. We don't. And why should we? And neither do you. You never liked him so don't go pretending you did."

"I wouldn't go that far. We had plenty of time for him."

"Well I would. You say what suits. You haven't liked this, us being here it's not fitted in with what you expected a family visit to be. Like you can tell all your friends about." She took a deep breath, "Oh yes it was lovely," she mimicked her mother. She went to speak but Christine carried on in a torrent. "So you think only if Steve had been here to mop up after us. As if. You must be joking."

At last her mother felt she could get a word in edgeways. Her Father had retreated to the table and was fiddling with a newspaper pretending he wasn't part of this. "Well, why did he leave? Where's he gone?"

"I don't know. He didn't leave a forwarding address. I don't care. Don't you understand?"

"I understand that you couldn't have been much use as a wife or he wouldn't have gone anywhere."

"How dare you say that? How dare you speak to me like that? You knew nothing about Steve and me. You didn't bother to find out."

"Because I'm your mother…"

"And a fine mother you are. Why do you think I don't visit? I don't want to see you. I don't like you."

Christine's mother took one pace towards her and struck her around the face.

"And that's what I think of you. You slut. You useless slut."

Christine got her bag, her children and phoned for a taxi from a nearby shop. They were unable to get a train back home until the following day so they stayed in the hotel that she had recommended to Jonathan all those years ago. They arrived home a day earlier than Rick was expecting and he was surprised to see them when he went over to feed the cat.

FIFTEEN

After Rick had been given his marching orders by Lesley and walked nonchantly down the road neither looking left or right he felt their neighbours eyes on his back. He was wondering where he was to sleep that night. He felt he had no friends. Elizabeth was already bringing Liam and Hannah back after giving them their tea. "Everything alright?" she asked Lesley as she entered the kitchen.

"Yes. You stopping?"

"I expect you could do with the company…"

"And a drink."

"What's wrong?" said Liam. "Where's Daddy?"

"Come in here children," said Lesley rather portentously inviting the children into their own living room, "I have something to tell you."

"I'll wait in the kitchen," mouthed Elizabeth over the heads of the children.

"Now. Sit down." Already tears were beginning to fill Liam's eyes. "There's nothing to worry about."

"Where's Daddy?"

"Daddy and I have decided to live apart for a little while," she said in the rehearsed speech. She could have given them a handout and said here you are read this. "We weren't getting on and it's best for all of us."

"Will he come back?"

"Perhaps..."

"Will we be able to go and see him?"

"Of course. As often as you like," conveniently forgetting to say as long as it doesn't interfere with my plans.

"Where's he gone?"

"He's got a nice flat in town," she lied.

"Can we go there now?"

"No. He'd want to settle in tonight."

"Can we go tomorrow?"

"Let's see what we can arrange for the weekend shall we?" She wanted to end this conversation now before it got difficult. She knew that the children were something that he wanted and that was why he wasn't going to have them. "We'll be fine and Daddy to." She wasn't going to talk about it anymore and the children realised that. "Why don't you go and play? I need to talk to Elizabeth."

They went from the room and went upstairs silently.

"Well how did it go?" said Elizabeth as she came into the room clutching a gin and tonic, "I took the liberty. Did you one as well."

" Thanks. I needed that. Oh fine. They were perfectly happy about it. Much better than I was expecting. They're at an age where they understand more."

"Yes. I know."

Hannah was sitting on the edge of her bed tears slowly trickling down her cheeks as though the flow was controlled. Her world had just ended. Twenty-four hours before she belonged to a family. Her father would not be in this house anymore. There would be no more silly games, chip butties, TV before bedtime on a Sunday night side by side on the sofa, going into their room at Christmas and birthdays and having two parents there. It had all gone. It was all out of her control. She would never have her childhood again. But she wasn't an adult either.

"They will be much happier now. You can make a happy secure environment here for them now."

Elizabeth had been reading her husbands National Geographic about keeping tropical fish that afternoon.

"Yes. You're right. I know you are. It will be much better. I should have done this years ago."

Liam was lying on his side in his bed curled up thumb in his mouth and convulsed in tears. Drying out. He wanted to know what was Daddy doing tonight? Would the bedroom door open and all of this have been a nightmare and his voice would say 'Wot Liam not in bed yet? You'll never be awake for school in the morning' and then kiss him goodnight whilst tickling him and Liam would sleep secure in the knowledge that Daddy would be there for breakfast.

Later on Lesley and Elizabeth went upstairs to look at the children. Hannah managed to smile and said that she was fine hardly looking up from her book. They couldn't find Liam until they looked into now Lesley's bedroom. Liam was lying asleep in his father's side of the bed.

"He must have been tired. Poor chap."

"I shall have to move him back to his own bed. Come on Liam. Wake up."

In the early hours of the morning Rick woke with a start. He felt around for the lamp switch and turned the light on illuminating a room that he didn't recognise. He had no idea where he was. He had dreamt that it was Christmas. The children were opening their presents under the bright lights of the tree. Lesley sat with a supercilious grin on her face saying 'these presents are from Daddy. Isn't he a kind Daddy?' As each child opened each present each individual toy was broken and they brought him the toys in a never ending succession saying 'But it's broken Daddy.' As he sat remembering the nightmare he cried.

He didn't go to school that day. Neither did he tell them or anyone else where he was. After a few days he went to the doctors with whom he talked. He was given a certificate for a month, which he sent onto school and was told to be careful about how much alcohol he drank. He found a bed-sit, paid the deposit moved in and realised that he had come full circle.

Perhaps that was the way to the truth. He thought about moving to France.

His children came down to see him and pretended to like where he was living. Lesley had dropped them off and so he walked them back. After he had left them at the house he went across to Christine's house.

"Hello stranger. How are you feeling?" She kissed him lightly on the cheek. "Want a drink?"

"No. Thank you. I'm trying to cut back. I'll have a coffee. Sometimes when you're by yourself all you can do is go to the pub."

"You can always come here." His face brightened with anticipation. "No. Let's make it clear from the outset Rick. You're a friend. I've no other feelings for you."

She made coffee and they talked some more and he began to feel more positive. As he left she said, "Why don't you come for lunch on Saturday. I have a friend visiting from America. I haven't seen her for years. She's staying with me for a few days."

When he'd dropped the children off Lesley had given him a large buff envelope. Rick didn't open it until he got back to his room. Inside were a sheaf of papers. He shook the envelope to make sure that was the lot and a photograph fell out. Whether it had been put there intentionally or by accident he never knew. It showed him and the children early one Christmas morning. None of them were dressed; they had their dressing gowns on. His was yellow. They were on the floor by the Christmas tree with the presents. Liam and Hannah looked happy and excited but Rick's smile is fixed as if he has been told to smile by the photographer, his wife. He notices that in comparison with other families whose trees he'd seen there isn't that many presents under the tree. Their Christmas day will be over, in about half an hour. After all it is the anticipation that's the significant part of Christmas Day. There wasn't any eagerness on his part. He would not have been allowed to buy the kind of presents he would have liked for the children, "We don't have the money." Where his salary went he never knew. Rick doesn't remember any presents that day unless it was a cheap label LP from Woolworth that he gave to his wife to wrap and give back to him.

Rick put the photograph on the shelf that had a couple of books on it. He sat and looked at it for a few minutes and then turned it to the wall.

He picked up the few pages and opened it out. It began with a letter, correctly addressed and dated as though it were written to a stranger it began:

' *Dear Rick, We obviously need to sort out quite a few matters. I'm sure that we can do this amicably like two grown up adults, friends. I do want us to be friends if only for the children's sake but also because we shared a lot together, happy memorable times as well as the sad latter ones. We can't put all that behind us and start again but we can go forward positively.'*

'*I have been in touch with my solicitor as I wish to proceed with a divorce. This raises financial questions but I know that you will want to continue to support the children financially as well as emotionally as their father. Both aspects are important. There isn't a problem with the house as it has always been in my name, as you remember I'm sure, my parents bought me the original terraced house we had all those years ago when we were setting out on the journey of marriage. So there will not be any divisions there. I know that you worked, but I stayed at home and saw to the children's needs and there was always a meal waiting for you when you got home. Labour was shared equally amongst us. I will continue to pay the mortgage with a contribution from you so that the children continue to have the roof over their head that they know and love. I am aware that your take home salary is £1500 approximately; we won't quibble over the odd pounds and pence! I think that £700 is plenty for you to live on so I would expect £800 per month backdated to the 25th of last month which was your last pay day. I shall be reverting to my former maiden name and the children will be doing the same. As there are no grounds for adultery, at least on my part, my solicitor tells me that the grounds will have to be mental cruelty as I don't want to have to wait around for a divorce and I'm sure that you don't either.'*

Rick put the papers down and brightened. At last she's admitting to something that she did wrong, how I've suffered mentally at her hands her tongue…but she went on.

'I have plenty of witnesses to the way that you treated me, belittled me, made me look stupid in front of others and so on. However rather than call these witnesses I have noted your attitude to me. You have said the following, and be aware that I can provide the dates to back me up:-
1. 'She's a fucking liar' to the children.
2. 'Fucking spoilt bitch' to Maurelian at a dinner party at his house when you were alone with him in the kitchen.
3. 'She is just nasty' to the Handsworths, when we were bird watching out at Wally's Wood.
4. 'Daddy just says your horrid' Hannah to me.
5. 'Daddy hates you' Liam to me.
6. 'Mummy's not normal' Liam to me on your birthday.
7. 'She's mental and needs locking up' to Philip and Elizabeth.
8. 'If she was a cunt she'd be useful,' overheard by Maurelian when you said it to another member of staff at your school.
These are just a handful. But even so quite a list! I have plenty of other evidence where that came from. Do you realise how hurtful it is to hear that you've been telling our friends that you think that I am mental when nothing could be further from the truth. I have often wondered about you, and I'm not alone in that but now is not the time or place to go into that.'

Rick put down the page and just thought, how can the truth work against you? He picked the paper up and read on.

'Obviously a person like yourself cannot be totally responsible for children and I shall be getting custody. I will of course want and expect you to have access and this will be, every other weekend, birthday, Christmas, and the new year equality of access. Holidays will be half and half with you having the latter part of the holiday so that you have the opportunity to buy them anything that they need for school.

These arrangements are made in the spirit of cooperation and we must agree to maintain communication regarding the children and to allow for flexibility on both sides.'

It was signed Lesley Newstead.

Who the hell's Lesley Newstead he thought. Then he remembered, Hannah Newstead, Liam Newstead.

Of course there was a PS which read, *'I shall expect the cheque for £1600 within a week from the date at the top of this letter. I don't want to have to take the matter to County Court. Make the cheque out to L. Newstead.'*

"Go fuck yourself," he shouted, so that a tourist passing by looked up at his window thinking that he'd left all that behind him in Birmingham for two weeks.

Sometimes, he wanted to tell someone a recurring nightmare in which 'I see my children old and realise that I am very old myself. I am about to die, my life has vanished and all those years have been wasted and cannot be recalled. Dying in its natural sense is not something that I am afraid of. It is something that I can accept. But I know I could never cope if any of my children died. What I am most afraid of is to regret not to have made the most of my life. Materialistically I want little. I had a wife, happy clever children, and a job. But should there be something more? When I am dead it won't matter but if, for that moment there is a sense of regret, it will be my hell.

FIFTEEN

Helen had been happily married. Now her husband was dead. She would not forget that he had kissed her sweetly as he had left for his work that morning. But she wanted to forget that he had said, 'see you about six'. The two kind policemen had just left. She couldn't imagine what they wanted when she had answered the door just an hour earlier. They stood looking almost embarrassed as if they did not know what to say. Well what do you say? She'd wanted to be alone. But the policeman had insisted on calling her mother, even looking through her address book for the number. She just let him. She was on her way they told her. She thanked them and told them they could go now and that she was sure that they had other things to attend to. He'd offered then to ring the local pastor. She told them that she didn't believe. How did he die they didn't really know all the details but a drunk driver was involved and had survived. They left wondering whether she will be okay. The mother would see to all that maybe they could go round to see her later in the shift.

A drunk driver. Who got drunk at this time of the day? Her mother would be here soon she'd better make up the spare bed. Not her father. He hadn't lasted the dream in America for more than five years till a heart attack took. She would have had a US flag draped over the coffin if they had only let her. If they stayed in England would it have been different? Or was Helen destined to be a widow, would Rick have been the dead one today. No she would have never married Rick. She wondered if Stevi would be able to come over for the funeral. It was a long way and it would cost a lot of money but she wished she were here to talk to rather than her mother. Her mother. Her mother would simper or just be too practical. She will want to know what was his favourite hymn. Do It Again by The Beach Boys. Helen found it would be a good choice. She had tickets for Yes tomorrow and she and Billy-Joe were going to see. Her mother would understand that she still wanted to go. She had to be the mourning widow and brave in the face of her husband's death. How would the toy industry continue without him? There'd be someone to take his place at tomorrow at 9am when he was due to start his work. They might have even replaced him today. Deadlines still had to be met, orders filled. She expected the phone to ring and she was hoping her mother would fence those. She'd better ring Stevi before that all started. She was talking on the phone. Stevi was going to come out straight away. She was laughing and tears were streaming down her face when the door bell rang, and the key turned in the lock and her mother walked in mistaking the tears for grief. Helen raised a hand partly in greeting and partly to silence her and her mother was surprised to see her daughter seemingly in total control. "Yes. It is true. But wailing and crying is not going to bring him back. Stevi will be here in a couple of days. And then she sat. Looking at the void.

At the airport Helen saw Stevi first and was waving frantically for sometime before their eyes caught. When Stevi was landside they looked at each other momentarily reading the emotions before holding tightly onto one another.

Helen was first to break the hold, "Come on. There's a cab waiting for us."

"Cab now is it?"

They drove through the avenues and blocks in silence both aware that what they needed to say was too personal to speak in front of a stranger. When they reached Helen's apartment Stevi was expecting to see Helen's mother waiting for them and the real conversation would have to wait until she went to bed.

"Your mother…"

"I told her to go home until the night before the funeral…"

"Which is?"

"Three days time." She sat down and put her hands over her face as if she needed to block the whole world out. "It's not that I don't want to mourn. I just don't want excess." She was barely audible through her hands. As if she realised she moved them and looked at Stevi. "I loved Billy-Joe more than any man, but my mother…"

"Your mother was over the top." Helen's face brightened. "Well what did you expect?"

"That people don't behave in a normal way in situations like this. Last week Billy-Joe and I were talking about our vacation." She smiled at the American affectation. "And talking about having kids."

"How many?"

"None." They smiled. "Though it doesn't matter now." She looked around the room. "Here I'm not a good hostess. Do you want some tea? I know you Brits only drink tea."

"My body tells me its about six pm so I wouldn't mind a glass of wine. If its not too early for you."

"No. These days that's a good idea. Red?"

"Like the first time."

Helen went into the kitchen and after a while returned with a bottle and two glasses on a tray with some biscuits. "You know I put three glasses out." She sat down and raised her glass. "To Billy-Joe."

"To Billy-Joe," echoed Stevi not quite knowing what to say. "He was a good man. You can't ask for any more." She paused and disliking the silence went on, "What were we listening to that night, oh so long ago?"

"Remember we thought that Rick was upstairs with his former girlfriend and that we had to be silent."

"Yes. I'd forgotten that." She saw that her friend's eyes were filling with tears. "I'm sorry Helen. Haven't you forgotten? I'm sorry. I must stop saying that."

"Yes you must."

"Of course you have. It's Billy-Joe. I'm insensitive at times."

"Yes you are." Speaking as if she were speaking to a child. "You don't forget first love, do you Stevi?"

Stevi looked into her glass as if she were seeing a scene from the past and said, "No, you don't."

SIXTEEN

Jonathan and Helene married on May 7th. After the civil marriage contract they went onto the church for a more traditional marriage. Jonathan had the church filled with forget me nots, 'so that you will always remember', he told her, as she looked on too overwhelmed to speak.

He had written to his parents and had hoped that they would turn up but they never responded. His grandfather had written and wished them both well but had declined as he was too old to travel now.

They honeymooned in Brittany. They began their holiday in Alencon. They shouldn't have been there but the hire car broke down leaving them stranded in the middle of a road whilst cars hooted at them from behind.

"Don't the idiots realise the whole thing has packed up?"

"You shouldn't call my compatriots idiots. It might lead to our first bout of marital disharmony after," she looked at her watch smiling, "Nearly seven hours."

Helene got out of the car and after waving her arms around as the French are prone to do made the queue realise why they couldn't move and they had help to push them into the road side.

"Right what do we do now," he said to himself, "Ring the hire firm I suppose. Wait there."

"Well I can hardly go anywhere else."

He went into a nearby café and explained what he needed, throwing in for good measure that he was newly married and this was supposed to be his honeymoon. The kind owner came over and gave him free access to the phone after he had brought Helene into the bar and given her a drink on the house.

Jonathan came back from the phone. "We're too far out for a replacement. They are sending a mechanic over to us straight away."

The bar owner and the rest of the customers were looking at them.

"You won't get anything done today," said one of them.

"And tomorrow is Sunday," added another.

"And everywhere is closed on Monday,"

"They're a cheerful lot aren't they?" Jonathan whispered to Helene.

"You could stay here," said a lady who they took to be the owner's wife.

The mechanic arrived and shook his head in a way that meant, 'Oh dear nothing can be done here.'

He told them he would need to take them on his truck to his garage where he could have a proper look.

Jonathan shook hands and Helene kissed every person in the bar and a few from the street who had just come to have a look. That seemed to take the rest of the afternoon. "They'll be back," remarked somebody among the villagers.

Fortunately for them they had had the spare part that they needed. Jonathan and Helene were soon on the road again and they drove about seventy kilometres further on before staying at a small hotel for the night so that they could continue their trip in the morning.

They then carried on with their journey to the Maine Loire, or at least Jonathan did. Helene was perfectly capable of driving; it just seemed the right action to be driving with his wife by his side. They drove past beautiful sights which Jonathan could only glance at like fragments from a film; a blue house set in its own land its shutters open and inviting, a small community of wattle and daub that genuinely looked as though it belonged to a century past, the massive church of Puy Notre Dame.

They reached their destination at lunchtime and their honeymoon could really begin.

"Give me the letter Helene then you can look for directions. I think this gite may be stuck in the sticks."

"What letter. I don't have a letter."

"The letter. You know the letter confirming our booking for this place. Without it we can't get there. I told you…" Then he saw it propped up on the mantelpiece in its white envelope waiting for him to pick it up and put it in his pocket. Now here they were in rural France without a clue of where they should be. "Ah yes. I think you're right…"

"Something else for you to find out. If you'd told me to look after the letter then we wouldn't be where we are now."

"Look let's concentrate. We got to get out of this. I know the name of the place. Find a bar and we'll ask there."

They found a bar and the owner not only gave them directions but also took them out to the gite.

"I thought you were to arrive yesterday," said the owner who had been waiting for them.

"Well, we had one or two adventures on the way."

For the week they walked, they drank the wine, they ate and they loved one another until it was time for them to go into reverse and return to a real type of life. But they had one another, and Jonathan had his life in France. On the way home she said, "Jonathan, I've been thinking."

"Well I expect you have. We've had the time."

"About us…"

"What you want a divorce already!"

"No no. You'll have to be a lot richer first."

"I think you could have a long wait."

"We have two houses. We have your little one and we have our family home that my Father has given to us. He put it in both of our names."

"Yes. That was very kind of him. It would have been to easy just to make it your house."

"No he likes you. Jonathan. Listen. I think we could make your house into a gite. I imagine the English would rent it for holidays even in its present condition before we did it up."

He nodded. "Okay."

"There's money to be made. Invite them for aperitifs once a week and a barbecue while they are here and they'll come back year after year. You see. It'll be easy. By the way, I think I'm pregnant.

"You can't be, not yet. We've only been married for a week."

"But we've been seeing each other for five months."

"That is the best wedding present I could have."

"Ah, that's a shame because I have another present for you when we get home. A new guitar."

"I can sing Cabral to you. Whoever said marriage only goes downhill is awfully wrong. This is getting better and better."

He stopped teaching and their holiday business expanded, as did their family to five children. And ten years later they were content as they had ever been and as deeply in love.

SEVENTEEN

The following Saturday Rick got into the shared bathroom early and made himself look his best and arrived at Christine's promptly as instructed at one o'clock. Christine answered the door and asked him in. "You're a bit early. Not that it matters, silly," she added quickly when she saw the look of sadness on his face at having done something wrong. "The children are in town with my friend from the States having a present bought for them." She smiled. He loved it when she smiled. Not many people seemed to smile at him these days. "When they come back," she added, "we were thinking about having a walk into town and having a drink outside one of the pubs and then coming back for a late meal. That okay with you?"

"That's suits me fine. Anything. It's good to talk to you rather than my four walls."

"Actually Rick, it'll give you five minutes while we're waiting to have a look at a letter that Lesley has been sending round to all her friends." He looked at her enquiringly. "I got mine last night. Here you are. Go and read it. Don't let it upset you or make you angry. She's not worth it."

He took the piece of paper and read: -

'To all our friends,

To those who care for us, from Lesley, Hannah, and Liam. I'm sure Rick would also want to share the feelings expressed in this letter.

We felt,' Rick felt anger rising inside him, *'That we should be open and above board about the situation at home at present.*

You may have heard rumours,' I expect they have been bouncing round like squash balls Rick wanted to add, *'That Rick and I have separated. These rumours are true, but I hope that its only short term,'* not if I have anything to do with it thought Rick, *'However should it become more permanent it will only be for the benefit of Hannah and Liam. Nothing more.*

'We've had a traumatic last year. We've had the demands of our jobs, the journeys for the children to and from their orchestras. Rick lost his Grandpa, for whom I was particularly fond. It leaves a tremendous gap when somebody you love leaves forever. Rick's mum has been a tower of strength to myself and the children.' How many times have I heard her say how much she hated the 'fucking old cow' Rick thought. *'Fortunately Rick seems quite unaffected, but that's men.'* Rick just felt that he wanted to beat the next person he saw to a pulp.

'I know that Rick loves his teaching career and he can now pursue that without the responsibilities of family life other than of course the contributions I know he would want to make.' Money money money Rick sang to himself.

'I shall be working part time from now on and in time after I've discussed it with my bank manager, I shall open a shop in the town selling high quality artistic goods. As you all know I am an excellent watercolour artist. Hannah and Liam love the idea of helping out in a shop.

'Both children are thriving. Hannah has achieved top grade four oboe and Liam top grade two clarinet. I'm very proud of them. I'm sure we are both very proud of them.

'Please come and see us. We are not to be avoided. We are not a sad family but a happy one,' Well good for you mouthed Rick, *'We still have a lot to do to heal the pain that has been done to myself and my children but we are making a positive step forward.*

With our love
Lesley Hannah and Liam.'

Rick screwed the letter into a ball, threw it, and paced around the room as if he were trapped. He knew that he had to calm down. Christine may have planned this lunchtime for him. He had to appear normal in front of her friend. He heard the front door open and slam and the children's excited voices showing Christine their new toys.

"Helen!" he heard Christine say, "You shouldn't have. They'll think its Christmas. You've spent far to much on them."

Helen was a name Rick knew.

"I don't get to see them enough. It's a big pond between you and me. Let me spoil them."

A voice Rick knew

"Well come in and meet my friend Rick. He needs cheering up." They came into the room. Rick could not turn. He was feeling numb as if entering a dream. "And," as if she were announcing the result of the Miss World competition, "All the way from America, Helen."

"Helen?" enquired Rick.

"Yes my cousin from America. You knew." Wondering what was wrong with him now.

"I think I'd better go."

Christine looked puzzled and wondered if she were witnessing Rick having a nervous breakdown in her own front room. Maybe the letter had been too much for him. Helen motioned for her to leave and she went closing the door behind her. Should he stay? Should he go?

Finally a voice said in a slightly sarcastic American accent, "I'd recognise those round shoulders anywhere."

"And I'd recognise that voice. I've never forgotten you. Your curse worked."

"Well maybe I'm here to lift it."

He turned and they stood facing each other.

"Helen..."

Christine came into the room. Hearing the voices and unable to bear her curiosity any longer. "So you two do know each other?" They both smiled. "Well it's been weeks since I saw you looking anything close to happy Rick. So you've done something useful."

"Yes and it's been a long time too since I laughed," said Helen.

"We were at University together..."

"I didn't know you went to Uni," said Christine looking at Helen.

"I didn't. It's a long story."

"Oh. I see."

There was silence. Nobody knew what to do next. Rick turned and looked out of the window and saw that the grass needed cutting. He wondered whether to offer to do it.   Finally Christine broke the atmosphere. "Look," she said, "You two probably have a lot to catch up on. I've had Helen for 24 hours now and I've got her for another day. Do you want to go off to the pub by yourselves? The children won't be bothered and I'll get the meal ready."

They replied at the same time. Rick with a 'yes' and Helen with a 'we couldn't possibly'. As they walked side by side into the town neither knew what to say. There was too much to talk about.

"Are you still teaching?"

"Yes and no. I'm on long term sick leave."

"What's wrong?"

"I'm getting divorced. It's not easy."

"No. But sometimes you just have to keep on going." They walked in silence for a few moments as he expected her to carry on. "My husband died nine months ago in a car accident."

"Oh I'm so sorry. I cannot say what I feel. Any words would be useless."

"Yes they would. I'm sorry I didn't mean to sound aggressive."

"Do you have children?"

"No. Fortunately. Do you?"

"I don't know what to say. Yes. Two. It makes my problems seem insignificant."

"Don't say anything. People react to situations in different ways. It's good to see you."

"I was horrible to you."

"Yes you were..."

"And you cursed me. And it worked. I never forgot you. Everyday I thought about you and wondered why. Why I had behaved in the way that I had. Did you think of me?"

"No." She shook her head. "Hardly ever. I lift the curse." They looked at each other and smiled. "We were very young."

"And I was immature."

They reached the pub and sat at a table looking down the river towards the hills watching waves wash against the hulls of the yachts. They talked and talked and as the sun finally began to go down over the hills and lights around them were switched on, they realised how long they'd been there.

"We should be getting back you know. After all it's Christine I've come to see. Not you."

That hurt him a little. "What are you doing in England anyway? Holidaying? Wandering all over London like a real American?"

"No working. Thanks to you I think you gave me the taste and excitement for working with live bands." Rick looked puzzled. "The Rag Ball and Richard Thompson? Remember?"

"Oh, yes. What do you do then?"

"I work in promotion for a record company. I'm over here promoting Greenday."

"Never heard of them."

"Exactly. You should have. Here I go. Seriously you would like them. I've a cd in my luggage I'll give you one when we get back to Christine's."

"Helen can I see you again?"

"I go tomorrow. I have to work. Anyway we are part of the past. You have to look forward."

"Can we write?"

"I don't know. Give me your address and I'll think about it. But I was properly in love. He has gone forever. The other, what ever you say, went through his own choice..."

"I sometimes wonder if it was my own choice. In fact I often wonder." Interrupted Rick.

"Anyway it doesn't matter now."

"Do we have any choice over anything? Or are there outside influences that we do not control that and make our decisions for us?"

"I don't know. I really don't care. I'd better be getting back."

They were silent for a moment, the close atmosphere broken by loud laughter from a nearby table. Instinctively they looked over. A happy man with his family?

"If..."

"There are lots of 'ifs' Rick. Too many. Forget them."

"I know. I know. But..."

"If the man who was driving the other car that killed my husband hadn't been drinking."

"I'm sorry I didn't know."

"No you don't know very much. You lived cotton wooled in this seaside town without really doing anything and now you expect to turn everything back. Except that you don't really want to make the effort. You just expect everything to fall back into place. To be as it was." She went to take a sip of her drink and seeing that her glass was empty put it down with an air of finality.

"Do you want another?"

"No. I'm going." She paused. "Rick. I never said I loved you. You never said you loved me. All these years you've just made that assumption. You've hung onto something that wasn't there. I loved my husband. I would not have married him if I hadn't. You can't just keep on assuming."

"I always thought that our love was something special."

"I'm sorry." She looked at him. "I am sorry Rick. Just think on that boy."

"That sounds like Stevi talking."

"Stevi?"

"Yeh."

"We write."

"You write? I didn't think that you were that close."

"Its called keeping contact with the past, whilst at the same time living in the present and looking to the future. You learn from the past after all. Stevi thought that you treated me badly. Underneath all that feminism stuff there was a heart." She

paused as if wondering whether to say what was on her mind. "I even hear from Malcolm once a year at Christmas."

"Malcolm. Not Malcolm the…"

"Yes and I'd marry him if he wasn't already married," she spoke smiling, "I certainly made the wrong choice there between him and you. He's a property developer. Millionaire. He'd still do anything for me. I could retire tomorrow." She grinned at the thought and looked around her as if she were seeing the world afresh. "Will you know where your children are in six months time?"

"Yes of course."

"Make sure that you do. I don't think you know where I am. I don't think I'm prepared to take any more chances."

"I'll walk you back."

They went back to Christine's in silence. He left her at the gate. She kissed him full on the lips looking directly into his eyes as if she saw and understood everything he had ever experienced. He went back to his bed-sit. He played a cd of Leonard Cohen's. Perhaps she would put the promised Greenday in the post. He poured himself some vodka, looked at the stars and waved. Yesterday was just another dream.

Acknowledgements
Anne Lamali. The cover painting is detail from a portrait of my wife.
 Ken Anderson for his technical help. SlingInk forums.
Hannah Taylor.
Most appreciation for her hard work though has to go to the editor of this novel Cindy Strunze. I could not have finished it without her, not just for corrections but for pointing out what was irrelevant, what didn't make any sense and what was just plain silly!
For more details of Anne Lamali the renowned French artist go to
anne-lamali.com
To contact me email
gjpopeuk@googlemail.com
I hope you are looking forward to the next one.
With love and best wishes
Glyn
myspace.com/glynpope